The Judas Inheritance

Also by James Collins

Other People's Dreams
Into the Fire
You Wish
Jason and the Sargonauts

Symi 85600
Carry on up the Kali Strata
Village View

symidream.com/james

JAMES COLLINS

The Judas Inheritance

THE JUDAS INHERITANCE

FOREWORD

The Judas Inheritance was inspired by the ruins of a village on the Greek island of Symi in the Dodecanese. The story is complete fiction, but I was captivated by the mysterious dates, numbers, and names that appear on many of these hauntingly strange buildings that seem to conjure up a curiosity about the lives of the people who once might have lived there. While the story is set on an imaginary island, visitors to Symi will recognise a number of features which I have borrowed. And in 2013 a motion picture adaptation of the story, called *The Judas Curse*, was filmed using these same Symi locations. It is important to stress that film adaptations, of necessity, are often markedly different from the books on which they are based. This is the novel version of the original story before it was adapted for film.

For more information about the island and the locations that inspired the book and which were used in the film, please visit symidream.com which is a site dedicated to information about Symi.

No book writes itself and I would like to thank Nigel Edwards for his input in the early formation of the film script structure and characters, and for his wonderful work in designing the layout of this book. I would like to thank Jenine Woodhall for her proof reading of the manuscript. I would also like to thank my partner Neil Gosling for his photography and encouragement, and our families and all those Symi friends, visitors and fans who made the filming possible. And you, of course, for picking this up and reading it.

JAMES COLLINS
Symi, Greece
February 2014

One

You are in darkness. Your eyes are closed. You can't see but you can hear. There is a strange kind of whispering sound, like voices from another room, frantically chattering, excited, hushing each other, gasping, begging, all mixed up. And behind all that but close to you, some kind of motor is whirring away, a small, tiny motor driving something on, steadily, slowly, growing louder.

What is it?

There is something in the room with you. Something or someone. You just need to open your eyes. You just need the courage to open your eyes.

A quick glance. Open. Shut.

You saw a photograph of a man. A priest was it? It was old, a bit faded, the colour drained, the edges tatty. And an album, the photo was going into a photo album, a small one, a red cover, a plastic wallet of old memories. Who was doing it? Whose hands were those?

Eyes still shut, ears still aware: thumping sounds. What is that? Sounds like books being dumped one on top of the other, a pile of heavy books being made, and… Someone crying? If the whispers would die down you could hear better but that's definitely someone crying. A man. An older man breathing fast, desperately, trying to control himself. A whimper of fear.

You dare another quick glance.

The crying man is pushing the red photo album into an envelope. His fingers are trembling. There is a name on the envelope. You can't see it. You don't want to know what is going on. You close your eyes again.

And hear the whispers rise in excitement, tumbling over each other madly, a crescendo, incoming chatter down an unseen telegraph wire, and the sounds of whimpering and the old man mumbling. You just wish it would all stop, all go away, leave you alone. Your eyes screw up tighter until your eyelids hurt, your face is distorted. And then a scream that holds within it all the horror and desperation of a man with no way out.

'I can't do it!'

You have to look.

You see Frank, a man in his sixties, in the darkness of a small, closed room at night. A candle on the table lights papers and books, and his face. It lights the lines on his skin as if his face is made up of crumpled shadows wet by the streams of his tears. His hands are over his ears.

The muffled thump-ker-thump of a heartbeat within a body. The rhythm of life or the sound of approaching death.

He takes his hands away. The whispers have changed key. Lower now and more conspiratorial. They have something planned.

Shadows jostle on the walls of the room like curious spectators as Frank looks down to the table before him. A small metal chest with its key, a small silver pill box, an envelope, a roughly drawn map and a book. He places his hand on this book as if he were about to swear an oath. It is a journal, 'The Judas Curse', and it is his life's work. Beside the book a Dictaphone whirs as it records.

Frank picks up the envelope now and quickly slips it inside the journal. This he throws onto a pile of other books in an old box, then picks up the pill box. It rattles. There's something heavy inside. He clutches it tight in his hand for a moment, drawing it towards his chest, and then he throws it, as if it just burned him. It rattles into the box of books.

And then he slumps down. Deaf to the sounds around him, or immune, he looks slowly at the map. Hand drawn, rough, tatty, it makes no sense to anyone but him. But it will. It has to.

It's useless. All of it. Desperate and useless.

He hesitates, picks the map up and is about to rip it in half when sudden screams shatter the gloom and the chattering falls silent. Frank stands still, his grip poised to rip the map, ready to destroy the clue. But a deep, low growl rumbles through the room and the sound of frightened children pulls him to his senses.

'No. Please,' they say, close enough that he can feel their ghostly breath.

'I am sorry,' he whispers back, and his grip on the map relaxes.

'Help us.'

'I can't!' And with that he swings around and grabs the candle. He thrusts it into the darkness, lighting up the walls, the shelves, the locked cupboard, the shuttered window, but no faces. He is alone.

The cupboard. He unlocks it, puts the map inside. He knows he cannot make this too easy. Too easy and it will not happen, it will not be finished. He has to make it a challenge or it won't work. It will not end.

He locks the door and pockets the key.

The only way is to lay a trap; he knows this, and, as much as it pains him, it is the only option left to him.

The voices are calmed, but the shadows loom up, crowd in closer. Frank spins, something darker than the rest stands in the corner, something with the stench of evil about it, death in the air. He staggers back, knocks a picture from the wall, upsets a small table as he thrusts the candle to the corner.

'He will finish it!'

The light burns the shadow away. Nothing there. No one there.

'He will,' he says, quieter now as he lowers the candle and looks at the desk.

It is finished. Words from a book he read once and believed in always. Into thy hands…

His work is done, all but the chest. The final clue to leave. Tears now pouring from his eyes, his heartbeat counting down his last moments of life, he drags the chest from the table and walks to the door.

The whispers follow him from the house as the Dictaphone blinks its red recording light on the table in the darkness. In the silence.

5

Soft, silver clouds scud by a faceless moon as Frank stumbles from the house and into the narrow, cobbled lane. Hard stones under foot, uneven, passing light, gathering night, he clutches the chest and half runs, half lurches his way along the path.

He stops at the corner, a church tower bearing down on him, challenging, disapproving, and he shakes his head at it. He laughs scornfully. He no longer believes in life after death.

He runs on; he knows where he is heading. Windowless ruins of a dying village look down on him like buildings blinded by history. He reaches out to the walls for support as his breathing becomes tighter, his vision blurring from the tears. The warm night air contrasts the cold of his heart.

As he passes a gaping doorway he reaches for that key.

'It must be a challenge,' he mumbles to himself. He takes the cupboard key and throws it into the ruin. It strikes a stone and then is swallowed by the undergrowth.

Frank staggers on, turns, follows the twisting path until he reaches a door. Metal, creaking open, clanging back as he staggers into a large lobby and towards an arch.

Clouds part, showing him the way as he enters the apothiki, the store room.

'This house,' he whispers. 'He will put it all together.'

The store is a large stone cellar smelling of damp and things long dead and best forgotten. The walls crumble as Frank attacks them with his fingers, pulling the mortar away from the rocks, freeing one large stone.

He looks back over his shoulder. No whispers. He is alone, and yet he knows he is not.

He can see it in the corner. So near and yet so impossibly far. It would be so easy to take his last few steps that way. Over to there, to that in the corner. If only he had the faith, if only he could find the strength within him. But there is nothing left inside now, any last strength withered with his hopes long ago.

'Why?' he shouts out. 'Why can I not do this one thing?'

But he knows why. He has always known. This is not for him. This was never his to finish, and that's the punishment for not being able to love his son enough. This is what he deserves.

The rock falls from the wall revealing a hollow. The chest slides in, the rock is replaced. He crams crumbled mortar around it.

'So close. So near.'

Near enough that he can feel the presence behind him, laughing at him, invisibly grinning and wringing its hands and winning, gloating, sneering.

Frank looks down, sees a length of rope amid a pile of clutter, work tools, cans of paint, a dusty baseball cap that reminds him of…

He picks it up. Places it. A smile creeps onto his face and then rushes away as, with his other hand, he picks up the rope and clutches it tightly.

The trap is set.

He takes the rope and leaves. Behind him, in the cellar, that thing in the wall starts to breathe and stir.

5

He stands beneath the withered tree, its branches white in the nightlight like cancerous veins in diseased lungs. The night darkens with the slowing of his heartbeat.

The rope swings and the noose waits.

'It has all come to this,' he says, quietly, resigned. 'I did what I could, but I could not do enough.'

'You could not give enough,' the unseen children whisper back inside his head. 'You have betrayed us all.'

Frank falls to his knees. Sobbing, he claws the earth, digging, his fingers catching on rocks and stones, bleeding. He pulls up the ground and frees a stone.

'I didn't know,' he shouts, and dumps the heavy stone to one side. 'I didn't mean this to happen!' Another stone, another rock, another step, the pile grows higher.

Until it is high enough and he stands. He places one foot and then the other on the stones and steps up. He balances on the stones and looks down over the edge of a wall. It's a drop enough. He takes the noose and places it around his neck.

A flickering light, like hope, steps out from the shadows and lights the pale face of a young woman. She watches through large brown eyes as Frank looks up and across.

'I can't,' he says again, and she knows.

She just stares back. There is nothing she can do, not now. But, all the same, she tries one last time.

'If you take this path,' she says, and her accent is as rich as the night is black, 'then he will slowly possess you. He will grow in you and thrive.'

Frank tightens the noose around his neck, the coarse hairs of the rope scratching his stubbled skin.

'You will still have to fight him.'

'Not me,' he counters. He looks away from her now. 'Not only me.'

The rocks beneath shudder as he shuffles his feet towards the edge.

She watches him, her eyes impassive, the candle dancing yellow across her face.

'I am sorry,' he says, and he is.

Frank lets his feet slip from the rocks and the rope burns into his neck as the noose grows tighter.

She watches and then silently blows out the candle and disappears back into the darkness.

Two

I don't know what was more disturbing. The fact that the old man died and left me all his stuff, or the fact that I actually went straight to the internet and booked a flight. There was, of course, the expected run in with Sarah as I was packing. It was my turn to have Ben for the holiday and she wasn't exactly chuffed that I decided not to take him.

'You think there's money in it, don't you?' were her exact words as she let herself into my flat with her key and moaned her way into the sitting room. (Note: change locks.)

I was rereading the letter in its broken English, postmarked from a country I had never been to let alone never knew that my father had lived in, or had been living in. The letter didn't mention money. It just talked about his possessions, his work, his 'things', which was all pretty vague. But yes, if I am to be honest, then I did hope there was money involved.

It was one of those kind of 'forget who you are' moments. I mean, put it like this: your father treated you bad all your childhood, and by bad I mean by never being around much, and when he was he only shouted and took a belt to you. Then your mother dies and he takes it all out on you like that was your fault. (This is over simplifying things, of course, but that's because of where I am writing.) So, you leave him and the house as soon as you can, sixteen in my case, and make your own life. He tries to follow you for a while, finally gets the message and disappears out of your life when you are eighteen.

Time passes, you get a girl pregnant, you marry her, you

realise the mistake, so does she, then a boy comes along and suddenly you are a father and there's this most wonderful thing in your life and you are now not only joined to this woman you don't care much for, but also to your father. He has a grandson, the boy is old enough to ask about him, now being eight, and you find yourself sounding like your dad when you tell him off for asking about his grandfather. I really am over simplifying this, of course, but then it's hard to write when resting the diary on your lap.

So then, after she cheats on you and lets you down at every turn, with the divorce finally coming through and the boy living half with her and half with me (at least that was decently arranged), you try and get back to making a living so you can pay the maintenance and all her bills while wondering why on earth she suddenly can't afford to pay any of her credit cards bills and does she really need a new kitchen and how will it benefit Ben anyway?

And then you get a letter from the far south east of Greece demanding that you come and collect your estranged father's belongings before they are destroyed and you do have to wonder if there is any money in it. Of course you do. Natural first reaction on the death of a 'loved' one. I mean, where there's a will there's a relative, right?

Actually, you have to wonder because you need to eat, Ben needs to eat, and she needs a new kitchen. Apparently.

So, my question is, do you feel guilty? Do you say 'I'm not going anywhere near that man dead or alive because he hated me'? Do you say 'Sod it, I'm going if only to make sure the bastard is really dead'? (Preferred option.) Or do you say 'No, I wanted nothing to do with him for the last twelve years, I want nothing to do with him now'?

What do you decide? A moral dilemma or an easy decision?

He wasn't rich, as far as I know, but then what do I know? Actually, what do I know of him these last twelve years? Not a lot. He battled with himself for years after mother died until he left the church, got himself un-ordained, if that's possible. I don't think it is, but he certainly gave up going to church and went off travelling instead. That gave me my out, and when he got back one time, I was gone.

Anyway, where was I? This bloody boat is bouncing around like some kind of fairground ride.

'You are doing this out of duty?' she asked when I told her I had to go.

'Yes. No. What's it to do with you?' I think was my reply. It was only yesterday but feels like a month away. Overnight flights and taxis, and strange languages, journeys, and now a rollercoaster boat ride have wiped the timeline from the streaming player I call my life.

I did actually check the envelope that the letter and stuff was in. You never know, old people sometimes put five pounds in cards and things. But not Frank, of course, not dear old dad. Dearer to me now that he is dead.

'Can you afford to go?' she quizzed on.

'No, but I had put a small amount aside for your split level hob and essential spice rack, so I can use that. Homes and Garden will have to wait for the photo shoot. Shit!'

Not given to swearing much I had, by then, bought my plane ticket and then remembered that I had a photo shoot in four days' time. 'I'll be back by Friday,' I said. 'I need the job.' But she wasn't happy about that either.

I could hear her foot tapping and her teeth grinding as

she looked around the room. What she was looking for I have no idea. No, I do know actually. She was looking for something to complain about. (Her complaining about how I live my life somehow helps her get some of her guilt off her shoulder, I'm sure of it.)

'Yes, it's a mess,' I said, reading her thoughts. 'But it's a clean mess.'

The only other thing that dropped out of the envelope was a small, red photo album, one for four-by-six sized prints. A tatty old plastic thing that I remembered my father owning. He'd sent me a photo album. Great.

It gets better.

There was nothing in it. Well, actually there was a piece of paper in it that read "1909, it all adds up" and a photo of four boys in what looked like Edwardian costume. Smart and with high collars, formally posed and with Greek lettering along the bottom; the name of the photographer, I guess.

It's there in my bag on the seat beside me. It's strange but it's got me intrigued. No words, no clues, just a photo. Perhaps they are some old relatives, my great uncles or something. Maybe there will be an answer when I get to the island. In about half an hour, I think.

Anyway, Sarah was not pleased that I had decided to go and had given her only child back to her for a few extra days' quality time. You'd have thought she would have been happy about that.

'Take him with you,' she pleaded.

'No way!'

'He's been talking about his granddad Frank a lot recently, even drawing him. He really should go and say goodbye.'

'He never met him. He has no idea who Frank is, certainly no idea how he was, so, no. And I can't afford it. Not if you want a new and indispensable MFI worktop.'

'He should go.' She can be very stubborn.

I shook my head and put the photo album and letter into my hand luggage. No need to take much, just a couple of cameras, the iPad, the laptop and leads. (Might as well get some shots while there. Chris Trelawney travel photographer, sounds good. Better than 'family portraits and weddings.' Yawn.)

She repeated: 'he should go. The Ed Psych says he needs to work through some issues.'

I stared blankly at her for a moment and saw nothing there that might once have endeared me. 'Ed Psych... Issues?' I snorted a satisfying laugh. 'And what American TV series are we watching right now?'

'His dreams...'

'Kids have dreams. Nightmares. He's got a lot going on.'

'Take him with you. Let him have closure.'

'Oh yes, closure. Now there would be a thing.' Of course, I mean regards her and me. She actually looked as if something was about to burst out of her chest. I zipped up my bag. 'The dreams only started a couple of days ago. He's too bright for his class, that's the...' I almost said issue, 'problem.'

I still played into her hands. She picked up a bottle of Scotch (empty) and dropped it deliberately into the waste paper basket. (To loudly clang against two others.)

'You have a way with words,' I said, but the sarcasm was missed.

'As you keep saying, fathers and sons need time together.

He needs this time with his father.' Her voice raised a notch, perhaps it wasn't missed after all.

'Four days and I am back. It was dad's work. I should go get it.'

'And suddenly you care about that?'

For some reason I did, and her questioning me made me snap, so I rounded on her with the bottom line. 'Someone's got to pay for his shrink.' And there was Ben right at the end of my pointing finger, standing in the doorway watching and listening and clutching one of his drawings.

Sarah glared at me to turn me to stone, but when that didn't work she looked our son up and down and said to me, 'you dressed him in this?'

I didn't see anything wrong with it, and was about to say so, when Ben spoke.

'I saw how granddad died,' he said in that quiet, distant voice of his.

I was a bit gobsmacked so just went back to my packing as Sarah crouched down to him. And then I had to listen to her side of the truth once more.

'We talked through this issue, Ben,' she said, and I am thinking she's been watching CSI Somewhere. 'People die for all different reasons, but you remember what we do for them?' Maybe Law & Order.

A stray glance in a mirror and there she is holding up her crucifix and there's Ben putting his hands together in an angelic, mind-washed, praying gesture.

'One day,' she went on, 'a long time from now, you will meet granddad again in heaven.'

'Castles in the air, Sarah,' I said. 'Remember, we did the workshop.'

'Daddy doesn't believe in heaven, does he?' Ben said it more as a statement than a question. It is, after all, true.

'You can leave me out of heaven,' I said, and laughed. She didn't.

And some fell on stony ground.

'When can I say goodbye to granddad? He wants me to.'

She looked from Ben to me and scowled at me. It was time to go.

'Let yourself out when you've finished,' I said, and hoisted my bags onto my shoulder.

'He needs closure,' she persisted.

I knew how he felt.

I fished out his favourite cap from under a pile of something and crouched down to him. That was when he gave me the drawing.

'What's that?' I asked, as he held it out. A really weird looking house, seen from the side, with a chimney and a balcony and lopsided walls. And three generations of stick men standing in front of it. Ben pointed.

'You, me, and granddad's ghost,' he said, simply, as if it was perfectly clear. 'Take it to show him. He will be there soon.'

'Hey, we talked about this,' I said, aware that I was now sounding like something on TV. 'There's no such thing. When people die, that's it. You don't see them again.'

There was always something about this kind of thing that unnerved me. It went right back to Bible-bashing Frank and his afterlife theories. It made me cold to think about it because it made me cold to think about him. I took the drawing Ben was offering, and was about to put it away (to throw away later) when she stopped me.

'That's what Frank would have done,' she said, knowing my intentions.

It's now in my bag beside me on this bouncing boat.

I put Ben's cap on his head and pulled it down with a sharp tug, the way I always do. I pretended to take a snapshot of him and said the customary 'I'll be seeing you,' to which he replied with a similar mime.

It's those kinds of silly little things you miss when you're hundreds of miles away from your child and heading off to a place you've never heard of to sort out the mess left behind by a father you hardly knew.

An announcement. We are nearly at my destination.

Three

Walk through these lanes, you have never seen anything like this before. There is more here than the crumbling buildings you see either side, more than the empty, windowless shells, the gaping doorways the rough cobbles and flagstones beneath your feet. There is more here than the weeds growing through the cracks of time and the rotting vegetation of long dead life.

People live here still. Some do; many more have fled. They stay on for their life, their property, their loved ones. They stay because they have no chance to flee. For some there is no time, for others the time has come and gone and they wait, as they all waited, for something else. Something next.

In this house here, the one where the old wooden shutters are closed, where the paint peels from the woodwork and flakes from the plaster. In this house where there hangs the remnants of a once proud country flag, now torn by the wind and rain and the burning heat of the last summer, here there lives a family. Once complete with mother, father and son, once a smile, once a joy. Now their lives are darkness and confusion, sadness and bewilderment. She has gone. She waits with the others. Only her men remain, lost without her, lost without reason.

That bell, clanging its slow rhythm, mournful for sure, is being rung for her today as it was rung for others yesterday. The living hear it, some go to it, others have gone to it too many times and there is no spirit left in them to go again. Another death, another funeral. The desperation of one has spread to become the desperation of all and the withered, blue and white stripes of the flag that led them to this point can do nothing to bring back their dead. That is how they see it. That is who they blame.

But there is more in these lanes other than death. There is hope and there is life. But it needs to be hope and life in the right hands or else there is nothing here but the cold smell of abandoned rock and the lingering bitter taste of betrayal.

Imagine a stage, set for some huge high opera but one to be played out amid ordinary lives. The ruins of the past are the scenery, dramatic, each one with its own story, each one historic. The occupied houses are home to the living characters, the houses still warm and bright, decorated against the myths and battened down with superstitions. The players wait behind their closed doors, the guarding hands and charms, their fires alight, their windows closed but with faces pressed against them looking out and down onto the stage, waiting.

A stage that now sees the arrival of a stranger. A second stranger. Who, like the first, has come to find something. But what this one comes to find is a thing he has not yet realised he needs. The one he follows, the one now gone, another one for whom the bells tolled, has put it all in place; what he needs to do, what he needs to find, and he has left behind the means for him to find it.

5

It seems me and my father had more in common than I like to think about. It wasn't until this afternoon that I discovered where I inherited my diary-keeping habit from. At first, I was tempted to be done with it there and then. Throw it away. But then I remembered why I keep a diary. It's a way to get my thoughts clear, it was part of the agreement, part of the 'therapy' as the newly Americanised ex-wife would probably say. So, after a morning of many shocks, the final one came with the knowledge that Frank had also been an avid diary keeper. But the stuff that he kept in his? Well, I am more convinced now than ever that he was ill. No other way to put it.

To make sense of what's going on here on this small, dead, island, I need to start right back at the start. After the madness that was yesterday, the rush for tickets, the flight, the taxi to the boat, the boat to the island and that character right out of some old Roger Korman film, after all that, tonight is positively dull by comparison, and yet, here I am, in my father's house, writing my notes by the one and only light, a candle, while the night settles in around me outside. I am not going to get any sleep here so I may as well write.

I could no longer cope with the diary open on my knee and there was nothing else to write either; I'd exorcised that last meeting with Sarah in a couple of pages and that was enough. My mind turned to the future and what was going to happen next, where I was heading to, what I might expect to find, and so I took my bags outside onto the back of the ferry.

Out there the wind was strong and the sea was spraying along the sides. The weather was rough at sea but had been fine when we left Rhodes. The island I was heading to is about twenty or so miles from the nearest big island (Rhodes) and lies between two places I'd never heard of, Symi and Tilos; two smaller islands. Apparently, according to the information on the walls inside the ferry, these islands were once on the Crusade route, hence the Knights of St John occupying them at one point. They were also good trading routes to the Holy Land, and they are still as close to the Infidels, the Turks, now as they were then. So they have, in their time, been Turkish, belonged to those Knights and also, if I remember right, Italy, and are now Greek.

Typical of father Frank to find such a place to settle in after his many travels; somewhere more or less inaccessible and small and yet with enough history to fill several books.

The back of the ferry was pretty empty due to the wind, and trying to take any photos was a bit of a waste of time: sea and grey skies. I thought I'd take another look at what the solicitor had sent me, my father's small photo album and the letter telling me to come immediately. I thought I might try and remember the name of the person who had written, but it was pretty hard to remember and even now I have to look it up. "Tzandakis" and I am not even sure if that's a surname or a mister or a what.

As I was swaying my way to a chair I ripped the airline baggage label from my bag as I don't like it when people can see what flight I've come with, or my home address, and I was just putting that in my pocket when I saw this old guy trying to get to a chair. He was wrapped up against the wind, a scarf across his mouth and was reaching out towards the seating some several feet ahead of him as if he was trying to magically drag it towards him. He was staggering as the boat lurched so I went to his aid. I took his arm and together we wobbled our way rather comically across to the seats.

He said something in Greek (I think) and then saw the letter in my hand.

In an instant he had grabbed it from me.

'Hey, what you doing?' I said and tried to grab it back.

He studied it carefully, squinting at it and then thrust it back at me. He pulled down the scarf from his face and then I saw that he wasn't old at all. He was only about twenty, but had lines around his eyes, his face darkened by the sun, his skin dry and leathery.

'Why you come there?' he said pointing to the address on the letter and the name.

I didn't feel like I needed to tell him, so I didn't. I just started putting it away again.

'Stay on the boat,' he said and started to get up. 'Not there. Not there.'

And with that he walked away crossing himself in a way that the taxi driver had done earlier. (We had passed a church at speed but the speed and traffic didn't stop him from crossing himself three times. The fact that his other hand was engaged in sending a text message didn't seem to worry him either. It worried me; I put my seat belt on.)

'OK, thanks!' I called after him, my words caught by the wind and thrown overboard. 'Will do. Not.'

Nosy old, young, git, I thought, and laughed. I opened the old photo album instead. Something to ponder might take my mind off the fact that I was suddenly feeling queasy inside. I've never been seasick before, or any kind of travel sick, but right then something settled in my stomach and made me decidedly 'not right.'

Seeing the inscription in the front of the album turned my stomach further: "For dad, love Chris" and a X for a kiss. In my defence, the handwriting was very juvenile and although I don't remember giving him this album I must have. In fact, I think my mother bought it and wrapped it after she'd made me write in it. I'd say the age of the person writing it was around four or five. She died when I was six, so that would tie in.

I flicked through the few images that were in it. The first showed dear old dad in his priest outfit, C of E, in the late

1980's, before mother died. The second showed him holding hands with someone, but that someone had been torn out. I assumed it was mother. The third was the one I'd remembered seeing yesterday, the four boys in Edwardian outfits. I mean, rather, that it was an Edwardian photo. It had that colour, that tone to it. One small child with what looked like blonde curly hair stood beside a chubbier one who sat in a chair; behind him stood two older boys looking much more grown up. All of them had the look of wealth about them. There was the Greek name but no other clues as to who they may have been. I took the picture out and checked the back once more. No clues, no numbers, no printer's stamp, nothing. I put it back.

The last thing in the album was the piece of card that read "1909, it all adds up." Which of course makes no sense and I wondered why I kept it there. I did though, but I also checked the back and found nothing written on the other side. The rest of the sleeves in the album were empty and there was nothing written in the back flap either.

I had flicked back to the photo of the four boys and realised that, yes, their costumes could have been from around 1909. I was just wondering if there was some kind of connection when my eyes were drawn to the youngest child. It was something to do with the rocking motion of the boat and the fact that my stomach was turning again, but I was convinced that his face had moved. Someone had pencilled in some CGI into my life and played a visual trick on me. His eyes sparked. Sunlight breaking through the cloud and catching a drop of spray, of course, but still my finger felt drawn to the image, and, as I looked closer, I saw my hand come into view and my index finger point to the youngest boy. It was like I was being lured beyond the image, into the room in which it had been taken.

The ferry's claxon screeched out about three feet from my ear and nearly surprised my last supper out of me. I slammed the album shut feeling a sudden ending of something as I did so. My guts were back to normal and I felt as if I had just awoken from a short, but nasty, illness. I looked up. I was alone on the deck and ahead of me was a small bay with a folded, dark hillside behind it.

The strange feeling returned.

ى

After the pounding of the engines and the shrill klaxon in my ears, after the sound of the clanking anchors and chains and the shouts of the crew, the bay where we landed was silent. I say we; just me and that strange young man who had told me not to get off the boat here and who had then got off himself in a rather hypocritical fashion, I thought. I watched him run to the end of the jetty and jump into a waiting car which drove away at speed leaving me alone.

And I mean alone. I had expected this Mr or Mrs Tzandakis to meet me, not that the letter had said he or she would, but I thought it would have been polite of them to. I had rung and left a message once I'd bought my plane ticket. They knew what boat I was going to be on, they also knew I only had a day or two here. After waiting for fifteen minutes, during which time I saw absolutely no one, I tried the phone number again.

There was no signal. I did that thing where you stand up and wave your phone around and look pretty stupid, but still, no signal. So I sat on a… what are they called? A bollard? A thing where boats tie up their ropes. And waited longer.

After half an hour my stomach started rumbling. I'd had no

breakfast, so I started walking. Ahead of me, at some distance up the hill, I could see houses, and, as I had seen nothing in the bay apart from empty buildings with closed doors, I reckoned there must be somewhere at the end of the road. That car had, after all, headed that way.

I walked, becoming hot as I did so, carrying my cameras and my bags.

It was a long road with a slow incline uphill and my bags, not that there were many, soon became heavy. The road narrowed, and after a while it stopped being a road. I came to a car park, of sorts, an open space with a few cars in it that looked abandoned. But then I saw the one that my odd sailing companion had been driven away in and realised that all the cars looked equally as battered and rusty. No one seemed to care for their vehicles here as they do back home.

There was only one way to go and that was up the steps, wide and rough, old and very uneven. As I climbed I had the feeling that there was someone following me. I looked over my shoulder and there was no one there of course, but there was definitely something making me feel uneasy again.

The path narrowed, the steps became more eccentric, some low, some high, some deep, sometimes a slope with weeds growing through the cracks in the stones, and sometimes smooth and well kept slabs, possibly even marble. And as I climbed, the village started to loom larger in my vision and the walls either side started to close in on me.

I am prone to claustrophobia and I put the uneasy feeling I was experiencing down to this; the walls were, at times, only a foot away from me either side. I mean, sometimes the lane was narrow and the walls high, but then I would come to an open space and breathe again. I say open. There were always buildings. Some looked relatively newly painted compared to others where layers of peeling paint had fallen away revealing what looked like ancient maps of the globe, in reds and blues, orange and yellows. But then I would be faced with another path, heading off in another direction, and then there were places where two or three paths met in one tiny opening and I had to decide which way to turn.

And then I realised what was wrong, what was odd. I had not seen a single person since leaving the boat, only the young man going off in the car. And I'd not heard a voice either, not a phone ringing, a beep of a mobile, not even a breeze or a bird.

I stood in this one square and looked around me, listening intently. Nothing. No sound. That was so odd it made me wonder if I had some kind of ear pressure thing going on, a blockage caused by the air pressure of climbing up the hill or something. I swallowed, held my nose and swallowed again, did all that kind of stuff, but no, I really was standing in the quietest place I'd ever stood in.

I lifted my camera and took a shot of where I was, just in case I got lost, and then headed off down a lane. This time I called out 'Hello?' But there was no reply.

I came to another small square, no more than a few feet wide, with tall houses on three sides (all crumbling and ruined), and one pink and shuttered house on the other. I banged on the door. To be honest, I wasn't expecting to get a reply. I just wanted to make sure I'd not gone deaf. No one came and I heaved myself up some more steps and turned into another, narrower lane.

Finally!

'Hello!' There was a tall, thin man standing right down at the other end and beside him stood a small boy, about half his height and young, probably around six years old. They were standing stock still and looking towards me.

'Hello!' I called again, but they did not move. I raised my camera, took a picture, thinking that might stir them into action. It didn't. I walked towards them and they turned and walked away.

At the end of the lane, where they had stood, I stopped and looked left and right. No sign of them.

'Hey, mister!'

The voice came from behind me. I turned on my heels, but saw no one.

'Hey, mister! You need a guide?'

Great, I thought to myself, the first person that I find and they want to rip me off. But how could they do that if I couldn't even see them? I looked around. There was no one in that lane, nor up in any of the empty windows.

'No!' I shouted out, angry for some reason.

'You need a guide.'

I spun around again and there she was, standing right behind me where I swear she was not standing a moment before. Reason fell into place quickly: the man and boy had told her I was there and she'd called from around the corner before I'd seen her. The maze of lanes had tricked my ears. I then noticed that I could hear a bird singing somewhere.

Any anger left me immediately. Large almond eyes (yes, now I understand what they mean when they write that in novels and describe someone Mediterranean with gorgeous eyes), and deep brown. A soft face, a warm smile and deep black hair tied back behind her ears. Slightly shorter than me she was looking up at me expectantly.

'Hello,' I said, and in an instant felt completely inadequate.

I managed to put out my hand and smile back at her but I must have managed a leer of some kind as she actually looked shocked, as if I'd suggested something filthy.

'I'm sorry,' I stammered, not knowing what I had said or done.

She blinked, her dark-skinned eyelids momentarily covering the glittering eyes, her head tipped forward, and she laughed. Her laugh was unnerving at first, none of that "like tinkling glass" rubbish, nothing high and girlie, but deep and rich and as deliciously tempting as dark chocolate.

'I am sorry,' she said. 'But you look so much like your father.'

'My father? Do I? Oh Christ.'

It didn't occur to me then to ask her how she knew. I simply blurted out what I had been rehearsing in my mind during the walk up the steps.

'I am looking for a mister Tzak...an...something.' Here I waved the letter at her and realised I was talking loudly, as if I didn't expect her to understand. 'Can you read this?'

'Tzandakis,' she said and it sounded like she was giving a secret password and unlocking the cavern full of treasure. 'Yes, you need a guide.'

'You know where he is?'

'Come, follow.'

And with that she was off, walking away ahead of me giving me just enough time to admire her figure and swaying hips before she rounded the corner and was swallowed up by the lane.

I double timed it to catch up, hoisting my bags to a more comfortable position on my shoulder.

'Look,' I said as I followed. 'I don't really need a guide, just directions.'

'You must come with me. No problem,' she replied.

'Er, listen.' I had a concern. 'I don't have much money. I can't afford a guide.'

She took me by surprise then and stopped, turned, and her glare bore into me. 'Why is it about money?' she said. 'I must have experience for my new work. You need a guide. We are good. Come, we walk up higher.'

I felt as if I had already walked up high enough but she walked on and I followed. Our transaction, whatever it was, was not yet complete but at least I had told her I had no money to pay her a tip or anything.

'Who are you?' I asked, aware that she had not given me her name.

'I am a tourist guide.'

I looked around at the empty lane, the shabby houses, the old stonework. Possibly picturesque but certainly not your ideal holiday resort.

'I don't see any tourists,' I said.

'There are reasons for this. I will explain. Come.' And she simply carried on walking as if the steps were nothing to her, while I started to feel my chest burn inside through lack of oxygen. I paused for breath.

She stopped and turned, looked down to me from her place a few steps up. She smiled and there was something in that smile that made me smile too, so she laughed, turned and walked on up. I gathered from that that our deal had been struck. Whatever that deal might be.

My mind was wandering as we walked. Distracted by our meeting (well, distracted by her), part of me fell to wondering who she was and why I had so readily agreed to follow her, while another part knew the answer and decided now was not the right time to go there. Much as I would have liked to. But even those thoughts were interrupted by the sights I saw as I followed her, up more and more steps. The first thing I saw that I thought odd was a bunch of dead flowers hanging on a door. They must have been there some time, they were dried and withered.

'It is Easter,' she said after I had asked what they were all about. 'They should be Spring flowers. But nothing is growing this year. These are left from before.'

'Decoration?'

'No, to guard against bad luck. We are a very superstitious island.'

We came to one of the open spaces where the path widened and wide stone steps appeared on the far side of the small area.

'These were called platia,' she said. 'Moments of breath in the narrowness of the lanes.'

'It's certainly a maze,' I commented. I stopped for a look around but there wasn't actually anything to look at. I just wanted a rest. 'Is there a bus?'

She laughed, and carried on up the wider steps and into another snaking lane with high stone walls. In this one I could detect bricked up windows, camouflaged, the edges showed to be lintels and frames of stone. One was half bricked up by stones and then a rusty bathtub blocked the remains of the gap. It looked like the ruin above was being held up by the tub.

A closed door, wooden, with another bunch of dead flowers hanging upside-down this time. The stems were wrapped in foil and bound with string. On the high doorstep a child's toy, an Action Man with one arm missing, naked. Beside it a newspaper, yellowed by the sun, being held down by a glass of what might once have been coffee.

I was about to ask where the villagers were but she spoke

before I had a chance to ask any of the many questions that were bubbling up in my mind.

'You are staying long?'

'No, only a couple of days.'

She stopped and turned to look back at me, giving me a chance to catch her up and rest a moment. She was waiting for more information. 'I need to find this Tzandakis person, see to my father's things, take them and go. I have to be back for a photo assignment.' This was not enough information. Her eyebrows were raised, expecting more. 'I am a photographer,' I said, and held up my camera.

She must be camera shy as she turned away and carried on walking when she thought I was going to take a photo.

'So quick a visit is not possible, I think,' she said rather cryptically as we set off again.

'What do you mean?'

'Your father. The Englishman.'

'You knew him?'

That laugh again, oozing out of her mouth warmly. 'Everyone knew your father. He loved it here. He was popular. For a time.'

That last part had a ring to it that I could well understand. Everyone liked Frank. For a time. Then they got to know him. My school friends could pay testament to that, if any of them had kept in touch with me. They hadn't since school, thanks to Frank. They all liked him at first, and then, before long…

My heart suddenly pounded, my skin turned clammy and my breath started coming in short gasps. I made a quick grunting noise, attracting her attention, and looked at my feet.

I was somehow standing on the edge of a precipice, a deeply cut river bed in the rock. The path had opened and turned left, I had carried on, my eyes fixed on the buildings above. I'd not seen it, but now I was on it. On the edge.

It's never easy to explain, and unless you've suffered from it you won't understand it. 'He's afraid of heights,' they say, as if it is something you will grow out of, something to mock, something like being scared of the dark or spiders. But it's not a fear of height I have, and it's not vertigo. My balance is fine. This isn't either, but I cannot stand on high things, in high places. Ladders are out, windows in tall buildings are kept at a distance, parapets, cliffs, even open-topped buses are a no go area. But it is not a fear of heights.

It is a fear of falling.

More. It is a fear of not being able to stop yourself from falling.

And here I was suddenly, in a strange place, with so much going on. Attention was not being paid, I had walked to the edge of a high cliff, with jagged rocks below me sloping down to piles of dirt and rubbish beneath, and my feet were on the edge. My toes were over the edge. I felt sick.

Worse, I sensed a hand behind me, coming closer. It was about to touch me, to push gently. I could feel the drop calling me, drawing me inevitably towards it and there was no way to stop myself from falling.

'Christopher.' A quiet, calming voice. Was that a hand on my arm? 'Christopher, close your eyes.'

In an instant they were open again and I was back, away from the edge, sweat running on my forehead and my shirt clinging uncomfortably to my back. My heart pounding.

She stood, watching me curiously, waiting patiently as I pulled myself together.

'It's a problem,' I said. 'It goes back a long way.' And I know exactly where to.

'Come,' she said, as if there was nothing to concern ourselves with. 'We go higher.'

Charming. Higher.

She walked on and I suddenly realised.

'How did you know my name?' I asked, but there was no reply.

My back to the wall, I followed and we turned another corner. Now I was happy to have the close-in walls, the ruins around me. Now, claustrophobia was a cure.

'Why so many ruins?' I asked, to keep my mind off long drops and falling. (Though the feeling stays with me all the time.)

'Wars, depression, people left.'

I saw another of those tatty old Greek flags, faded and hanging. 'And now the economic crisis?' I asked.

A church bell started to toll somewhere around us.

'More people are dying.'

On hearing the word 'dying', my mind leapt to thoughts of Frank and I said, 'And more flowers?' to try and dispel them.

'More superstitious residents.'

'Are you superstitious?' I asked. I don't know why. Fishing for personal information from my guide. A sign that I was feeling comfortable with her.

'We all do what we can to keep away the evil.' She said it so earnestly it made me laugh.

'The evil, of course.' I could feel the laughter deep in my throat. Had I been back at school with my old classmates we would be stifling laughs and kicking each other under the desk.

'Where we live,' she said, and her voice was steady, designed to make me realise how serious she was, 'where you go, it is better to have an open mind.'

'Sorry,' I said once again and sought to change the subject.

I looked up wondering how much further there was to go and heard the wind. We were higher up the mountain now. It felt colder, the air was more active, a breeze was at play above me, and yet that was still the only sign of life. If there had been any signs of activity down by the sea (and there hadn't, apart from the man getting a lift) there were certainly none now that the boat had left. Only the whine of wind through overhead cables, and higher, ruined houses looking down on me.

'So, tell me. What can I expect from this person I have to meet?'

'This person?'

I pulled out the letter, the summons to the island.

'I mean this old mister Tzan... Tzandakis.' I read: '"Come at once, it is imperative that you deal with your father's inheritance." A bit difficult, is he?' I was thinking he would be something like one of our old teachers, strict, by the book, old fashioned.

'Difficult?' She stopped again and turned to watch me as I joined her on the same step. 'No, not difficult. She is dead.'

Four

This young man has hurried back from his job on the island of Rhodes. He took the last ferry of the day, not that many come to this small island any longer. Petros, a man in his twenties, recently married, was working at the electricity station when the phone call came. Not, as he expected, from his new wife saying how much she missed him and asking when he was coming back, but from her sister. Come home now. There is bad news.

Petros is standing in the doorway to their bedroom. It is a small, humble house high up in the village. It is simply furnished. They are a poor family. His wife is no longer here. She has been taken away.

He kneels down by the bed. There is a small table on which stands a framed photograph of his wife in her wedding dress. A lit candle sits beside it. There is a small bunch of flowers. A hurried gesture, it seems.

Petros mumbles. His words are incoherent. He has come here fast to find answers and heard only rumours and stories. But there is also truth: His wife is dead, and he, at twenty five, is a widower.

He turns his head, forcing himself to look at where they both once slept. The bed is made neatly. She did that before… She put on the new cover that was a gift from her mother. It is cream and hand embroidered.

On it lays the empty shell of her blood-soaked nightgown, spitefully mimicking the shape of her young body.

5

'Just how much further is it?' I was really starting to feel how unfit I was.

'Not so far now. Nearly there. Tell me,' she said, 'you will not stay for your father's Panikhida?'

'His what?'

'The ninth day service of his remembering.'

'Church?' I think I actually shuddered. She saw and her face fell. To cover myself I said, 'I believe in the camera. In things that never lie.' And I held it up to take her photo.

'No,' she said, and she sounded worried and turned away from me. 'No, I hate it.'

I lowered the camera.

'Here we are,' she said.

We turned a corner and came to yet another lane. But here there were blue doors brightly painted and metal. There were several bunches of flowers on this one and letters painted on the wall in red. Two large letters, initials I think.

She stepped up to the doorstep, which was pretty high, and watched me. I stopped walking. I suddenly felt heavy, concerned, ill at ease. There is no easy way to describe it. (I usually deal in images not words.) It was as if something had occurred to me that had been hovering around outside my mind all this time and now finally settled in. All this time! It had been no time. Just over one day since I'd decided to come, only two or three days since he had died.

That was it.

I suddenly realised that he had died, and this, seeing his house, was like seeing his coffin.

You can pretend death is not around you until you see the coffin. This building, this blank wall and its brightly painted blue doors were his coffin. They made his death real.

'We buried him,' she said. 'The same day. It is what happens here. Within twenty four hours.'

'Sorry?'

'You will have time to visit his grave.'

I shook my head. 'Get the things, see to any papers, leave.'

'You must pay respects to your father.'

'Why? He paid none to me.'

Again I seemed to have offended her and she drew in a breath. I realised that I was letting out all kinds of personal stuff, things I hardly ever even told Sarah about, not even when we were being civil to each other. There was something about this girl that was making me want to talk to her.

I shivered. She gave me an enquiring look.

'Someone just walked over my grave,' I said without thinking.

'Ah,' she said, and smiled. 'Now this is good. Here, we say the same thing, but when you feel this it means you will come into some money.'

'Well, that's what I came for.' She looked blank. 'I mean, I got a calling to come and deal with an inheritance. My father had money, he used to travel, so I kind of came to pick some up.'

'It also means that your guardian angel walks beside you.'

Now I must have looked blank. 'Guardian angel. O-kay.' And just when we were getting along so nicely she turns the conversation to religion. I turned it back to the house.

'What's with these?' I indicated numbers stencilled above the front door. I was stalling. I did not want to enter that house.

'Registration numbers from a previous occupation,' she said, and put her hand to the door.

'And these?' Here I pointed to the two initials on the wall.

'Your father's initials.'

I looked again. The second one looked like a T for Trelawney,

35

but the first looked like a circle with a line through it.

'Fi,' she explained. 'The closest we have in Greek to your F.'

'As in Fee Fi Fo Fum, I smell the blood…'

Like I said: Some fell on stony ground.

She pulled a wire and the latch behind the door gave. The door creaked open a fraction.

'Why?' Stalling

'Why what?'

'Why paint your initials on the walls of your house?'

'To claim it.'

'Who from? Who else is going to think it is theirs?'

She didn't answer, she just opened the door further and invited me to cross the threshold.

Now or never, I thought, and stepped up. But as I did so I noticed she was looking over my shoulder. I turned and looked, followed her gaze. She was looking off down the lane, back the way we had come and there I now saw the old man and the young boy watching us. Hand in hand. They somehow looked hopeful.

'Father and son,' she said under her breath. Then more loudly, 'Please, enter. This was your father's house.'

Five

Whispers in the room. The empty room where so much happened and where there is so much more to play out. The dust has settled through the shafts of window light and coated the surfaces with memories. Books wait to be read, boxes wait to be opened, their contents wait to be discovered, and the whispering voices wait to be heard.

He walks into the room tentatively, uncertain of what to expect. Did he think he would see a body lying there? Did he think he would be able to smell death in this room? He falters at the door and looks around. He looks but he doesn't hear.

Not yet.

ʃ

I don't know what I expected of this room, this house, but it was not what I saw.

I am at the table now, the boxes of his possessions on the floor beside me, some on the table before me, the journals, the books, the papers, all neatly stacked and tidied by someone else. The table is against a wall, a white, blank wall with nothing on it but some marks where things were once taped, I guess. The table is large, a dining table really. Some smaller boxes serve as drawers. Pens, pads, pencils, a tape machine, some tapes, a book of maps, a map of the island showing only the one main road, nothing about the lanes we walked through. Nothing to show me where I am.

I have my back to the room and behind me is the door to the hall. The floors there, I noticed, were bare boards, creaking and old. It looks like there has been water damage in one part of the hall at least. There is a small bedroom off this hallway and a kitchen at the end. The bathroom is outside and she tells me that this is quite common around here. It was as recently as thirty years ago that there were no bathrooms here, not indoors and private at least. The whole island, from what I have seen of it, is stuck in some slowly limping time warp.

The rest of the room is simple: a chair, a small table, some shelves above a cupboard making up an old, oft-painted over cabinet, a window that looks directly onto a lane. No one has passed recently.

I think my first feelings when entering the house were nervousness and a slight underscore of interest. I mean, to come and find your father's belongings, to see what he left you after twelve years of not caring, it's a bit of a step. I was almost glad to be here. It meant the journey was over, what with its taxis and planes, boats and endless climbing up stone steps to reach a dead village. At least now I could sit and unwind a bit, have a wash, in the outside bathroom, and then, later maybe, tomorrow perhaps, I would gather up his things and head home.

That had been the plan.

I don't know what I expected of the room, the living room I think you'd call it. But it was nothing like I remember from our house when growing up, nothing that I would remember as my father's taste. A table, a chair or two, a small table and some boxes. It was like someone had been through and completely taken away anything of character. Apart from the painted ceiling which, she told me, was done a hundred years ago. Ships, swirls, a landscape in the corners, bright colours now faded, very impressive and completely out of keeping with my father's tastes, as I remember them.

I think my first words on seeing all this were, 'Is this it?'

'It has been cleaned,' she said, but I could see that.

'Did he...?' Those words just came out and I looked at the floor expecting to see something. What? Blood? A white outline, perhaps? (Too much CSI Somewhere-or-Other. I huffed a laugh.)

'No,' she said, 'not here.'

Like someone considering a purchase, like someone being shown a property by an estate agent, I walked to the cabinet and the cupboard, ran my finger over a ledge. A little dust. I looked about the room, the ceiling...

'Traditional,' she said flatly, no hint of enthusiasm.

'Nice.'

I went to the window and looked out into the lane. I was looking at a stone wall, high, with a dying tree of some sort hanging over the top of it suggesting an abandoned garden beyond. Withered, dying... My thoughts flashed back to the man I had once known.

'Do you know how?' I asked, and turned to her. 'They didn't say.'

She looked like she was gathering herself to tell me something very nasty. I expect it wasn't easy for her. She was, after all, pretty young. Only in her early twenties, I'd say, and new to this job of guiding people. She would make a very pretty tour guide if not yet a confident one.

'Whatever you need to say,' I said quietly, 'will not affect me. We were not that close, Miss...?'

She looked up at me from under those great big lashes, the kind of look that makes your heart skip a beat, in a hurry to get to the next moment.

Had she mentioned her name before? Did I hear it spoken

already? It didn't matter. She was capturing me, at least, that is what it felt like for a second.

But then her expression changed and she looked at the boxes, in particular the one on the table. A simple cardboard one like you'd pick up groceries in.

'We have much history here,' she said and then looked up at the ceiling as if the painting up there told a story. It probably did. 'Your father looked for it.'

'He was always keen on finding things,' I said, more to put her at her ease than anything else. 'He would go away searching for all kinds of things when I was a kid. He was hardly ever at home, and when he was…'

I stopped myself. Why was it so easy to talk to this woman? I was about to bring out things that I'd not even spoken to Sarah about.

She was once again looking at the box on the table.

'What he found he should have returned,' she said.

'O-kay.' This was not what I was expecting. 'And what was that?'

She suddenly turned to me, stepped up close, her eyes burning with some kind of fear.

'All that is happening now is because of how close your father came. It is because of what he could not do.'

All her charms left her in an instant then, and I suddenly felt very uncomfortable; she was too close. I stepped away towards the table.

'He was not strong enough,' she went on. 'You need to hear the stories. You need to know what you must finish.'

I started looking through the box. What was in here?

'Finish?' I said, mainly to myself, I think. 'He's dead. That's pretty finished.'

I wanted to block her out now. Only seconds before I'd wanted her to look at me that way again and now I felt uncomfortable with her in the room. It's hard to explain the feeling. Like someone you have just met has seen right through you and knows that secret, the one that even you don't think about. She knows you.

I picked up a small pill box, silver, possibly valuable, and something heavy inside rattled.

'Clues,' she said, her eyes flashing to the thing in my hand.

I looked at her, looked at it, could not see a way of opening the box so I held it out to her. She backed away.

'He was the only one to come close.'

'Close to what?'

She was talking in riddles, it was starting to confuse me.

'He was a religious man?' she asked and walked to the window where she looked out.

I dropped the pill box back into the box and noticed a Bible in there.

'He had a calling,' I said, and it was true. 'But then one day…'

She looked at me, a quick turn of the head, her hair falling onto her shoulder, her eyes alive with questions.

'Then one day God stopped calling,' I said, and went back to looking through the box. 'So he went hunting for myths. He read books about ghosts and hauntings, he studied the occult, but not to worship it, you understand.'

I was aware of her moving around the room, like some kind of shadow, a blur in the corner of my eye. She was studying me and keeping one eye on the lane through the window, her head turning to me when I spoke and back to the window when I paused. And me? I just found it pouring out.

'He had this thing about myths and legends and how

everything was based in truth. The Truth is the word, he would say. Not the word of God but just the word. Truth is all that mattered. Once the spiritual side went it was like the factual side took over him. He would say things like, Noah's Ark was a true story and he would one day prove that there is a wreck somewhere up on a mountain. I would repeat this at school and my friends would laugh at me for it. But my dad says that it is all true, and there really was a man who lived to be four hundred years old. The bullies would beat me up for believing it. My dad is a vicar, I'd say, he knows these things. And behind my back he would be off to Borley Rectory on a ghost hunt, he would be off to some far flung place looking for everything mythological from the real Dracula to the tomb of Pontius Pilate.'

I have no idea, now or then, why I rattled all this off to her. One moment she was making me feel like I could tell her anything, the next she made me feel ill at ease. I was probably just exhausted from the journey. I even doubted that I was making sense. I stopped talking and realised she was not in the slightest bit interested. She showed the same expression, picked up the same thread as if she had simply been waiting for me to get it off my chest.

'This is why you see the flowers,' she said. 'This is why you see the letters on the walls. This is why the villagers will fear you.'

'What?' Confused.

'He found it, brought it back to the surface, people started dying…'

'No, hang on,' I said, and folded my arms, leaning on the table. 'I heard your country was in a bad way but you can't blame him for that, not even Frank.' She stared back, her face blank.

I laughed. 'This is stupid,' I scoffed, and went back to the box.

I started emptying it on the table. 'I mean, yes, he was forever trying to prove Bible stories and other myths, always had a thing about the Holy Land and what was under the sand, Jesus and Judas, the Twelve, where they went, where they ended up, the ones we don't know about. But if people around here are superstitious and if their government is making a pig's ear of things and they get depressed, well, you can't really blame old Frank for that now, can you, eh?'

Turning back to her, a smile on my face, being reasonable. She had not flinched.

'Please!' she said, and it was a plea. 'He made it stronger, he left it unfinished, it will come back to us, all of us. More will die.'

'Oh, now come on!' I said loudly. This had gone far enough. 'I have no idea what you are talking about, or why you are doing this, but all I want to do is get what I must and head home, okay? Anything else is between you and your government, your council, whoever.'

'In here,' she said, and pointed a slender finger towards the box. I noticed then that her nails were newly painted, red. 'What you must do.'

'I'll sort it all out when I get it home,' I said. 'Obviously I won't be able to take all these books and Bibles, and things. So I'll sort it tonight and head back with what's important. The rest can be thrown.'

'In there. It is why they called you so urgent.'

'Urgently,' I corrected her. 'They said it was to do with the house. I had to get the things, the inheritance, before it was thrown away.'

I looked back at the box, a load of junk.

When I became aware of silence in the room I turned back

again and there she was, right behind me. She had silently stepped up close again and that look was back on her face. Vulnerable, pleading with her eyes, a simple feminine ploy.

'I can offer you so much if you will only help us,' she whispered and it was like there were a thousand other whispers around her in the room.

Offer me what? Heart skipped. Thoughts of Ben came to mind, home, work, an assignment, money.

I shook them all away. Back to the task in hand.

'I am just here to collect my legacy,' I said.

Why did I say 'legacy'? It's not a word I've ever used before.

She held me in her stare for what seemed like an age as the word I'd just spoken floated around inside my head. 'Legacy.' What he left behind. I finally opened my mouth to speak but she was there first.

'From father to son,' she said simply. And with that she turned and left the room.

A few seconds later I heard the front door shut and then a few seconds after that the gates clanged and she passed by the window, heading off down the lane and into the maze.

'Well,' I said to myself, 'at least you're here.' I looked around the room, the shelves, the cabinet and cupboard. 'I don't suppose he left me anything to drink, did he?'

Six

The answer was 'no.' There was nothing in the house to eat or drink. I thought about settling down with the books and papers and going through what was there. Checking the time I saw the afternoon was wearing on. It would be night before too long and I didn't fancy being out there in the lanes after dark trying to find a shop, let alone trying to find my way home again. Food and drink first, get supplies in for the night, and then sort through the junk. Find anything of value, any deeds or paperwork that might be my inheritance, and head towards the boat in the morning.

Instinctively I picked up my camera and headed for the door.

A picture paints a thousand words, they say, and so I took several. There's no real way to explain what this village is like except to say that it is confusing. I know I am in Greece, but there are none of those blue and white cube houses I thought they had here. There are small houses with classical looking fronts and pitched roofs. There are some that are like boxes with the roof slanting down on one side only. There are some that are just empty shells, there are plenty of ruins, as I've said, and there are lots of stone walls. Behind some of these are, I suppose, houses, but some are simply walls, and over the high tops of them you can see trees growing. I recognised palm trees and fig trees, surprisingly sparse for spring. Some of them grow through derelict windows like some kind of cancerous growth developing through a blind eye.

I walked back the way we had come and took a right, as that was the way we'd been before and I remembered seeing a shop of some sort lower down in the village. But when I came to the end of that second lane I didn't recognise a thing, so I turned back and came to another junction. I didn't recognise this one either. At least, I may have missed it before, but now there were steps heading up to one side and a twisting, high-walled path to the other. Straight on now took me to a dead end. I must have missed this earlier as well, I decided, and so turned right and followed the twisting lane thinking that I did recall it after all.

I was deluding myself. I had no idea where I was and a mild panic started to set in.

But, after a few minutes, I came to an open area and immediately felt better. I realised that I had been holding back my breath due to the closeness of the walls and the dimness of the afternoon shadows they created. Once out into a lighter area, a small square, I felt better.

And then I saw him. Out of the corner of my eye I caught a movement. Someone was off down another long lane and a flash of a red jacket made me turn and look. It was the guy from the boat and he was heading towards me, fast. I called out hello to him but stopped when I realised he was shouting and running.

Straight at me.

And he was holding a knife.

I turned to the way I had just come, and started to back into that lane, ready to run. But as I turned I saw her, the Greek girl. She stepped out from somewhere on the other side of the small square. She shouted out, 'Petro!' and then some words in Greek.

The guy, Petros, was almost on me and his eyes were wild and wide. His hair was flowing, his face taut, his eyes narrow, and his hand held out with the blade glinting. Flashes of light, his red jacket, the knife, and flashes of voices, hers calling to him.

And when he looked her way he stopped running. He pulled up short like some kind of cartoon character and the knife dropped immediately from his hand. He looked petrified. Suddenly, the anger had gone and there was nothing but fear. He looked at her and then at me, shouted something, shook his head, turned and ran.

My heart was pounding as I looked down at the knife. I kicked it away like you see them do with guns in films, and looked over at her.

'They blame you for what your father did,' she said. 'Go carefully.'

'What did he do?' I managed to ask, breathless for some reason. The after-effects of some kind of shock.

All she said to that was, 'Read his book,' and then she was gone. Not a great help.

I checked that the madman had completely vanished before setting off again. I crossed the square and headed after her but when I came to her turning she was nowhere to be seen. With all these lanes I am not surprised. It's so easy to get lost, to hide, to vanish.

But, after several more minutes of wandering and hoping, I found the small shop. It looked empty apart from one crooked old man sitting at the till (a wooden drawer) and trying to mend a telephone (cradle version circa 1950 I'd say). But he did have several bottles of whisky which he eagerly sold to me along with some cans of food, some biscuits and other things which, I realised later, were all things that would keep. Thinking back, there was nothing fresh in that store at all.

Heading back the way I thought I had come, I came into

an open square. This felt refreshing after the dark and damp smelling narrow lanes. There were ruins on all sides, a great round stone in the centre of the square and an impressive looking building with high double doors guarding over it. The rest of the square was in ruins, a pile of rubble on one side, four what looked like bombed out shells at a lower level to the round stone, and a large odd looking house behind me.

I shot a few snaps and was just about to examine the buildings in more detail when a young boy walked into the square. He was dressed in baggy black trousers and a white shirt, a round cap on his head with a tassel hanging from it. And on a stick he carried a small national flag, slightly ripped. His face was drawn, his eyes drooping down and sad.

I was struck by the contrast of the blue of the flag against the dull grey of the ruins behind him.

I crouched to take a photo.

'May I?' I asked, but he made no reply. He didn't move. 'I've got a son around your age,' I said, to put him at his ease as I clicked away.

I took a couple of shots and then stopped. There was something in his expression that started to unnerve me. He had something about him similar to the man with the knife. Something accusing in his look.

I stood up and stood back. I felt unwelcome suddenly, and then... well, it's hard to explain, but it was like there was something on my back. Fingers were lightly scuttling up onto my shoulder and I spun round to see...

No-one, of course, nothing, just the square. But I was sure someone had been watching me.

I turned back to the boy only to find him gone as well. What is it with these people? I laughed to myself and headed off in the rough direction of the house. But then, rounding a corner, I could hear the boy crying. At least, I could hear a young person weeping.

'Hello?' I called out. Perhaps he'd met Petros and got scared. 'Hello!' No reply, just the sound of sniffles and weeping.

A little further along the lane and the sound became louder. I was approaching a ruin on one side; there was nothing but rocks on the other. The sound was coming from inside that ruin. I could see, as I came closer, that the door was off, the roof was off, but the ground floor walls looked immaculate. Like someone had taken away all the woodwork and upper floors, leaving a smart, stone downstairs. The only blemish were two Greek letters painted on the walls.

'Hello?' I called again, almost at the doorway now.

But the sound stopped as I turned into the building. I stepped onto the threshold, and saw the old stone floor of what was probably once a shop. The walls were stone, there was an arch further in leading to another room which was now overgrown with weeds and trees. No way out that way.

(I reason now that the sound here carries far. It bounces around the stone walls through the maze of lanes which is the village, and which is itself, as far as I can make out, in the bowl of an amphitheatre-like valley.)

But what then caught my eye was a small shrine at the far end of the room. A candle floated on water in a bowl, there was a photo in a frame standing against the wall, a small one, and some incense of some sort burning, smoking away and wafting towards me in grey clouds that smelt of the churches of my youth.

And around this photo were pieces of paper, stuck to the stone, resting on the floor, propped up. I stepped closer, the incense filling my nostrils, and knelt to look and read.

Someone had died here, the face in the photo, I assumed. A young girl, angelic in death, eyes closed. The notes were written in Greek, apart from one:

"I will help you. Frank."

I suddenly felt an overwhelming need to cry and swallowed hard against it.

I felt a cold hand touch on my shoulder and I knew I was in the wrong place, that I had done wrong. I leapt to my feet, turned to see whose grief I had trespassed on. But there was no one there. It was just a trick of the mind but I was left with a feeling that I was intruding on a very sad place.

I hurried away, back the way I had come.

All this mystery, this non-communication, these strange feelings, the ruins, the strange letters on walls, the superstitions, all played through my head as I picked up my pace and concentrated on getting my bag of shopping home. Frank found a very strange island to die on, I thought. Why here? Why in God's name did he land up here?

I turned confidently into the lane leading to the house and found myself back in the square with the large stone in it.

Now, on the other side of the square, sat the boy and the old man I had seen outside the house when I arrived. They were sat on old, wooden chairs at a small table that was laid out for a meal; salt and pepper, some plates, and a glass each. They looked to be, for all intents and purposes, like they were waiting to be served.

By who?

Nothing but ruined buildings all around and no one else in sight. I expect it was some kind of child's game. Whatever was going on I had to get a photo, which I did. It was only when lowering the camera from my eye did my heart skip a beat.

I thought we were alone in the square but Petros was there, just around the corner, hanging by his shoulder on the wall, slouching, smoking a cigarette and looking at me with cold eyes.

I turned to go and as I did so noticed a plaque on the wall above the tall double doors of the only almost complete building in the square.

The number "1909" caught my eye immediately and so much so that I momentarily forgot about Petros and the father and son at the table. There was other writing on this small plaque, in Greek, so I couldn't read it. I photographed it so I could ask my Greek guide what it meant next time I saw her.

Seeing it set off those questions again: what was the meaning of the note in the photo album, 1909, why?

I heard the sound of a foot scrape on gravel behind me, remembered Petros was there and moved off, quickly.

5

That was a few hours back now and the afternoon is now turning to night. My camera is downloading to my laptop and, as the darkness settles in, I have an evening of Frank's books, my photos, and the shopkeeper's best whisky to look forward to.

The card is now copied from camera to laptop so I will have to pick this up again in the morning.

Seven

I have to get all this down now and not just before I forget it all. I need time to stop and think, and figure out what happened. How did I come to be in this state, in this mess, in this confusion? I have a fear that there is something at play here that I do not want to understand, that I will never understand, but something that will force me to try to understand it. Whatever is taking place here should be happening without me and yet I seem to be in the centre of it all. And this is all due to Frank.

But first, to get things down logically and in order, to help me clear my head and think through these things as I remember them.

For some reason my images took longer than they should to get from the camera to the laptop and I could only assume it was to do with the diminishing battery power. I'd forgotten to pack an adapter, not that I could see anywhere to plug into the mains, so was relying on the battery packs, and they were old. My eyes kept getting drawn to the box of Frank's books and things on the desk. I didn't want to go there. My intentions were to take them back with me and sort it all out from the comfort of my own flat. But as the darkness started to creep into the room last night, bringing the cold with it, I couldn't stop myself from taking an interest. It was like there was something in that simple cardboard box of books that was pulling me towards it.

It was the nagging question I'd had since the letter arrived at home. What was '1909' all about and who were the four boys in the photo? I assumed there would be a connection.

I turned on the light when the evening became too dark, and sorted through my bag for another jacket, or a jumper or something. There was a damp chill in the air now, a smell of wet earth and rock. As I pulled a jumper from my bag Ben's drawing came with it. Slightly crumpled, but still, a warm reminder of who was waiting for me back home.

I dug out my mobile as I looked for a place to put the drawing, a comforting reminder in this strange place where someone had tried to attack me, where families ate at ruined cafes in deserted squares, played games, hid in lanes, and where people were mourning for those who had recently died. And all to do with Frank?

But I'm leaping ahead now. Facts, events, first.

I took out the mobile and tried to ring Sarah to see how Ben was, to see if he had missed me yet. As I waited for the call to connect I spied a roll of tape on the desk, behind the box. I reached over to pick it up and tore a strip with my teeth. The phone started to ring at the other end and then cut out. I checked the signal. Very weak. I decided to come back to that later and stuck Ben's drawing up on the wall over the desk.

Suddenly there was something strangely familiar about it. Of course, I had only seen in the day before, two days ago now, but there was something else. Something in what he had drawn was sparking off a memory, a recent one. But what?

The images were still downloading (I hadn't taken that many!), and now it looked like they were going to take even longer to process. Like the whole thing was winding down. Checking my phone again I found the signal had now gone completely.

And that box of books was still waiting for me.

I gave in to them. Taking a decent swig of the whisky, I

grabbed the top book in the pile, drew up the only chair in the room, sat at the table and opened the journal.

The title: "The Judas Curse", the first page a row of quotations from, according to the notes at the bottom, the Gospel of Judas. I nearly threw it away then; too much Dan Brown, the world had done that craze. But no, there was something in the text that held me.

"Jesus answered and said, 'You will become the thirteenth, and you will be cursed by the other generations — and you will come to rule over them. In the last days they will curse your ascent to the holy [generation].'"

And then scribbles of explanation lasting several pages. A drawing of a man hanging, a doodle no more, no less.

Pages of Greek text, scribbles and notes, the jottings of a madman, I'd call it. But was Frank mad? It's easy to see how he may have been turned so by this place.

Towards the back of the book:

"It takes some slowly as the depression builds."

Nothing to do with Judas but more to do with madness. What takes them? And who are the some?

A page later: "It is spreading through the village like a cancer. It infects all." What does?

A page later: "No, not all, not at first. Just me, at first just me and those who I care about. I see this now. As I fight it, those close to me it takes first. But now I realise what I have done. I have cared for too many people. Judas was the same."

The same as what? Or as whom? This was my father writing rubbish as he took more drink no doubt. I was swigging away merrily, I have to say. (He'd cared about too many people? That made me laugh out loud. I raised my glass to him.) I read page after page of scrambled thoughts.

"Some linger, with others it is instant. One moment a smile, then the plunge of a knife."

I think I was talking out loud at this point, 'what are you on, Frank?' as I read the stupid scrawl, squinted against the light to read what he had written. And drawn. There were more quotations with illustrations. A chest by the looks of it with the words 'The Vessel?" and a row of question marks.

"Potter's field."

"Guts spilled out."

Things became more graphic at this point and I flicked through the pages faster and faster until:

An envelope spilled out from between the pages. A simple white envelope. It just slid out and landed on the desk right there in front of me. And it had my name on it.

"Christopher" was written in the same hand as the rambles in the journal, and the envelope was unsealed.

Curious, I took out the note written inside. I am not going to write it here. I have forgotten it already. It was some kind of twisted, vicious stab in the back. No, that's not the right word for it. It was some kind of mind game he was playing, and just the sight of those few words left me feeling sick. The realisation hit me then. My father had lost his mind.

I like to rationalise things. I like to know why things happen? That's what got me into trouble with him in the early days, in my earliest memories. 'Why, dad?' And his rants about trust and faith and not asking why. The usual childhood questions about God, I mean: if he was so nice to everyone why let wars happen? We've all asked the same things. I needed to know what, and when I asked Frank he would first shout at me and then, if I persisted, lock me in a room alone, for hours. I soon learned not to ask.

And now this? Now this note to me? I chucked it on the floor and slammed the journal shut. Or so I thought.

No, I did. I am sure I did.

As I threw it into the box one of the pages must have caught my hand with its edge. I felt the red hot brush-past of the paper and a hair thin cut opened up at the base of my ring finger.

I swore. Well, it hurt. It is hurting now! I slammed the book down on the table and I marched out to wash the cut. Angry at the book, at Frank, at myself for even coming here let alone delving into Frank's 'work'. I went to wash my hand and see if by any remote chance there was any antiseptic in the house.

5

And as he leaves the room you are left in it, alone in the dusty light from the one bare bulb. Outside, the night has closed in, settling thickly against the window, the shutters open, leaving you unprotected against whoever might be out there looking in. The air chills further, becomes damper and still. The room is waiting.

Why does the light dim now, and why flicker? There are shadows on the wall, crowding up, and falling back, but what creates them?

Somewhere else in the house a tap runs, water splashes. You wait.

And while you wait, the journal on the table draws your eye. You want to see what the writing says, you want to know what the note said. You want to know why this young man, handsome and strong, is starting to feel ill at ease. What is written in this book and in these notes that upsets him so?

What has caused him to remember the worst of his past?

Come closer to the journal, read the title, "The Judas Curse."

The book opens. An invisible hand turns a page, or is it a draught from the window? The window is closed. The light flickers again but now grows brighter. The page you look at shows nothing but a barely legible scrawl. Notes about the Bible, New Testament, places and travellers, merchants and journeys. It makes no sense.

The light settles again, the room feels slightly warmer.

He comes back in, sucking at the cut on his hand. He heads straight for the glass he was drinking from and sees the book is now opened. He must imagine that he left it that way as his eyes fall instantly to the page, and, as if suddenly caught in a trance, he sits to read.

He needs to turn to the next page, but he realises, and is, at first, confused. He is sure that when he left the room he left the book closed. Maybe that sudden flash of his father, himself, memories of growing up, that cold, empty room, maybe all of that had cut through him at the same time as the paper cut happened. He doubts his memory. But whatever he feels he can't stop himself from going back to those pages and those strange drawings.

He turns the page and reads aloud.

'Aged Five.' And there he sees a photograph, slightly blurred, of a boy. A colour image, but cut from a larger photo, a child cut from its family. A boy all alone on a blank page, aged five. It reminds him of being left alone in that blank room at the same age.

Another page. Another photo. A girl. 'Aged ten.' He reads his father's scrawl and wonders what this all means.

Another couple of pages. Another couple of photos. Young

men, older women, older men, teenagers. About eight people in total. No names, only ages and seemingly nothing in common apart from one word. The same word written beneath each photograph:

'Suicide.'

Behind him the shadows hang thickly at the window, still and silent. Watching and waiting.

Until one moves. Not a shadow but a face.

The Greek girl, his guide, peers in from the lane outside. She sees him reading the book. She sees him reach into the box and take out a second journal. She sees him turn back a page.

She draws in a deep breath as she turns and walks away from the glow of the house and into the darkness.

She leaves behind only the shadows, and now the sounds of whispering voices. An invisible cluster of young children share a secret. Their delight is hushed, their voices bubbling over with barely controlled excitement.

The sound is becoming louder as if the children are running along the lane towards the house, ready to swamp it with their enthusiasm. But their shrill shrieks maybe not laughter after all but horror, rising through a crescendo to a united scream that pierces the steel-cold night air.

Eight

I woke with a start, a jolt more like. You know how it is when you're half asleep, half awake, and you hear someone right in your ear say your name? They don't shout or anything, they just say your name really clearly and you're wide awake, heart thumping, thinking there is someone in the room with you. It was that kind of moment. Strange dreams of chattering children all locked in a large, empty room, all running around me in circles like they were playing some kind of game, each saying the word 'suicide' over and over again, and then, suddenly, 'Christopher', and I am wide awake.

It was early morning, the light was weak but there was light, and it was coming in faintly and shining onto the table. I had fallen asleep, slumped over open books with photos and notes, and scribbles, charts and diagrams I had no chance of understanding, and right in the middle of it all the little red photo album opened at '1909.' I'd fallen asleep trying to work out what Frank might have left me, what he had been writing about, and why had he suddenly taken an interest in me after all these years of estrangement.

My head hurt too much to even worry about it right then, and, as I righted myself, I knocked the near-empty bottle of whisky, just managing to catch it before it fell to the floor.

I'd forgotten all about my camera and the laptop, but the download had finished at some point through the night and then the camera had cut itself off. I unplugged the leads and checked the laptop; the battery had finally gone flat. I looked at the overhead light and tried the switch. Sure enough, that had been on last night and now there was nothing. At some point while I was asleep the power must have gone off, or been cut.

I was standing in the bathroom staring at my unshaven face, checking my tongue and wondering if it was worth saying 'never again', when I heard a clock strike, far away but clear enough, a dull thud of a bell from some church somewhere. I idly counted the clangs, seven, eight, nine.

Nine!

I scrambled madly for my ferry ticket to check the time and found it in a pocket of my jacket. The boat was at nine thirty and I had a way to go to get to it.

It took me all of ten minutes to bundle my things back in my bag, pack away my equipment and head for the door.

A last check around the room, the box of stuff on the desk, paper and books open and the album lying there. What was it to me? I decided then that I had a choice. I could stay and sift through it, spend time working it out, packing it up and miss my boat, the last boat back of the week, so they had said in Rhodes. Or I could make a run for it, grab the boat now and be back in time for that photo assignment, a decent and guaranteed pay cheque. Not some kind of wishful thinking hunt for Frank's leftovers. I'd been through it all last night, whatever he had decided to leave me. Books of scribbles, words that made no sense, and nothing of any value. He could keep the lot of it. I decided to go, leaving the no-show Tzandakis to deal with it, or at least any partners she might have had in his firm. It was their problem.

There was nothing there for me and nothing here for Ben. His granddad had crapped out big time and I would tell him so when I made it home, only in different words.

I pulled the front door to behind me, but it didn't want to

close. I just left it and crossed the small courtyard. The metal gates opened with a groan and I avoided the wreaths of flowers hanging from them.

I heard whistling. Someone was coming down the lane cheerfully whistling some light tune. The sun was shining and the day felt warm after the damp and dark of the house the night before. It was good to hear, a simple whistle, and good to feel the warmth of the sun as I stepped into the lane.

This guy, well dressed in a suit and open necked white shirt, with neatly kept white hair, carrying a black briefcase and smiling, said something to me as he passed by. It sounded like 'kali' something, and by the way he nodded his head as he said it I took it to be a greeting of some kind. I was still a bit wary after that idiot with his stupid knife the night before, but this guy meant no harm. He certainly didn't blame me for whatever Frank might have done, which, as I had seen from the notes the night before, was absolutely nothing.

I checked my watch and set off in the vague direction of the square with the millstone in it, about the only point of reference I was able to recall.

How long had it taken me to walk up yesterday? I realised I had no idea. It could have been ten minutes, it could have been an hour. We'd walked slowly and it was uphill, so if I headed in the right direction I should be able to get back down that road in no time and be there when the boat pulled in. I had twenty minutes. I just needed to find the road.

I turned left, picking up my pace a little, and there ahead was the girl. I saw her long hair catching the sunlight, it gave her a kind of glow around her head.

'Hey!' I called to her as I approached.

She turned to me and was smiling.

'Which way to the ferry?'

Her smile faded. 'You do not stay?' she said, and her brow knitted up.

'This way?' I pointed towards a lane that I was pretty sure ran down to the square, then from the square to the steps.

'But your father's work?' she said, and looked over my shoulder.

'He was crazy,' I said. Saying it aloud confirmed it for me. 'This way, yes?' I started off towards the square. 'Thanks for your help.'

'Another family has died,' she called out after me.

It wasn't my problem, not my affair, nothing I could do. I carried on at a trot.

'Manos, Ana and Lefteris,' she called, her voice sounding more pleading. 'All by their own hands.'

Suicides.

I slowed a pace, caught off guard. Something resonated inside.

'And all children,' she added, and her voice was clear.

I turned and she was coming up behind me. 'You must stay,' she said. I carried on walking but she was not going to let me go that easily.

'If you do not stay then why do you not take his work? It was his life.'

I slowed again.

'Think of your own family. Won't they want to know what he did, how he lived? What he wrote?'

There is no other family other than Ben, but it was Ben who wanted to come and say goodbye. The boy has never known his grandfather and yet he felt something for him. Wanted to do what was right by him. Wanted to do what I could not.

Did I owe it to Ben to take Frank's books and pictures back for him? No, I thought, and I don't owe it to myself either. I owe nothing to no one. But then again, maybe there would be something in those books, maybe another letter I'd not found, maybe something like a will. Maybe there would be something for Ben after all. If so, I could take it and deal with it when I got home.

Growling with frustration, I turned back to the house and heard the distant klaxon of the ferry as it approached the island.

I ran. Barged back in, threw everything, including Ben's drawing, into the box, picked up the album and that note, and ran again.

I ran from the house and turned right, headed towards the square, found it, ran through it, down the steps and around to the left. I kept running until I reached the end of that lane, a T-junction. Directly ahead, the walls of a dead house, the window frames gone, two dark red letters painted on the walls, a wreath of dead flowers lying on the step. I headed left, towards the sound of the ferry, again sounding its horn.

But this lane was narrower than I remembered, and it twisted to the right. I came to anther T-junction; a right would take me round in a circle. Surely, the lane to the left was the right way to go. I took it, and nearly stumbled on its uneven cobbles. Up ahead I saw a lane I thought I recognised. There was a house there.

Sure enough, a house I had seen before. I turned right into this lane and saw a white sheet hanging from a window high up. A large house this one, with green shutters, and from inside the sound of someone crying. I mean really crying, keening they call it. The metal gates clanged shut as I passed and I could hear the sounds of more people weeping inside. I shut my ears to it as the klaxon sounded. Closer.

Ten minutes and still no sight of the road. My heart was starting to pump now, my breath coming fast and my lungs beginning to burn. These were old, familiar feelings that took me back to my childhood. Running home from school, when I was schooled nearby, not daring to be late for father. And then, when he'd sent me away to school, when he went traveling and hunting, running back to my house so as not to be late for meals, or inspections. My life, always running, always in fear of someone older and bigger and more powerful right on my tail, always there to catch up with me, beat me, scold me, shame me for being late.

Another right, a long lane, high walls, narrowing, plants drooping down from above, another stone wall at the end, and a left turn brought me to:

The same ruin, the same dark letters on the walls, the wreath of flowers on the step.

Exasperation; the panic level cranks up a notch.

Turn right this time. A tiny lane, I almost had to go sideways to get through it. Claustrophobia taken over by panic; less than ten minutes. Another twist, up some steps. No, I should be heading down.

Turn, go back, take a right. Sideways lane, that's right, then left at the end. But no house. No wreath, no keening sounds, no white sheet. But a tatty old Greek flag hanging from a closed shutter. I remember that. Yesterday. Follow this lane.

The ferry klaxon again, and I can hear an anchor dropping in the distance.

Blood pressure rises, skin on face tightens and sweats cold.

Down steps, yes, down is good, around the corner and I

am in a tunnel. This is not right, but there's no way back, no point. I run on, down the steps under the tunnel which closes down on me as my shoulder brushes the wall. Dank smell, dark crevices between rocks. What lives in there? How close are those stone to my head? How heavy are the rocks above? Don't let a stone fall loose, the walls will crush down on me. The box of books is getting heavy. Leave it.

Five minutes. No road.

Sweat on my face and a scream in my throat. Dark tunnel, stone lanes, narrow, no sunlight in here. But, there! A light ahead.

Daylight, and someone standing there, someone to ask.

I stumbled from that tunnel, from that hellish narrow lane, and there was the open air, a small clearing amid the houses, a view down to the sea below, and a man standing with his back to me. The man with the briefcase, in the suit. Still whistling.

'Thank God!' I said. 'Please, the quickest way to the...'

He turned, still smiling. The sound of the boat.

'Kalimera,' he said, and raised a knife.

I stepped back, dropping the box, holding my hands out before me, but it wasn't me he was aiming the knife at. It was himself.

He plunged it down, hard, into his own stomach.

What the...?

There was no one else around. I didn't know what to do. In fact, I didn't think what to do. Before I knew it I was reaching forward, grabbing his arm, acting on some kind of impulse, grabbing his hand to pull it away, but he wouldn't give it up. I couldn't get to the knife but I could grab his hand; warm, rough skin, taut muscles as he gripped the handle. I gripped his hand just as hard and pulled it back. The knife freed with a slicing sound. He held it firm. He just stared at me and carried on smiling, his eyes wide and blue, sparkling. And used his strength to plunge it down again.

'No!' I cried out, feeling myself pulled towards him as I gripped his arm.

My momentum pulled us both down and I fell onto him, the knife slicing deeper into his stomach. I could feel hot liquid on my hands, his blood, now spilling out. We rolled over and I rolled off him. I let him go. He lay there on his side looking at me, his face paler now.

'There is no other way,' he said.

And stabbed himself again.

'Someone help me!' I screamed. But there was no one.

I saw him aiming for his gut again and once more tried to stop him, but for someone bleeding to death this man had strength. I wrestled with him some more, desperate to get the knife out of his body and something over the wound. It was spewing out dark red, almost black, blood, and still he had that smile on his face.

'I didn't believe,' he said, and now he was only able to whisper.

'Hold on,' I cried, but his eyes were closing. He stopped struggling.

'Christopher.' A voice, close and calm, reassuring and soft. 'Christopher.'

The man dropped from my grip, fell completely to the ground, eyes staring into the sky. Dead.

She stood behind him, the Greek woman, and knelt down to me. She looked at me with compassion, I thought, and I realised I was crying.

'Christopher,' she said again, 'there is nothing more we can do for him.'

Through the shock, through the horror of realising what I'd just witnessed, through the sight of her sorrowful look and the wild thumping of my heart, through the smell of blood and death and the warmth of both evaporating around me, I heard the boat sound its horn. It was pulling away out to sea.

Nine

I demanded she called someone. She said there was no one to call. My shouting must have attracted attention because that slimy guy with the long hair appeared at some point and started dragging the body away. I told him to leave it. He didn't understand me. She persuaded me to get back here and calm down.

And that's all I remember of what happened straight after the man stabbed himself. I remember feeling sick, and angry, and totally confused. And then all that changed to frustration when it sank in that I had missed the only boat off the island for several days and I would miss my photo assignment. Somewhere at the back of my head my brain made a note to call them about that, and while it was doing that, cutting clean and sensible through the mayhem of the early morning and the sluggish thud of the hangover, it also suggested to itself that I call Sarah and tell her.

But then, after washing and changing into my only other shirt I have with me, I came back to the living room and found she was still there. I was putting a decent covering on my hand, on the cut, and I felt weak, then hungry, and still sick. Faint, you might call it.

'This is how it is,' she said. She was standing by the window and there was sunlight streaming in. Throughout the horror of the morning, the pain in my head (now subsiding), and the confusion, she managed to stay calm. Her impassive face brought no focus to the world around me.

'What's the number of the police?' I had my phone out and was testing for a signal. There was one bar showing.

'They have left,' she replied.

'Don't be ridiculous, there must be someone here.'

She shook her head. 'Either dead or gone.'

'The number?' I demanded. She shrugged and told me. I dialled, and sure enough, an answer machine cut in after two rings. Some long message in Greek. I listened in the hope of a translation but none came.

'This is how it is,' she repeated, and looked out of the window. 'It will not let you go.'

'What?'

'It will make you stay until you find the way to stop these things.'

'The lack of damn boats off this island is what's making me stay,' I replied. I was still bubbling inside with some anger. But thinking about it now, it was more out of frustration. 'There's got to be something I can do.'

'There is,' she said, turning to face me, her eyes wide and hopeful.

'A fisherman, perhaps? Someone with a boat.' I, too, was hopeful.

But she ignored me. She was on a different tack.

'Your father spent much time at the museum,' she said.

'What?' Not what I was expecting. I thought about the box of Frank's books, now back on the table. I had this idea that somewhere in there would be some kind of address book, and in that a name, a phone number. Surely if he had lived here for some time and got to know and like the people, as his diaries said he had, there would be a contact. This Tzandakis firm for example. They must have had an office, there had to be someone around who could help.

'I can help you with the work,' she said.

I started rummaging through those books again, ignoring her. She was going to be of no help.

'Frank came to the island to find something,' she went on. I was only half listening but her words did sink in. 'When people first came to know him he was asking questions. History. He wanted to know much about what has happened here in the past. He knew what he was looking for and he became convinced that he had found it. He called it a treasure.'

I think I laughed out loud then.

'Yes,' I said, 'that's what he did. He followed leads, read books, went away, always trying to find that one elusive thing that would either make him rich or happy.'

'This did none of those things,' she said. 'It only brought death.'

'You don't say.' Flippancy is a cover for nervousness.

'I can help you. I am a guide. I know the history, I know the stories, but I can't help you if you do not want to listen.'

Something had registered with me. 'You called him Frank,' I said, turning to her. 'How well did you know him?'

Better than she was prepared to let on, I would say, judging by the way her eyes fell and she dropped her head. She moved gently to the table and stood on the other side from me, looking at the box of books.

'My family helped him buy this house,' she said.

A morning of surprises.

'He owned this?'

I didn't know why I'd not thought of it before. I had assumed he rented the house, that he wouldn't need another. As far as I knew he still had the old family house back in England. Family? Did I really remember it as such?

'And now it passes to you,' she said, and gave me a swift smile.

'You didn't tell me.'

'Is it for me to tell or you to ask?'

I felt like a new game was beginning. If I could keep her off talk of Frank and on talk about what he'd left me then maybe being stuck there would have a purpose. Perhaps I wouldn't need that photo assignment after all.

'You didn't tell me your name,' I said. I have no idea why that suddenly popped out of my mouth. I can only think that it was her smile encouraging me.

But she didn't reply. She just waited with that delicious twist in her lips until the penny dropped and I knew she was waiting for me to ask. Point taken.

'What should I call you, miss?' I asked, returning the smile.

'Stavroula.'

A name I had never heard before. Greek, obviously, and said with a deep, rich lilt to it, like she was singing it.

'Stavroula,' I repeated it to make sure I had heard correctly, and then I went far too far. 'Can I take you for a drink?'

She looked shocked for a second and then shook her head, sadly, I thought. I felt like I'd overstepped some mark but after what had happened that morning I also felt like I could do with a drink. Hair of the dog. The whisky bottle still had some in it but it didn't feel right, drinking at that time of the day in front of her. I took more interest in the room.

'What's the value of the house?' I asked, as I looked up at the ceiling. I hadn't noticed this before, but in the corners of the design, and around the edge, there were faces looking down at me, bodiless faces with large, round eyes staring vacantly towards the room. Had they always been there? This eerie collection of disembodied people clustered above my head. I looked away, towards the window. The window frame looked sound; the woodwork seemed to be in good condition. The house was small though, just this one room, a small, dark sitting room-come-study, a small kitchen across the hall, a bedroom next to that, towards the front, the courtyard and an outside bathroom that was little more than a shower block. Small, but old.

'What do you think I could get for it?'

She ignored me. 'He promised me something,' she said.

'What's that?'

'Are you willing to listen?'

'Is there someone who deals with property sales?'

'Are you prepared to listen?'

'Sure.'

She followed me into the hall and over to the kitchen where I inspected the cupboards more closely.

'Frank said he had faith in you.'

That gave me pause for thought. 'Faith in me?' I said through a laugh. 'Now that I find hard to believe. He used to kick me down when I was up and then kick me some more.'

'I don't understand.'

'I never did, either,' I said.

'I was some kind of disappointment to him I guess. There was... stuff.'

There is plenty of 'stuff' but nothing that, at that time, I was prepared to stop and think about, and certainly nothing I wanted to talk to her about. And yet I felt I could. I shivered, and ran my hand over the worktop. I wondered what repairs might need doing here; it was a way of derailing thoughts about me and Frank.

But her mind was clearly still on the same train of thought.

'He let us down. But he said you would succeed.'

Outside, distant, a bell started to toll.

'Succeed in what? Oh, in selling the house? You're right, I should go and find someone.'

I can't now think how it is possible for that sweet face of hers to look blank, but that's the only word to describe it. It was as if everything had gone from inside her, like all hope, all enthusiasm, any spark of joy. Sad, dull eyes now returned my hopeful smile.

'What's up?' I said, wondering what I had done to upset her.

'Maybe you will not succeed,' she said. She raised her head, listened to the bell. 'I go now to mourn with my friends.' She stepped back into the hall.

'What did I say?'

And then she left. I heard the door open and close and then the gate clang shut. I was left standing there, derailed myself. Bemused in this house. On this island. In this place, where seemingly cheerful, happy men stabbed themselves to death for no reason.

Leaning there against the sink, the whole situation felt so ludicrous to me. My long estranged father came to live in this place and care for its people, and they for him. And then, according to what I had read the night before, things started to turn nasty, people started to die, and yet he carried on living here until he himself died. And then, the strangest twist of all, he left me his few possessions, his work and his house. Me, of all people. Why?

Remembering Frank as I did, I knew there would be more to it than that. And I decided to go and find the lawyer's offices and ask for myself. There would have to be papers to sign, the deeds for example, so I made my mind up there and then to go and sort this out. I mean, I was stuck there. There was nothing to do in the house, the hangover was thankfully fading as the thought of owning a house crept in.

I got my camera gear together and headed out to seek someone in authority who could explain to me more about my inheritance.

5

Just when you thought a day could not get any stranger…

I was convinced that if I went slowly, if I took photos, then I would be able to use them to find my way back to the house again later. I was also convinced that I would have no trouble finding the person I was looking for, a lawyer surely, someone who knew what I needed to do about the house. I was also wary of anyone coming up behind me, thinking of the long-haired idiot and his silly little knife. On more than one occasion I was sure I'd heard him as I approached a corner, but turned it only to find another deserted lane ahead. I even once imagined he was running up behind me, convinced I'd heard his footsteps, but no, there was no one there.

I photographed several houses and ruins that had those numbers painted on them. They looked to be in the same style, the same font I suppose. All done with the same colour paint, uniformed. Relics of a previous occupation, she had said. Or something like that. I wondered which occupation.

The numbers were all out of sequence, but the sequence of photos would act as my route home. Who lived in building 1279? Was it a family? Number 2366 looked like it had once been a large building. Possibly someone rich lived there. What would they make of it now, the roof gone, the upper floors missing? And 579 was stencilled at an angle, hurriedly, a botch job on a stunning, grey stone lintel over an impressively grand doorway that led to a pile of weed-infested rubble. House number 1926 looked like it was still inhabited. It had, like my house (I like that, 'my' house, it has a rich ring to it), metal courtyard doors with grills in them and a bunch of dead, dried flowers hanging from it. The doors were orange. There was a large Greek letter, in metal, on the bottom panel of each one. I was crouching down to take a shot of one letter when, from the corner of my eye, a movement caught my attention.

Along the lane, right at the far end, just before a bend to the right, stood that old man and his boy who had, earlier, been waiting outside the closed café in the square. He, tall and gaunt, serious looking, was holding his son's hand, and the boy, angelic and round-eyed, was gazing at me. I turned the camera to them. They were silhouetted and had a wonderfully soft halo of sunlight behind them, and I just caught them as they turned and walked away.

There was something poignant in that moment. Being there among the ruins that spoke of wealth and happier days, seeing the hollow faces of homes tattooed with official numbers and painted with letters of hope and superstition. It was tranquil, mysterious and sad, like one big graveyard.

I pulled myself together and stood. One more shot of the door knocker and I'd move on. I switched to macro and came close in. The knocker was in the shape of a hand, a slim, slender, lady's hand with a ring on one finger. It was made of brass which needed cleaning, and there were small flecks of paint flaking off around it. A layer of paint fallen off revealed another colour beneath, like many layers of history on one door. I focused, my finger over the shutter release when:

'The Khamsa.'

A voice directly behind me, right in my ear. I spun around, flattened myself against the door and cried out.

Totally shocked. Not only by the fact that I had not heard this person creep up behind me, but also by the person herself.

'Yes,' she said, studying my reaction intently and very close up, 'I do this to people.'

Ten

She held out a hand and I wondered how on earth she kept it up with so many rings on her fingers, so many bangles on her wrist. I looked from them to her face. It was pale, a stark contrast to her long and wild, deep red hair. Her green eyes were piercing, searching, and her lips were the brightest red, the colour of a sports car.

'The Khamsa,' she went on. 'The hand of Fatima. Placed here to ward away evil, to bring luck and prosperity to the house. Yes?'

She had an accent. German?

A jangle of light metal, her hand was waiting to be taken. I took it, shook it and let it go. It was cold.

'You believe the superstitions?' she asked, looking over my shoulder now at the door knocker. 'You collect them. You are here to study the events as well? No, you are not.'

She looked back at me again, and looked me up and down, blatantly.

'But it is true. They use the Khamsa here. It means, literally, five; five fingers, sometimes up and open to the palm, here downwards, but still five. Numbers, always numbers in superstitions. It came from across the sea, Israel, the Holy Land, Muslim countries, Arabia, they all have the similar thing, the same superstitions. It is Fatima's hand, or Miriam's, or the hand of Mary. Here on this island they truly believe that this will keep away the bad luck. Is true, yes?'

'I guess,' I stammered. Who was she?

'No.' Her expression changed. She had been jovial before and now she was serious. 'Is all trash. It is simply here to knock on the door. Yes? Simply this. Knock, knock, who's there? Hello. It is Helen.'

A brief silence between us. I was expected to do or say something. To be honest my heart was still pounding and my brain was still trying to settle after a quick shake-up.

'Ah yes.' I got it. She was introducing herself. I did the same. 'Chris.'

'Christopher,' she said, and closed her eyes tightly for a second then opened them. 'Who carried the Christ across the river. Saint of travellers. Are you a saint, I wonder? No matter, is all pappekak, as we say. Some of us.'

She turned to face the lane and as she did so she slipped her arm through the crook of mine with what looked like well-practised ease and started to lead me away.

'Walk with me,' she said, and there was no arguing. 'There are no handsome men left alive to be seen with.'

I wasn't quite sure how to take that.

'I am looking for a lawyer,' I said.

'I am crazy to you?' she cut in. 'Yes? But this is good. It is good to be a little crazy, especially in these days, in these times. Let us be crazy while we still can, yes?'

I couldn't place the accent. Whatever it was it was tainted with British. Once German, or Dutch, maybe even Danish, but now watered down.

Her arm gripped mine tighter as she led me along the lane.

'There are many crazy superstitions here,' she went on. 'They love to scare away evil things. The flowers? You see them? Dead on the door. They are alive in May, usually, they stay on the door until a feast day, August, I think. It is all to do with pagans and churches. I don't follow it. But it is a national pastime, keeping away evil things. At Easter, here, they blow things up. Ker-boom. Dynamite. They even burn a man as Judas.'

'What?'

'Oh, not a real one. Not yet at least. It is Easter soon. You are staying? I hope so. Look, it is spring but nothing grows, have you noticed?'

'Well…' It had crossed my mind. 'Look, Helen..?' Was that her name?

'It is spring, and yet everything is dying when it should be coming to life. Bad things.' Her face fell then and her eyes lost their focus. It was as if they were looking inside and not out towards me.

'Door knockers not working then,' I quipped, to lighten her mood.

She loved it. 'Ah, good, a fellow cynic.'

We stopped walking. Actually, she stopped us and stepped in front of me, looking once more into my eyes very deeply. I could see wrinkles around hers. She appeared young, but thanks to her artistic makeup interpretation, and I was convinced she was older than she looked. She spoke with the cheerful enthusiasm of someone who is hiding something, almost believable, not quite false, yet with a cheerfulness that felt as if it had no foundation; a façade built on sand, as Frank might have said.

I could tell she loved life from the way she took an interest in what she saw. There was something dynamic about her presence. Normally I wouldn't like someone standing so close 'in my space', as they say. But with her it felt fine.

'Not a tourist,' she said. She crossed her arms over what I noticed was a freckled cleavage with a string of beads resting around it, framing it rather neatly. The top she was wearing was bright, patterned, and with that and the beads and bangles she looked like a market stall selling accessories.

'Not a tourist, no,' she went on. 'None come these days. Here to live, perhaps, but then, why? Why? Why? Why?' She repeated it as if she was trying to figure out a riddle. 'Not a fellow investigator… Possibly a journalist?'

'I am a photographer,' I said, and held up the rather obvious camera.

'Everyone is a photographer in these digital days.' She dismissed my profession in one clattering swoop of her arm.

'And you?' I was rather taken aback and was ready to put down her own profession in a moment. Artist? Writer? General busybody? Man-eater. All came to mind.

'Ah,' she said, pointing at me. 'Do not run screaming.' She stepped in even closer, whispered in my ear, intimate and invasive. 'Psychologist. At least I was, I still research and learn, observe and investigate.'

Not what I was expecting.

'Investigate what?' I whispered back.

She stepped away, looked me up and down once more.

'My God!' she said, as if suddenly realising something really obvious. 'It is you. Christopher.'

'I'm sorry? What do you mean?'

Her hand went to her mouth and she ran a long, purple, fingernail across her bottom lip, looking at the ground, thinking.

'I'm sorry?' I repeated, but she hushed me with the palm of her hand.

She looked back up, into my eyes. 'Come with me,' she said. 'I will show you.'

5

Along that lane further, around a corner or two, starting to lose my bearings again, we came across a house. Shutters closed, gates closed, the building blanked out and silent. A lone, white sheet fluttered from a window. A sign of some sort? Helen saw I was looking at it and wondering.

'A death. Sit,' she said, indicating a low wall, wasteland behind it.

I sat and looked at the house, noticed how the sheet was rippling in a very faint breeze, noticed the wreath of dead flowers on the door, the dripping, painted letters on the wall.

'You have heard of the deaths.' She said this as a statement not a question. 'So many deaths and all by their own hands. So many and in one small place.'

'I see,' I said. 'And this is what you are studying? So, what is your conclusion?'

'That some kind of ancient evil has been disturbed and is stalking the island, growing stronger with every life it takes. Gaining strength with every suicide.'

I looked at her, startled. Like I keep saying: not what I was expecting. She didn't look at me but her face was serious now, almost stern. She looked across the lane to the closed up house.

'A curse has returned to the island,' she began. 'A force that grips people, takes them, makes them kill themselves. They fall into depression first, and then finally give up. They kill themselves horribly. Violently. And eventually the island declines and nearly dies.

'Last week the woman who lived in this house, a mother, not old, with a child, she too gave up. You are going to die, you have had enough, so what do you do? How do you do it?

'She was prepared. She put down something on the floor in the kitchen, a sheet, plastic from the table cover. She sat looking across her neat kitchen to her fridge, the pictures drawn by her child, the magnets, the bright letters. The child learning to read, the signs of hope and future.

'She picked up the knife for bread. You can see her face, blank, nothing there, all life already gone, all hope left. Perhaps a tear on her cheek because inside us we all know that when we do this we do wrong. We all know that it could have been better. We could have taken a different path. Somewhere we have hope still flickering inside like an ember of a fire that has been left untended through the night. But she cannot find this dying ember, though she wishes she could. She cries for her loss of dignity.

'She moves her arm out, over the bucket she has put on the plastic. She takes her knife and rests it on her wrist.

'She starts to saw, back and forth, she feels nothing. Back and forth. Deeper into her arm. First the skin, it breaks, it splits, it bleeds into the bucket. And then into the flesh deeper, through the veins, through the artery, into the bone. Back and forth. Back and forth...'

I was watching Helen now. She had a tear rolling on her cheek, she was looking blankly ahead, she was making the sawing movements across her own arm with the side of her hand. It was as if she was that woman. That quite clearly mad and suicidal woman who had killed herself in that house.

'She was not mad.' It was like she'd read my thoughts. She turned to me, shook her head, shook out the story, and smiled again. 'She was quite sane, they say. She was a practical woman, of course. She was practical, she was a woman. And yet... We must ask, why? Why do people do this now?'

She was expecting an answer. 'I have no idea,' I managed to say.

She reached into her pocket. I heard money jangling in there.

'Because,' she said, fixing me with those eyes, 'because hell is missing a soul. An ancient, foul soul that escaped hell. And now that restless soul has been woken, and its evil is taking hold of the island and will not rest until that soul is put where it has always belonged.'

She took hold of my hand, pulled it towards her, gripped it tightly with cold, bony fingers.

My heart was beating fast in my chest and, I can admit it now, she was actually scaring me.

I felt her open the palm of my hand, felt something cold placed there. But I couldn't take my eyes from hers.

'It will kill us all,' she said, and let go of my hand.

I looked down at a palm full of money. She'd placed several euro coins there, too many for me to hold, and as she moved her hand away some fell to the ground, clattering on the stones. I looked back at her.

And now she was laughing. 'No.' She shook her head and touched the coins in my hand with a long finger. 'No ancient evil. No hell missing a soul.' More laughter. 'The economic disaster of this country is causing people to die. Everything else is pappekak.'

Relief. I had almost started to believe her.

'You were starting to sound like that Greek woman, Stavroula,' I said.

'Who? I do not know this person. It is never mind. But this is fascinating, yes? These stories they are telling. This is what they are believing.'

'I know. She thinks there's something here that I can help with, some stories in the history of the island, something like that. She thinks there is a...' what would the word be? '...a supernatural reason that the island is dying.'

'Oh, they are right; it is dying, for sure. Yes. Oh, my God!' Again Helen surprised me with the change in her voice. Back to serious. 'The whole country is dying, and yes, there is a curse.'

She was playing with me. I didn't know what to make of her, one moment solemn, the next cynical, then laughing, now thoughtful.

'You believe there is a curse?' I could hardly believe I was asking it.

'Yes.' She nodded. 'There is. I can tell you what it is. Do you want to know?'

Did I?

'Go on.'

'It is the curse of bad government,' she said. 'That is all. That is what is killing these people.'

'Your academic conclusion?'

'One, yes. I saw it on the news; the country is given lots of money, they give it away, pay too many wages, employ too many people to do nothing, the state looks after everyone and everyone is happy. Utopia. But money must be paid back and back it comes, from the same people, who have spent it. And so we have people with no money and lots of debts and no way to pay it back and we have big pressures. So we see deaths in Athens and the main cities, and I ask why this happens, and does it happen more now because of this reason? I find that, yes, a little in Athens it is higher, and there is more people so more poverty, more hardship, and so more people take extreme measures. And then I look at the islands and see alarming number here, in this one small place, and my mind is hooked, you say, yes? So we... I come here and I look and ask, and I think there is value in this study.'

She gripped my arm again and a few more coins fell from my hand.

'But here I can find no reason. This is not Athens, this is not the same problems here, so why?' She let me go.

'What you must know, Christopher, is that suicide is a solution. It is just one solution to many problems and it is the one that people are choosing. I tell this to Frank, but he is not listening. Was not listening. Did not hear me. This village, this island, has many problems, I think, and so it must find a solution. Yes? It has found this one. There it is. It is so.'

She took the coins back from my hand, then, leaning in too close, I could smell her perfume in the breeze. I couldn't place it.

'We will have drinks later,' she said, and stood up. 'You will find the main square, the one that still has a kafeneion open. Now I go.'

And with that she went. I mean she just upped and started to walk away, didn't even pick up the coins that had spilled onto the ground.

'Wait,' I called after her. 'You knew Frank?'

'Of course,' she called back over her shoulder. 'Everyone knew Frank. As crazy as the rest!' She rounded the corner and was gone.

'You're not wrong there,' I mumbled to myself as I picked up the last of the coins and counted them; only a couple of euros' worth. I decided I would give them back to her later when we met for a drink, which, apparently, we were going to do. There was no arguing, clearly. She was like a schoolteacher who decrees this is what you will do, but forgets to tell you how, where or when.

I looked back at the house. Did someone really choose to kill themselves in that way, and leaving behind her child too?

The thought, or the breeze, or a cloud passing the sun, made me shiver with cold then. I realised I was hungry. Not only that, but I had failed to ask if she knew of this solicitor person. I decided food was needed and headed back to the house. I'd not travelled too far but it still took me a while, and several looks at the camera and photo record, to retrace my steps and find my way home.

Once there I plugged the camera into the laptop and changed the laptop battery for the spare I'd brought. This was pretty low on juice as well, but at least there was something there. I set it to downloading. I'd still not been through yesterday's images and there were more I wanted to look at. My mind mulled over superstitions and 'hands of Fatima' as I waited. The progress was strangely slow again so I reckoned that I'd leave it and use the time to find something to eat.

Had I known what I was going to see on those images I would have switched it all off there and then.

Eleven

Looking around the kitchen, I was wondering who had cleared up after Frank, or whether he had really lived such a Spartan life. I was going to make a cup of coffee with some of the meagre supplies I'd bought but there was something not quite right about the kettle. There had been something in it at one point but now there was just a bed of furry stuff and a very unpleasant smell. Then, as I was dumping it in a bag ready to be thrown out, I remembered that there had been no power in the morning. Trying the switches I found it was the same now.

Checking in the hallway I found a fuse box, but all the switches were in the same position. I tried them the other way, in case, but still no power. It was still daytime so I wasn't yet unduly worried, but decided I should find some candles before it got dark, perhaps even a torch.

Looking in the kitchen again, I found a calendar in one of the otherwise empty drawers. It was produced locally, a church fund-raiser by the looks of the images of saints, icons and churches that came with each month. I flicked through it idly until I came to June.

What I saw made me stop in my tracks. A red circle around 6th June and the words, in Frank's hand: "Ben's birthday." How on earth did he find that out? I'd not spoken to him since I was sixteen and walked out. He'd not made any contact with me, not even then.

I flicked over to the following month and there, again circled, was, "Christopher's birthday."

Perfectly reasonable signs of domesticity and family life. I imagined the calendar hanging on Frank's kitchen wall and him looking at it each time he passed, or opened the fridge, or made a note on his shopping list. Like that was at all likely.

I chucked it across the room and let it flap itself into the corner.

And that's when it suddenly struck me. The date, or rather the day.

I headed back to the sitting room, dug out my mobile and saw two bars on the signal line. Dialling quickly, I wandered the room in the hope that the signal might get better, but no, still weak. But the line did connect. I waited for Sarah to pick up, which she did on the third ring. There was a brief moment of static and I said 'Hello?' but then nothing, just the echo of my voice coming back at me, bounced from some satellite overhead I guess.

I checked the bar; no signal again. But at least the call would register on her phone, she'd know I was trying to get hold of her, perhaps she'd call back and leave me a message. Perhaps she would know something was wrong. Well, she would in a day or so when I didn't get back as planned.

So, what to do? My eyes fell on the books and papers on the table and then moved swiftly to the empty bottle. I wasn't going back into all that without a drink inside me. It wasn't too early for a drink and Helen had said she would meet me for one later, so there must be some kind of bar open.

I switched memory cards on the camera, set the last load of images to download and headed out.

5

The lanes and crumbling ruins of this village capture you in some strange way. When she, the Greek girl, said that they wouldn't let me out, or whatever it was she did say, she was right. They have some strange kind of hold over you. I set out from the house and had no trouble finding the shop, and then a simple, straight road-come-lane led me right into the heart of the village. No problem; as if the village itself wanted me to find my way this time. I say the heart of the village, but I am only guessing because this square was larger than any of the others I'd seen. There was an open space with houses around that didn't look completely ruined, apart from one. And there was a café with some chairs outside it. It looked a bit run down and unloved, but there, outside, was Helen drinking something orange and vibrant from a tall glass and writing in a notebook. This was about an hour after I'd last seen her. She waved me over cheerfully and I sat, ordering a beer from a tall, disinterested boy who could have been no more than fifteen.

Sitting, I tried the signal on the mobile again, but if anything it was worse there and the one bar kept coming and going. I gave up and put it on the table.

'It's a curse,' Helen said, not looking up from the notes she was making. 'It is the same with the power, on off, on off. I have the same. Everyone has the same. No phone service at the moment, so thus, therefore, and here we have the answer: an evil curse is invading from somewhere. It grows more angry, excuse my English, and so it cuts off communications for the island, yes?'

'Pappekak?' I said with a smile, but she wasn't smiling.

'No. It is so. This is how it is.'

'I don't know when you are being serious and when you are not.' I didn't.

She made it easy for me. 'Let me face you with a choice, then,' she said, at last putting her notes aside and looking up. 'We have no telephone network right now. A supernatural curse, or repair work to the radio masts?'

'Repair work, clearly.'

'And there we have it. But for some here this is too modern an answer. They don't understand. Either that, or they prefer to see a curse of some supernatural variety than to realise a problem with the power company or the phone services. I ask myself, can it really be superstitions like this, still, today? But which way you swing we still have no signal. It is only just one of those things, yes? One of those crazy things.'

She winked at me.

'But,' I said, pulling in my chair, 'is there something else? A way to call home? A landline, the internet, something? I have this job to get to and I'm going to miss it, and I need to let them know or I screw up a whole contract.'

'What day?'

'Friday.'

'If there is a boat it will come on this day. Where is this appointment?'

'London.'

'Then you are, as you say, right royally screwed up.'

'That's not the half of it. She is going to kill me.'

She laughed. I didn't. She clearly had not met Sarah. I had said I would be back by Friday and now there was no way I was going to manage that and, currently, no way of letting her know.

Helen must have seen my blank expression.

'You don't find this funny?' she asked.

'No, not one bit. You don't know my ex-wife.'

'This is true. But how easily we take death into our joking. How easily we talk about death, and yet... It fascinates me, yes?'

'Clearly.'

'She is going to kill you. Is she really?'

'Well...'

'No, she is not going to kill you.'

My beer arrived with a heavy clank of glass against metal as it hit the table. The boy wandered off and I could hear a television or radio inside playing a sport event of some kind.

'We take death so easily for granted,' Helen went on. 'Think, how often do we say, I am going to kill you! Or, I nearly died! Or, I would rather kill myself than... You see? I would rather stick pins in my eyes. Would we really?'

I got the impression that this was her favourite subject.

'We say things like, I would rather...' She put her drink aside with distaste and indicated it. 'Rather drink this *stront* than do X and Y. You see? Would we? Really?' She lent in closer to me, infringing on my space again.

'No,' I answered her, feeling slightly uncomfortable.

'It is the hardest thing to do, to take your own life. Imagine, how would you do it?'

'Well... I've never thought about it.' More uncomfortable now.

'There is no other solution, no other way out. You must end your life. So, do you take a knife and cut a wrist? This way, by the way.'

She cut lengthways through her arm with an imaginary blade.

'Not this way.'

She cut across it.

'This way you must dig in, gouge out. Very complicated. This way is for show only. So you cut your arm this way. Good, you do not mind the blood, you are mindful of the mess, like our mother in that house, who did gouge out by the way. But this way is too long, you give yourself too much time to regret your action, to change your mind. So, you take poison. Also very brave. Again pain, again mess. Vomit.'

Feeling distinctly queasy, my mind desperately trying to block out the flesh-crawling pictures she evoked, I looked away and around, hoping no one else could hear this. She was speaking more enthusiastically than quietly.

'Or you fall from a great height.'

She had my attention again.

'A very great height. You look down, rocks below, the sea perhaps, the street, wherever. It is a long way and you wonder if it will hurt. Should you close your eyes? Take off your glasses? Most people do.'

I could picture that too. It's always been the way I thought I would go. I would confront my fear of heights, the vertigo, whatever it is called, by standing there and doing that thing which, when I think of it, jolts me back to the real world. I would jump, fall, just to see what it was really like, just to see what the attraction was.

And in a flash I was back at that place, on that day, the day it all changed. The sun, the stones, that little innocent plant alone among the rocks, bending slightly, silently, in a breeze…

'It takes so much strength to do this,' she was saying. I took a breath to clear the flashback from my mind. 'And yet we take death so easily into our joking. Sad. It is so.'

I noticed again that finality to her debate; always there. Always it was so. It was as she has stated. So let it be done.

I sipped my beer. It was lager, and warm.

'How many suicides have there been?' I asked.

'Many, many. The island has many troubles, so it needs many solutions.' She shook her head. 'And so, also, they make it easier. There are many troubles, so this difficult task of dying is made easier by putting the blame over there.'

She meant nowhere in particular, just away.

'Over there with Frank's meddlings which woke their evil. It is just another solution.'

'So, you mean...' This sounded particularly stupid to me. 'So you mean, people are pissed off at the state their country is in, so the only way they can cope is to kill themselves, and so they... No, this is ridiculous.'

'It is how it is.' That statement of fact again. 'They have only this way out and so they find a reason to justify it. In other places in the country they blame the government more openly, they riot. In some they blame the schools, the church, who knows? I do know there has been a huge rise in suicides in Greece since the economic problems. I have the numbers at home, I show you if you like.'

'OK,' I said, 'I can understand that. But, blaming Frank? Blaming my father?'

'Ah, yes, but because of what he discovered. This is their way out. They believe in what he discovered, what he aroused.'

She had moved right in, her knee was touching mine. It didn't feel right and yet it felt interestingly dangerous. Like something I wanted to respond to, something I wanted to do, and yet it was something I knew I shouldn't do.

Her knee pressed against mine.

A signal?

I was about to respond when she said, 'But I do not

understand this strange thing.' I realised she was still on the same tack and probably hadn't even realised she was touching my leg.

'What strange thing?' I said, sitting back and reaching for my beer again. I moved my leg away from hers.

'Frank,' she said, looking up and out. 'Why him as well? He had money, he had means, there was no crisis for him as there is no crisis for me. This is not how I believed the man to be.'

I could feel my stomach turn over and I turned cold inside.

'What do you mean?'

She looked back at me. 'You do not know?'

'Know what?'

'You are his son and yet you do not think to ask how he died? Your father also took his own life.'

That was just plain ridiculous. That was not Frank, pure and simple. Frank would never be so accommodating. He was too precious to himself, too selfish to take his own life. He was too important.

All kinds of feelings started bubbling up inside me at that moment when I realised that she was completely serious. This man, my father, who had spouted all kinds of doctrine about everything from communion to Catholics, had always maintained that life was sacred and to take one's own was the ultimate sin.

'No way,' was about as fluent as I could manage at that moment.

She remained calm. She sipped her drink, grimaced, and slid one jewelled hand over mine as she lowered her head and spoke conspiratorially.

'He made me wonder,' she started. Not a word of apology for throwing that shocking news at me. 'Maybe what is happening here is not just "one of those things." Maybe there is some explaining in his work? Perhaps, yes? Maybe you should ask the Greek lady you mentioned. I think so.'

She gripped my hand tighter. 'If nothing else, it will help you understand his death, and this you must do. For your own sake.'

I didn't know what to say. I didn't need to. She looked at her watch and at the sky.

'It is a nice day,' she said. 'A little cold, but good day for a walk. I say, go and find your Stavroula and do what she wants. Listen. Ask her some more questions. You need to come to terms with this, and this way may be of help to you, yes?'

It seemed to make sense. I was shocked, and I had had enough of her teacher's voice her telling me that everything 'was so.' A walk sounded good; clear my head, take some shots, find out more about Frank.

In a way, I knew then that I had no other choice. I knew I had started on a path to somewhere and there was no way off it until I understood why my father had taken his own life.

Twelve

On the mountainside high up she walks silently through the makeshift graves, the small shrines, the roughly hewn wooden crosses that mark places where her friends now lie. She looks down to see the face of a child she once held smiling back up from a photograph placed there for remembrance, a photograph taken when the child was happy, unaware of what was about to come. Candles are alight inside tin lanterns with glass windows, oil, wicks, matches, all supplied in case a flame should die. Flames mean memories, and they stay burning, protected by the glass, to keep the dead living in the minds and hearts of those who remain. She kneels to the dead flowers that lie beside it, withered and dried in age as they do and should, flowers plucked young and sweet. She remembers, they were the last few flowers of winter; none have grown this spring.

She kneels among the graves and wonders what will become of her as the soft breeze lifts from the valley below. It sidles up the hillside to toy playfully with her hair. She looks out towards the sea, far distant and glittering, the sea that protects and feeds the island but also holds it captive. Then, she looks back to the graves, the suicides' graves hurriedly dug here, outside the grounds of the church, here at the end of the path above the village, away, out of sight. Away from the parents who have buried their children, away from the fathers who have said goodbye to their sons, away from the children who, like her, have all too soon seen their parents taken from them.

Standing, she walks softly towards two wooden crosses and looks down at the photos. Two simple images, one per shrine.

They move slightly in the breeze, the dried flowers protecting the souls who cannot yet rest. She is sad, the whole island is sad, and yet, looking back towards the village, she knows there is hope. Just a faint glimmer of it, just a small light in a long, dark night-time, but a hope nonetheless.

She stands and waits for him to come.

5

He makes his way through the lanes, more confident now. He knows where he is going. He knows where he walks but he has no idea what he is walking through. What he has walked into. His mind is reeling; he has finally let part of it open up and is now starting to think about what he has here. He has questions. So many questions. And when he turns to someone for help he simply gets more.

You can hear his thoughts: 'Frank killed himself. Why? He'd never do that.'

Images flash into his head: Frank in his vestments, spouting, shouting, spitting words of Christ and God, and things the boy Chris who is too young to understand. An image of a woman, his mother, high on a cliff edge. Why? What is she doing up there? Why is father shouting at him? He should be shouting at her to come down. It's dangerous up there. So high. But why? How can it be Chris' fault?

'It wasn't my fault. It was nothing to do with me, I was only six years old.'

His troubled mind turns fast to things long forgotten. Is it the lanes that make him think this way? Is there something in the stone that draws his worse memories from him, or is it this talk of Frank?

'Why here Frank? What were you doing buying a house and living here?'

He turns a corner. He looks up briefly, he is looking for her. But where? Where would she be? He knows nothing about her except her name and her job. Where would she be?

'Searching? What truth was he searching for this time? And why?'

He remembers how Frank left. First his mother, then his father, both gone in separate directions, both gone in different ways. First one and then the other. Where did Frank go all those years? No contact. 'All these years, no contact and then suddenly...'

A house, his now, with nothing in it apart from research. Journals he doesn't want to read. Books he can't be bothered reading. His father's legacy is a pile of notes and papers, and tapes and images scribbled in a bad hand on pages of words that make no sense.

Research into what?

'Maybe some explaining in his work?' she had said. What did she mean by that? Helen admits to having doubts and she's a scientist. She came to look for truth and found superstition, and now, now, she thinks here's something in Frank's work. What was he doing here? What drove him to kill himself?

Again that knowledge: 'Frank would not kill himself without a very good reason.'

Ah, the thought has taken root and started to germinate. He is starting to be doubtful too. It started with 'Frank wouldn't take his own life,' and now he has added, 'Without a good reason.'

What was that reason?

The cracks are starting to appear in the thin veneer of his

scepticism. Fault lines begin to show in the delicate outer shell of his reason, like crackle glaze running in frantic, confused patterns.

'Listen. Ask her some more questions,' she had said. He knows she is right.But where is she?

He looks at his feet as he walks, careful not to trip on the uneven stones, on the unmatched steps as he climbs higher into the village. There is no one to ask. Houses are shut up and those with open shutters have closed windows. He passes one, a white sheet hanging from a closed window as if the people inside have surrendered.

Surrendered to what?

Another turn, another lane, and still his thoughts tumble over. 'Why leave me a house after all this time? What do you want from me?'

He asks it in his head as if he is talking to his father, the man he has not seen for so many years. He wonders how it would be if this was twenty years hence and he was Ben, and Ben were here. But that would never happen. Chris would never become like his father, he would never leave his son all that time. He would not be like Frank.

He might not be able to live with him every day now, but at least he and Sarah kept some kind of civility so that Ben would not suffer. 'But he has been suffering,' he thinks. 'Thanks to her. Okay, so me too. Thanks to us, Ben must have suffered.'

Thanks to us.

The cracking continues.

He thinks of his son's bad dreams of late, his nightmares, his strange drawings. He remembers the drawing he has with him, the one he nearly threw away, just as his own father would have done. The drawing rings bells, lights a spark, a flame.

Something flickers at the back of his mind. But that's not for now. These dark thoughts are for later. He knows he must keep the house, for Ben. He must return Frank's work home, for Ben, for his future, for when he wants to know about his grandfather. He must see through the next few days until the boat returns and then he must go home to Ben, taking Frank's legacy with him. Ownership of a house on a far-flung island in a dying country, and… and what? Some journals he has only yet flicked through.

His thoughts go round in circles.

'Some explaining in his work.'

Explaining of what? These locals killing themselves? What's that to do with him?

'A supernatural curse,' she had said. These people honestly believed that Frank had found something on their island that was, what? Spreading among them and making them take their own lives?

He laughs out loud to cover the cracks and realises he is near the very top of the village.

His thoughts are so loud they echo in the lanes and bounce back at him. He stops dead in his tracks. There are no thoughts in his head now, and yet he still hears them. He hears something. He looks around sharply behind, as if he knows we are following him.

Keep still, think quietly, he is starting to doubt things usually certain. He doesn't know it yet but the creeping fronds of acceptance have started to grow within him. And so we must whisper quietly or he will scare. See, he waits, breathing hard, fast, nervous. Don't scare him. Keep still.

We need him.

Thirteen

One of the reasons I am taking so much time to write all this down is for Ben, so that he will know what happened when I went to his grandfather's island where the house came from, what my "adventure" was like. At least, that is how it started. Now I find I am using the pages of this book (one of Frank's old journals, ironically enough, one he only wrote a few pages in, perhaps his last?) to clear my head. Put my thoughts in order. Get things out of my system. To try and understand the history of this place.

But, in order:

I found her outside the village at the start of a path that inclined slightly up hill. The looming, dark mountain brooded above me and the last of the claustrophobic village lanes fell away behind me. I have no idea why I walked up that way. My mind was full of other stuff, but, before I knew it, I was on the very last set of steps from the village and there she was, standing above me on the path as if she was expecting me. I clambered up the last few steps, out of breath and sweating.

'You are ready to hear the stories?' she asked, as soon as I reached her. It was like I had kept her waiting and she wasn't best pleased.

My chest was sore and all I could do was nod. I tried to make it look reluctant but it was an urgent nod and made me look enthusiastic. It was urgent because I was gasping for air, but she gave me no time to wait. 'We walk,' she said, and that was it.

We walked a few paces and she seemed nervous, like she was unwilling to start on whatever it was she was going to tell me.

She opened her mouth to speak and looked at me, closed it, and smiled.

'I am sorry,' she said. 'Shall we sit for a while?'

We sat on a low wall and she seemed happier then, looking down to a fertile valley that sloped gently away to the small bay where I had arrived. There were fewer boats; more people had left, I assumed. The sea was polished, the sun reflected from it, the air was brittle and cold against my hot face, and everything suggested spring, except the valley was brown, still barren from the previous hot summer.

'You have read about the history of our island, you have read what Frank discovered about the legend? What is happening here?' She could see I had not and her face fell, stern. 'Have you read his books?' She sounded like a teacher asking if I'd done my homework.

'I glanced through them,' I replied, and it was not a lie. I had done just that. I've noted a couple of things that I saw in them, but to be honest, at that point, I couldn't remember what they were about. 'A jumble of notes and history and theories, drawings of stuff, dates, it made no sense to me.'

'It will,' she said, 'if you let it.'

That felt like a telling off. She was taking a bit of a strict tack with me I thought, and, to be honest, I didn't mind. There was something cute about the way she was trying her hardest to chastise me. I saw the sun on her face, wisps of her long hair catch in the breeze, and a faint flicker of a smile on her lips.

'Yours is a very attractive island,' I said, not looking at the view.

'It is a small island with a big history,' she replied. 'Will you hear some of it?'

'And a bit mysterious,' I said, wondering if I dare touch her.

The breeze had blown that delicate wisp of hair across her eye. 'Mysterious but somehow captivating.' I reached out to move it away for her.

She immediately stood up and walked off a pace.

Too much too soon, I thought.

'Sorry, I was only...'

'No,' she cut in. 'I am sorry. This is not possible.'

So, she knew what I was thinking, then? 'Not on this island, not for a local girl like me. It is not possible for unmarried girls...'

'I understand,' I said, and stood up. 'Sorry, I was wrong. I didn't mean anything by it.'

She flicked the hair away from her eye and gave me that smile again. A small, faint but deliberate movement at the corner of her mouth that seemed to suggest all kinds of things and yet gave nothing away.

'It is a shame,' she said. 'But this is how it must be.'

'A shame?'

She didn't reply, just looked down modestly.

'It is a shame,' I agreed. 'Because I see an... island I could so easily fall for.'

She looked down onto the village below, the jumble of old houses close together, brown roofs, silent church towers, gaps in the maze where the ruins stand, and no order to anything.

'But our island has much history,' she said. 'And, unlike your father, you do not care for our history.'

'I am starting to care more for it,' I said, feeling that there was at least some hope here. I didn't feel as if she was playing games, just that, well, that there was some attraction and she felt it too.

'That is good,' she said, and I could see her smiling to herself as she surveyed the houses below. 'Because I think our island sees you in its future.'

'Really?'

Did she mean she could see me in hers?

'Yes.'

She opened her hand to the valley below, indicated it and the sea in the distance.

'If you would learn some of its many mysteries. Solve its troubles.'

Before I could think of a reply she said, 'May I ask a thing?'

'Sure.'

'Why do you not honour your father?'

I didn't want to go there. I didn't want her to know, but she turned directly to me and her smile caught me off guard.

'It's a long story,' I bluffed.

But the flashback was already hitting me: the rocks, the cliff. Where were we? It was warm. A camping trip? An adventure, a treasure hunt? What was it? Warm day, warm feeling, everything running smoothly. After church. A Sunday, Frank looking down at me, but he is not smiling.

'See what you have done!' he is shouting at me. What have I done?

'Pray for her.' Why, what? Pray for who? I look up, and there, high up on the cliff, is my mother looking down at me. A small speck at the top of an impossibly high wall.

'A very long story,' I said, and Stavroula simply nodded.

'Whatever it is you must close this history,' she said. 'Do something to help you forgive, forget. Honour him. Finish his work.'

'His work? You mean... what exactly?'

'Frank found the truth buried in a legend. He found the clues through history, but he did not live to complete the journey.'

'What journey?'

'Remember this,' she said, 'an open mind is of more use than a closed book.'

She started walking, up the slight hill, away from the village towards a bend in the road, a fold in the mountain. I walked with her, listening reluctantly as she spoke.

'Your father came here before many years.' (She meant 'some years ago'. I like the way she speaks but sometimes must translate her sentences.) 'He had been travelling, he said. He had been to Israel, and around Jordan and other places, I think. He arrived one summer evening on the ferry with one suitcase and a big bag full of books. My family helped him find a place to live and then helped him to buy the house. He said he was here to work and had much to do. He became friends with the museum curator. It is now closed. The curator's only surviving son has the key and no one goes there. The ministry will not pay for it to be opened when there are no visitors.

'Frank worked hard. He went into the churches, he spoke with our Papas, he knew our language. Not our dialect, at first, but he learned that as well, and he became part of the community. But all he did was work. And read, write, walk the village, ask questions about our history. We all assumed he was a historian working on a book about our country. It was nothing special.

'Then he became more agitated, for a while, and after that he locked himself away in his house.

'And then it started happening. It started with one or two businesses closing, doing badly, bringing down the owners to despair. The crisis, we thought. But then, more deaths, and such ways to die! And people who had so many things to live for. This started before only a few months, and the closer we come to Paska, Easter, the stronger it becomes.

'Frank knew what it was. He told me that he had discovered something and he realised too late what it was. But he did not share the knowledge. He said it was guilt. He said he had caused this and only he could stop it from happening. And we in the village are saying no, it is not you, you are not to blame, but he takes the guilt and says he is. He insists. And he locks himself away in his house, he makes notes and he only comes out to look up at buildings, to talk into his machine and record his thoughts.'

She stopped and looked at me intently. 'And that is where the answer lies. In his thoughts. His books, his machine.'

We were at the bend in the road.

'Answer to what, exactly?'

'He believed that something came to our island many hundreds of years ago, when there was trade, when the Roman empire extended here, when Emborios was the main port and the island was thriving, teaming with life, covered in trees, when we built ships. Something was brought here for gain, for the wrong reasons, something powerful and dangerous that no one understood. Something that he was trying to find. A thing of great value.'

She looked straight into my eyes.

'He found it. And now our island is dying.'

There was something over her shoulder in the near distance, something I couldn't quite make out. I felt she was blocking my view on purpose.

'This is what he left for you to discover, to work out, to find. He told me himself that only you would be able to finish this. You have to accept what he wanted.'

She was starting to become desperate now. She was pleading.

'I don't understand,' I said. What was that behind her? What were those?

'The longer it lives the stronger it becomes.'

'What does?' A collection of... something, a group of, what?

'The longer it lives the closer he comes to us and the more will die.'

I stepped past her and saw.

'Oh, my God!'

She had led me to a graveyard. A muddle of rough wooden crosses, small and surrounded by candles, pieces of paper, flowers. A makeshift cemetery up here, on the edge of the mountain.

The edge of the path. Height. I looked to my left. The path dropped away steeply. It ended at the edge of the cliff.

A cliff. My mother, high up above me. The clouds racing over her head. Rocks. A long way down.

My legs weak. She had brought me to his grave. It was suddenly real.

Frank was here. He was in that ground. Just there. Dead.

'I'm sorry,' I muttered, backing away from the edge of the drop, backing away from the graves. I did not want to see his grave. I did not want to go anywhere near it.

'Please!' she pleaded. 'Please read his books.'

That look in her eye, that vulnerability. She needs me, I thought. These people actually believe that I can help them.

'Easter is coming,' she said. 'He is coming.'

And the rest I didn't hear as I was walking away from her, fast down the hill. Away from his grave, away from him.

5

But that was earlier. That was when my mind was dead set against all this talk of suicides and something coming that's driving people to kill themselves.

As Helen said, suicide is a way out of a problem, it's not much of a choice, but if it is the only choice then what else is there? It's also pretty final. Frank wanted to die. And when you're dead, you're dead. Okay, so Frank, Sarah, and millions of others wouldn't agree with that, but I hold fast to it. Death is the end of the line. You get off the train and no one hears from you again. There is nothing after it. No afterlife. 'The rest is silence.'

But that was earlier.

Now I have worked through the day, now I have cleared my thoughts on this paper, now I have an image in my mind of Stavroula, her beauty, those unspoken words hidden behind a smile that promises so much, now I have thought things through I have softened a little. At least, if I read Frank's books I will have reason to talk to her more, and for longer. After all, I have time to kill. (Still no phone reception, still no way of finding an exit from the island.)

And by sitting here and reading his books, it might help me come to terms with the truth I faced earlier.

It was such a final thing, realising that he was there, dead in the ground. I didn't see his grave, I had to get away from there. I had to get away from it. And that was more to do with the thought that she had tricked me into going there. She, like Sarah, thinks I need closure on his death. Well, I don't. He's dead. That's closed.

But these books. There are a lot of them and I keep putting it off.

There is also a tape player of some sort. A Dictaphone with

a tape in it. This must be what she called his machine, a place where he recorded his notes.

Okay, then. A glass of something to ease me into the afternoon, feet up and make a start, for her sake, on his 'research.' And that can all start with whatever is on this tape.

Fourteen

I have transcribed the recording from Frank's tape. The one that was still in the machine. There are others, but they are blank.

Transcription of Frank's tape:

Not a day for being inside among dusty books. Have decided to try out this machine. Found it at the stationer's shop. Speaking aloud is not a problem and I can talk faster than I am able to write. It fits nicely in my hand. I will accustom myself to it.

Tuesday twelfth. I finally gained access to the Italian records that are kept in the Sala, the mansion house. To not open that building to the public is a crime. Typical of this country. They spent a fortune on renovating the old house, so the curator, Costas, tells me, and it was indeed available to public scrutiny for a few years. But now there is no person who is capable of selling tickets and so it must remain closed.

This is ludicrous, and I told Costas so. He agreed, and in return informed me that the Ministry of Culture will not pay for someone to work there, but that it can be anyone. An unemployed school leaver? A retired person wanting something to do. I would gladly volunteer if I was not so involved in my research.

My research, yes. I digress. It is so easy to wander from the point when talking to oneself. I am rather enjoying it. Don't know why I didn't think of it before. But then, I do still enjoy the art of writing, the slow speed of think and pen, thought and paper. I am digressing again.

Italian records. Unsurprisingly, in Italian, with some very early Greek and Turkish entries. But from what I can ascertain via my Latin and a dictionary, I am still on the right path. But there is nothing definite yet from the occupation of 1912 onwards. And the books say nothing about 1909. This was, obviously, before the occupation so I suppose it must stand to reason that the Italian authorities were not that impressed with things past and Ottoman. Still, there is much work to do.

Er, what day? Thursday. I am told that the last of the summer visitors left today. I hardly noticed anyone visiting, so engrossed am I in this history. I have a theory to put down, which I have written, so no point to repeat here. There is folklore. Stories. Stories.

What are stories but truths once told? True to the teller, to the storyteller. Myths? [*The tape clicks off here but I believe the next is from the same day.*]

Myths lead me to stories that lead me to this square. Why the millstone? Is there significance in its circle? Circles protect through mythology and lore. Is there some protection to be sought at this circle? Was it here for a reason other than decoration? And why here? What is the significance of this square? Is it this kafeneion? 'First of April 1909' and the name of the first owner, George of the Cross, roughly translated. A stone put here to mark the opening of his business. What hopes did he have?

'Kalimera, Papa. Kala efharisto.' [*Said to someone passing?*]

In 1912 the Italians occupied this and surrounding islands. In 1909 it was Ottoman, and it was from around here that the decline started. This decline. It's still happening.

Why? Can it be related? Note, check back to Roman.

January. Sunday. Cold.

She tells me the stories. I ask her about the Romans, the Knights, the Turks. And she says what?

What do I feel, she asks? I do not know what I feel. I do. I feel close to finding something. To some thing, not to someone, not to her. Not any longer. But she asks me to stand here and see what I see, feel what I feel.

What do I see? 1909. George of the Cross, poor George. All his hopes and dreams in this kafeneion, the island at the height of its success, divers, trade, this the main square and George taking over a new business, something to pass on to his children. And then. The bloody Italians. Enforced language, change in religion, schooling. At least the Turks left them alone for most of the time. And people left. Why? Why such a decline? The Italians did, after all, give them electricity, draining. They made improvements, so why the decline? The War? Yes, of course, to a certain extent, but it was before then that it started, wasn't it?

Remember, 1909. This is the most recent. This date is key. What do I see around me? Empty buildings. What do I feel around me?

History.

I feel... I see the child on the balcony up there. He wonders what I am doing, talking into a small machine. Kalimera! Ah, his father. Morning! What do they see from up there? What am I not seeing? [*The next part is very jumbled. It's hard to hear. It's like he is running.*]

Oh, my God! It was staring me in the face. There. Right there.

Of course. It was in the numbers. [*Something I can't hear.*] I know... the numbers. And the value. Can it be? Really, can it be... [*Inaudible*]... After all this time. To be proved correct. To finally hold it. [*Panting, gasping, running?*] I must get it back and look at detail. Oh, Jesus! What power does this bring?

[*Clunk of the recorder hitting a table? Static in the air, hissing, Frank's breathing. A whimper.*] Something is taking me. [*Scraping sound. Muffled noise like the thing is now in his pocket. Door slamming. Rhythmic scratching, the machine recording in his pocket as he runs? Two minutes or so. Rustling. Then:*] The tree. The field. So possible. So simple. [*Deep breathing.*] It is starting to kill.

It has me now. I am caught. I know what it wants to do, I know what I have started and what has to be done. But I can't do it. [*He starts to cry.*] I can't do this! Who can do this? When it comes to it who can actually do it? Oh, God, why did you set me this task? The price is so high.

I think I have found out where it is. I am sure. It's unbelievable but yes, this is the only explanation. Leave me alone! Voices. Is it madness? Are they real? Am I worthy? I need help.

In the lanes. There she is. Helen! [*Rustle of tape in pocket again, the next very hard to hear, sounds like:*] Where is he? [*Muffled female voice.*] No. Oh Lord, no! Helen, I am so... [*Muffled voice.*] I had no idea. Helen, no, please don't go. Help me! [*A minute of walking. Rustling.*] Back in the square. It has taken him now. [*A bell starts to toll somewhere.*] And now more. Where is it!

I am calm now. This horror is around me and out there and I know what must be done but I know I cannot do it. I am not the one. It passes through me only. It is close, it is here, I know it. Grows stronger each day. [*Papers being turned.*] Clues. For him. [*Scratching of nib on paper for several minutes.*] They have rested so close to the place where they must be taken, but can he do it? It is in the numbers. It all adds up. I am sure of it but a better man than me must take this on. I am sorry. Maria, I can't care enough to be able to do it. I never asked for him. I am too weak. If only I had been able to care more. Christopher, and little Ben. I am sorry. But I know what must be done. [*Click off. Click on again.*]

He won't. Not if I tell him. [*Shouts:*] He killed her! [*Calm:*] Well, curiosity killed more than the cat.

[*The dull thump of heavy things landing one on top of the other. The journals? Frank breathing in short, sharp gasps. In the background that static noise, something in the air. Imagine the sound of dust if it could whisper. Frank crying now, and paper being moved. He's writing. More books moved. More gasps and sniffs. Inaudible muttering. He's packing the box.*] Christopher. [*I am sure he said my name. Was he writing the envelope? Leaving me the photo album? A scream.*]

I can't do it!

[*Sounds like: paper being ripped, something torn down? A creak, the cupboard door opening?*] I'm sorry! [*A scraping sound. Glass smashes. A picture from the wall perhaps? Something gets knocked over. Frank sobbing. More paper rustling, he is writing me that note. The one he left in the journal for me to find. He knew I would be here. That bloody note: 'I love you.'*]

Sorry.

[*Something heavy on the table, a book slammed down? The*

rattle of a metal handle. He moved something, dragged it across the surface – there are scratch marks on this table.]

[*Frank's sobs. Fading. Footsteps leaving the room. The front door slams. Only the sound of the dust in the air. The tape runs on recording the silence of the room. And then what could be another voice, more like a growl, more like the tape stretching, being chewed, but if they were words then they said:*]

Bring it back.

Fifteen

He sits in the empty room, his eyes fixed on the machine, the tape is playing through to the end and he has not yet stood to switch it off. He tries to take in what he heard, ties to make sense of the jumbled words, the brief exclamations. Can't do what? What voice was that? What was happening? There are too many questions in his mind, too many threads to work together. He can make no sense of any of them.

He has been affected by hearing his father's voice, probably his last words. And although he cared little for his father, or so he thinks, and hardly knew him, he feels something now. What he feels is not clear.

He reaches for the book and starts the tape again, writing down each word, listening in carefully for clues.

He finally reaches the end of the tape, hears that bestial, otherworldly voice and convinces himself it is not a voice.

Notice, he doesn't ask 'what was that?' He is starting to accept, starting to learn, though he is not yet ready to admit that to himself.

He reaches for his glass but it is empty. He leaves the room, leaving the dust to whisper and the light to play across the table. The journals wait. The photo album lies unopened.

The pill box moves slightly of its own accord.

He comes back into the room, his face less flushed now, his recovery from hearing Frank's words nearly complete. Now he has listened and listened again and written it down it has become research. He himself is researching. This is now fact and cold detail, not personal, not a desperate father's last words. This man, Frank, left him something to fathom out.

He has the job to understand it. That is all. He picks up a journal and sips as he reads. A shadow passes the window, the sunlight briefly blocked out. Someone stands looking in. He doesn't see.

The room has dimmed. He backs to the window for better light and slowly realises he is being watched.

He turns and drops the book in surprise.

5

She gave me the shock of my life, standing there waving a mobile phone in one hand and a book in the other.

'I have old news, and I have good news,' she said, her voice muffled through the glass. 'I come inside now.' And she was gone.

I did a quick scan of the room. Out of habit I tried to hide the empty whisky bottle, but the only place was the cupboard and that was locked. I placed it under the table at the back as I heard the front door open and she called in, 'It is not locked. I come in.'

Helen appeared in the doorway and looked around the room. She saw the table and the collection of books.

'Ah,' she said, 'this is the work station, yes? You have started on the reading?'

'I've just transcribed a tape,' I replied. 'But I have no idea what it means.'

'I have this.' She held up the phone and also, in the other hand, a large book. The cover was dark in colour, almost black, and the spine had a gold glint to it. It looked old.

'But first,' she said, narrowing her eyes, 'I smell a drink in the air. You have something, yes?'

I headed to the kitchen and poured us both a reasonable measure. When I got back to the room she was sitting in the chair flicking through the book.

'What is that?' I asked, handing her the glass.

'It is from the museum. I found the surviving son and he just about told me to take what I want. No one cares for nothing out there. Here.' She handed me the mobile. 'This is a different network, I think. It is a Greek one. Maybe yours does not work well because it is a foreign company? I don't know, try it. You have power?'

I flicked on the light switch to test it and yes, the overhead bulb lit up.

'Then perhaps the radio mast is fixed. Try.'

I had a flashback to the voice on the tape then, the part when Frank had met her.

'On that tape,' I said, and she looked up at me from the chair. 'Frank used the tape recorder to make some notes. I think he meant to do all his notes on it but there are actually only a few things. At one point he is out and about, it sounds like, and he meets you.'

'Me?'

'Yes. He says something like… Hang on.'

I picked up the book (this one) and read the section I'd noted down.

'He had given up stating dates or days even at this point. He just says "There she is. Helen." It sounds like he was calling you over and then he must have put the Dictaphone in his pocket. I can just make out him asking you where he is? He?'

Her face fell. She lowered the book and fixed her eyes on me. 'Go on,' she said.

'Well, then he says, "No, oh, lord no, Helen I am so…," and

then I can't make it out. "I had no idea, Helen. No, please don't go." Do you remember that?'

She nodded, her expression grim.

'"It took him," he says.'

She started shaking her head, side to side.

'What did?'

It took a moment before she answered. She ran her hands over the pages of the book and looked away towards the floor.

'He did,' she said quietly.

'Who? Frank?'

'No. He did. My husband. He took himself. A month, maybe two, before. The time makes no odds now. He was one of the first to die. He killed himself.'

I didn't know what to say. This kind of intimate, counselling thing isn't really me. I don't have a clue what to do, what to say. I said 'Sorry,' I think, and hoped we would leave it at that. Luckily for me she snapped out of whatever place she'd suddenly taken herself to and looked back at me. Her eyes twinkled slightly and she smiled. It was unconvincing but it caused the creases around her eyes to wrinkle up and betray her thoughts. There was still something she was not telling me, something deeper she didn't want to discuss.

'He had problems,' she said. 'And as I explain, where there are problems we seek solutions and this was his.'

'Frank goes on...'

'I know,' she said, interrupting me and raising a hand. 'Tell me, he goes on to talk about horror and more people killing themselves? He talks about legends and curses and evil?'

'Well, no, not really. Not on the tape.'

'Then in the books?' She turned a page and squinted at the book in her lap. I noticed she tucked her top lip into her bottom. Thinking, I guess. 'He always said the answer was in the island's books.'

'Was my father crazy?' I asked. It was a question that I thought hardly needed asking but it occurred to me that she knew him better than I did.

'We are all a little crazy,' she said and laughed. 'But what is crazy? Frank obsessed about old stories, things from the past of the world. He tells me more than once that he had struck upon a legend and wanted to prove it was not a legend but fact. Legends, facts, we could discuss for hours! Day follows day follows day. He looks at the village, the land, the buildings. He would ask everyone about the past and families, and he spent time at the museum. But I think he found little there. The books were locked away then and the older, older books that he needed were not available to him. They had been destroyed over time. So he was left with lots of questions and only some answers. This started to drive him, not mad, perhaps, but to be distracted.'

'Yeah, well I am kind of starting to feel that way myself,' I admitted.

'Ah yes,' she said. 'What our parents start spreads to us and captures us, eh?'

I didn't know what she meant by that but she seemed to have said it more to the pages of the book. I sipped my drink.

'What is that?' I asked.

'Just stories,' she replied. 'Try the phone. Your wife must be worried.'

'Ex-wife,' I corrected her, feeling the sting from the cut on my ring finger. Some kind of ironic reminder of the pain of our marriage.

'She will always have been your wife. The network has been

on and then off, like the power, but you might get a, how would you say? You might find a window?'

She carried on studying the pages of what I then noticed was Greek text and I realised she must be able to translate it. Otherwise she was putting on a great charade of pretending to. The book had certain illustrations as well, engravings or woodcuts or something.

I peered over her shoulder as I dialled Sarah's number, then turned to look out of the window onto the lane.

The sunlight was weak now. The sun was starting to fall towards the hills over to the west. The buildings along the lane, the walls, and ruined doorways, the overhanging dead tree, a large fig tree closer to the house, all cast shadows on the stones. I can admit that I found the sight of the light on the lane quite beautiful. A kind of dreamy image of something I never expected to see, in a place I'd never dreamed of being. A weird, slightly pink light hung over the walls like a see-through material that is barely noticeable, yet there. It was captivating in some strange way I couldn't figure out.

And it was spoiled by the way I was feeling. I was confused, and, to be honest, annoyed about what was going on, the mess Frank had left me. Feelings I could not shake off, now compounded by the thought that I might actually have to speak to Sarah and let her know I would not be getting back as promised.

I heard the numbers beep back at me once I'd dialled them, a short, random tune.

And behind me I heard Helen say, 'I would not believe all this if I was also not so crazy, yes? They record the stories and here they are.'

I looked over at her. She wasn't looking at me though she

was holding up the book. An illustration of some hole in the ground, it looked like, things going on above it, flames.

I turned back to the window. The line was hissing and I wasn't sure if that was a good thing or bad.

'In Ottoman times they are writing them. Not all have been lost.'

'That's great,' I said. I didn't mean it of course.

'Something evil lies sleeping.'

'Yeah, my ex...' The phone connected. It was ringing.

'And here again in 1909, "Evil and ancient awakened." You say awakened? Oh, sorry. It is working?'

I nodded and she fell silent.

She must have looked back over her shoulder and realised.

I heard a voice, Sarah's, but the line was still hissing and there was interference.

'Sarah? Hello?'

I did that thing of putting a finger in your ear and pressing the phone harder to my head. It didn't help much.

'Hello, Chris?'

I heard her clearly for a second, then more noise on the line.

'Can you hear me?'

'If it works, don't waste time.'

I heard Helen call out from across the room, and she was right of course.

'Sarah, I can't make it back. There is no boat for a few days. Did you hear me?'

Static, hiss, a loud crackle.

'Did you hear me?'

I heard what I thought sounded like, 'Ben,' and my heart leapt.

'What? What's the matter with Ben?' I said, loudly.

Another short tune made by numbers being dialled, like someone else was cutting in on the line.

'Sarah?'

'Soon.'

'What?'

'Ben... Must.'

At least I thought she said 'must'. It could have been dust, or, well, anything I guess. I heard no more. The phone simply fell silent. Not even any static or hiss. At the same time the overhead light dimmed and went out.

'That will be that,' Helen said.

'She was trying to say something about Ben,' I said as I tried dialling again.

'He is your boy, yes? I expect he is missing you.'

I looked at her for a second, just a second, and her expression was again far away, distant, as if she had suddenly taken herself back to somewhere she wanted to go to again. Thinking of her dead husband, maybe. But, within a moment, she had snapped out of it and was back to being practical again, scientific.

'The number registers on her phone, I think,' she said. 'She will call back. This phone has a message box. You dial a number and it plays you messages. If she leaves one. And she will. It will not work now.' She pointed to the light, still off, and I gave up trying the phone. I went back to the table and dumped it down, drained my drink.

She was watching me.

'What?' I said, rather bluntly. But I was thinking about Ben at that point.

'I train for many years,' she said. 'And I learn many things. Years of study, reading, counselling, my own therapy, lots of work. And after these years I come to learn when a man is in need of talking. And when he is in need of drinking.' She held up her glass for a refill. 'My diagnosis.'

I brought the bottle back from the kitchen, no point in hiding it, and poured her a measure with water. I took mine neat.

She held up her glass and looked at the drink within it. 'So many years training to learn this,' she said, with half a smile, and took a healthy swig. 'Yamas. Proost.'

I raised my own glass half-heartedly and rested back against the table.

Helen was looking over my shoulder and her brow started to furrow.

'What is it?'

She waved me out of the way and sat forward in the chair. Then she looked at the book in her lap and flicked some pages.

I realised she had been looking at Ben's drawing of the strange house, stuck to the wall with some tape.

'Who did this?' she asked.

'Ben.'

'Your son? Oh, my. How…' She looked back at the drawing, squinted, chewed her lip and then went back to the book.

'What is it?'

She didn't asnwer. She stood up, walked to the table and placed the book down.

I glanced at it; all in Greek, no images. And then she looked more closely at the drawing. She used her glass to point to the stick men.

'Who are these?' she asked.

'They are meant to be Frank, me, and Ben, I think. He's never met Frank so he drew stick men…'

'Father and son,' she said, and it was said under her breath.

'I guess. But you know, kids.'

She wasn't listening. She had turned her attention to the books on the table. She moved me out of the light, the dying afternoon light that came from the lane outside, and started flicking open books.

'No, no,' she said, and her eye moved across the table top, scanning it.

Her fingers touched the Dictaphone lightly then moved on to the journal titled 'The Judas Curse.'

'Ah,' she said in a whisper. 'This is the one he talked of most. This story.'

She opened the book carefully, as if it were some valuable artefact, as I watched. I'd flicked through it before, started to record things from it and then given it up as mumbo jumbo, which, as far as I am concerned, it still is.

Frank's handwriting at the start of the book is neat and small, his words are perfectly formed and he always writes in ink, I noticed, never biro. The drawings are in pencil and then the outlines are also made in ink.

There are pieces of paper, cuttings, things from newspapers and books, all stuck into the journal with the same tape that now holds Ben's drawing to the wall.

But the journal is all over the place, headings underlined, paragraphs ringed in red as though they were important.

'Look,' Helen said, and I leaned in.

She was pointing at a title of a page that read 'The Potter's Field' and the first few lines were ringed in red:

With the payment Judas received for his wickedness, a field was bought, a triangle of land to be called 'the Potter's field.'

She turned a page. More circled text:

And they conferred together and with the money bought the potter's field as a burial pace for strangers.

125

He stabbed himself… His bowels gushed out.
And for this reason the field has been called the field of blood.
Blood money.

'I don't understand,' I said. 'It's just signs of his obsession, isn't it? His madness?'

She opened up the museum book to a certain page.

'This,' she said, pointing to it, 'this is a very old story from the island. Before the Turks there were the Knights of Rhodes, of Saint John. They were here, fourteenth century, fifteenth. This story is from then.'

She was running her fingers across the Greek words.

'What does it say?'

She looked at it for a moment, and then, 'In modern English, as best I can: "It starts with he who finds it. It spreads from one to the next. It spreads its evil outwards through the world, like…" I would say, like ripples. I think that is what is meant. "Out it spreads and all will succumb."'

'Cheery,' I quipped. It fell on deaf ears. She was back at Ben's drawing again.

'From one to the next,' she said to herself. 'Like father to son.'

She was about to touch the drawing with one finger. She was pointing to the house in it, but then she suddenly turned and jumped back. She was staring at the window and there was fear on her face.

'What is it?' I asked.

She ignored me and walked across to the window. She looked out, steadying herself against the wall with one hand.

'It is not to be believed,' she said quietly. 'No, I cannot do this.' And then, suddenly, perky and smiling at me, 'I go now.'

And she did. She left. Simply walked out of the room and out of the house.

'Well, thanks!' I called after her, not knowing quite what to make of it all.

I stood there for a moment looking around the room. My eyes fell to the books of course, and the museum book she had brought with her and left. There was no chance of me understanding any of that. It was not in English, but it did have illustrations, and she had seemed to imply there was some relationship between Ben's drawing, this book, and Frank's journals.

Day was fast fading now and night was falling quickly outside. I used the last minutes of daylight to set up some candles and switch the light switches to the on position so I would know what the power was doing. I put the borrowed mobile on the table beside me in case it rang, sat down with my drink and once again started to note it all down.

It is now pitch black outside. I have something to eat, I have something to drink, the room is chilly and I have a blanket around my shoulders.

I have also made a decision, while I was writing up what happened this afternoon, today, and I, by reading through my own notes now realise that there is a mystery here. There is at least something I can do while I wait for the next boat. I can try and figure out what it was that drove Frank mad, what made him kill himself.

And I am pretty sure that the answer is somewhere in the journals I am about to read. In earnest, this time.

5

The shadows gather unseen behind him, reading over his shoulder, crowding him as they look on. The voices stay silent.

He is on the verge now, about to let himself look over the edge into the madness of his father's mind. He could step forward and onwards, or he could step back, turn and flee. The voices need him to stay but they know it is going to take more than accepting that there is a mystery.

He is going to need to believe.

Sixteen

A morning of strange events and numbers. I worked into the night. I call it work. I read his notes, and I started to get a glimpse of what it is like to slowly turn mad.

His journals are not so much a diary of events but more a list of threads. Parts of stories, ideas, words people once said to him, and legends from the island's history all mixed up with his own views on life and death. Example:

"15th century, prosperity dwindling. Why? There is life after death, I am convinced of it. I know it. I pray for it. Perhaps the castle?"

I mean, does that make any sense to anyone? Certainly not to me.

There are other notes as well and some caught my eye, so I jotted them down on a chart and stuck that chart to the wall. I don't know why this list appealed to me so much but something made me write it down. It's still stuck there now:

"Romans, rise and fall. Mid-4th century on the island? (It arrives? Buried in catacombs until found: 1222?)

1224: Nicean – rose and fell

1261: Byzantine – rose and fell

1278: Gifted to Cavo/Genoa – passed in 1282 (he knew)

1309: Knights of St John, capture, built 'Castro' again found, used, grew until:

1522: Defeated by Ottomans, buried, calmed, business boomed, success continues until:

1860: discovered? (Find references.) Skafandro = start of a long decline. Buried. Too late.

1909: Discovered (Well?) Decline again to:

129

1912: Italians. Buried. Safe. Too late. Decline, decline to 1970s.

It exists."

Numbers. Dates. That note in the album 'it all adds up.'

I stayed up into the night adding those dates together, searching through other books he has in this box, other notes. I found out that what he had listed were the times, some rough, some apparently documented, when this island had changed hands. He seemed to think that each occupying force came, gave the island prosperity, or success, or hope or something, and then, after *it* was found, declined, or was lost. (This involved a diving suit, as I found out that was what the 'Skafandro' was. If there is ever any doubt that he was going mad than surely this is it?) It was like he was saying the rise and fall of each occupier who took the island, was due to something it found, or buried. The Romans, Niceans, the Byzantines, the Genoese, Knights of St John, Ottomans, Italians, Germans/British, all had the island under their control at some point in history, and all rose to fail.

Why?

That's the other word he kept writing in his books. Why? Why and how. I quote: "How did they find? How did it destroy? Why not kill it? Why?" Then later. "I understand why not, why it can't be physically destroyed now, but how can it be defeated?"

I don't understand any of it. I find it intriguing, now I have taken time to sit and read and start on the stories, but it's all a jumble of madness, surely?

I worked into the night until the power flickered and failed again, like someone 'up there' was telling me to sleep. But I couldn't sleep then, I was into it, and so I lit candles and finally must have dozed off in the chair in the early hours, one of the books in my lap. It was light in the room when I was woken sometime after dawn by the heavy journal sliding from my hands and hitting the floor.

My hand.

I should see if there is a doctor. I think there may be an infection in it; it's more painful today despite the dousing I gave it with Scotch this morning.

I washed my hand and face after that but it felt too cold for a shower or shave, not that the water was working properly. Without electricity there is no water, only what is left in the pipes.

I tried the phone again but with no luck. Again, no power means no signal, which must have something to do with the masts I can see up on the top of the mountain. I don't see why they don't have generators to run them during power cuts, but then, I am not in England so who knows what goes on?

Half awake and feeling grubby from a night in my clothes I thought a walk and fresh air might be a good idea. I thought I might find someone to ask about the house (surely there must be papers to sign?), and about the boats, and when the next one is actually due. See if I can get a definite time. Get organised.

As I was packing up my camera stuff I looked at the flowchart I'd made. It's there by Ben's drawing, and I also saw how many other pieces of paper I'd stuck to the walls with that tape. Some loose leafs from books that I didn't want to lose, some I'd written out myself on scraps I found in the box, and some on a large piece of paper I found, unfolded and stuck up. This is the main sheet of my research, the main dates and numbers. There are a lot of them and they make no sense at all.

My biggest question, it seems (I hardly remember writing it, I was so half asleep), concerns a well that Frank mentioned several times. This well seems to be of importance to him as do a few specific dates.

And I did find out the relevance of the photo album. It seems this is the most important clue to whatever it was Frank was working on and wanted to pass to me. "The things that are needed to answer this riddle are now in the album." He had written that in a book somewhere. The books are still scattered across the table. Some have fallen to the floor, I notice, and I am not going back through them again, but I have charted what I must have thought were the most important facts:

1909 > Number of the Well? > Four brothers.

Looking in the album, there was the photo of the four boys and the card reading 1909. And I knew where that square was, so I collected my gear and headed out for another look.

I took the album with me and found my way easily through the completely deserted streets until I came to the square. I have to say it was pretty eerie this morning, no sounds at all, not even birds, just the wind high up in the electricity cables that criss-cross the lanes and the village. It's ironic; there's no power again this morning and yet the cables themselves seem to be alive with chatter, whispering, high voices, which is, of course, only the wind. But still, it made me imagine how voices might actually travel along cables, like telegraph wires, of which there are also several around this place. Like when people call each other on the phone, their voices become physical and actually move quickly down the lines from one pole to another making connections all the way along.

Not enough sleep. I am rambling. My hand is hurting. I think I might start using Frank's tape recorder, his Dictaphone, to keep these notes. Why am I keeping notes anyway?

Right. I reached the square and had seen no one. I had the album with me and I was looking up at the plaque on the wall wondering what the other writing might mean. It's Greek, of course, and I can't read that.

As I stood there I became aware of footsteps coming closer and turned to see Petros. I was still wary of him but today he looked comical. He was carrying a pair of old trousers that were stuffed with straw and newspapers. Half a bonfire guy, you could say.

He saw me and for a moment I thought he might attack again. He quickened his pace towards me, his face falling into a scowl. He lifted his arm as he came close and for my part I simply squared up to him. Normally I would have run away if someone was starting to come at me like that but today I felt confident, so I just squared my shoulders. I had the stone building with its plaque behind me; it felt like protection.

I didn't need it. Petros stumbled anyway. He lost his footing and his enthusiasm and staggered against the wall beside me. He slid down it to his knees as if completely done in, and yet he'd hardly covered any distance. He was gasping. And then I realised he was actually crying. He looked pathetic. He looked up at me. I didn't know what to say and was about to leave.

But he banged his head hard against the stone wall.

'Hey!' I said, shocked. 'Come on.'

He did it again and I actually went to help him up. But he fixed me with his eyes and pushed me away. He shook his head in a 'no' and then slammed the side of it against those stones again with a sickening crack.

'Stop it!' I shouted, and he did. He looked at me, a slight trickle of blood starting to appear beneath his hairline. He grabbed the wall and pulled himself to his feet. A hand went into a pocket, and I prepared to defend myself, but he pulled out a photo. Tatty, bent, creased, often-held, I imagine, and he showed it to me, held it up defiantly.

'I loved her,' he said, in heavily accented English, and thrust the image towards me as if something was my fault.

'I don't understand,' I said, and I think neither did he.

He waved the photo at me once more and then limped away, dragging that ridiculous pair of stuffed trousers after him. I watched him go. He headed off around the ruin that is in front of the strange lopsided house.

I looked up at it and there was the father and his small son high up on the balcony.

An idea occurred to me and I waved up at them.

'Hey!' I called, and the father looked down at me slowly. The boy was staring off into space. 'Hi there. Can you help me?' The boy looked down at me then, holding on to the high balcony railings as if he was behind bars. I pointed up at the 1909 plaque.

'Can you tell me what this says?' I called, and turned to look at it, to make sure I was pointing in the right direction. 'This writing here, what does…?'

Turning back I was surprised to see they had gone. Bloody rude if you ask me.

But I did know someone who would know, if I could only find her. Stavroula knew about the island. She was, after all, a guide. I thought she might have ideas as to why Frank was interested in the history of the island, and particularly 1909, and, it seemed, this square. Also the four boys. Who were they? A tourist guide must know, and, if I am to be honest again, I was after any excuse to spend time with her.

I headed off into the maze of lanes to try and find someone who might know where she was, where she worked.

As I walked I also wondered what had happened during the night to spark my interest like this. Why was I starting to wonder so much about what Frank had been up to? Going stir crazy, I decided. It was better to do something and have my mind occupied than it was to sit around getting annoyed about not being able to get home.

5

My search for her proved fruitless but I saw some really weird things along the way. I found one old lady trudging with shopping, taking the steps one at a time, one leg up and then the other, then a rest. I offered to help but she didn't understand me. One eye was completely white with a cataract, the other only half open. She had two teeth showing at the corner of her mouth and her head was wrapped in a scarf. She pulled away from me as I approached, and when I asked if she knew Stavroula she simply shuffled on her way.

A few lanes later and I came across a young guy, around fifteen I'd say, standing outside a house painting Greek letters onto the wall. The paint was red and glistening in the sunlight. He was healthy looking, dressed in decent clothes. There was nothing decrepit or shuffling about him.

'Hi!' I called out as I approached, and he turned to face me.

He, like Petros, was crying, his eyes puffy and red, his face screwed up, and I noticed that the letters on the wall were uneven, like he was having trouble seeing what he was doing. The paint dripped down, like blood running on a wall at a crime scene. The youth just looked at me and wiped the tears away with the back of his sleeve. He left a smear of red paint across his face.

Before I could ask him anything he had turned and gone into his courtyard, slamming the metal doors with a resounding clang of finality.

Frustration suddenly hit me like a baseball bat then and I threw up my hands.

And something else hit me too. A thought.

There was a book, one I'd looked at the night before, and in it there was something about a well. I have no idea where that thought flew in from. You know how they sometimes do? It's like suddenly you hear a tune in your head that you've not heard for years. Your mind kicks it out at you for no reason. Your subconscious says 'don't need that anymore, you have it' and it leaps to the front where it is up to you to get rid of it.

Well, I had one of those thoughts then, one that wouldn't go away, as if someone else had put the idea into my head. I had to get back and look at one of Frank's books that would tell me all about the well he had deemed was very important. I had to go and read more about it, right there, right now.

Back at the house, hunger kicked in for a second but was soon dismissed as I started going through the papers again. There was something driving me now and I realised (with a surprisingly good feeling) that I'd just been out, found my way around and found my way back to the house again with no hassle. Almost like I'd been guided.

'Hey, you're getting good at this, Chris,' I said to myself, and right then my hand gave me a stab of pain. It reminded me that I probably needed antibiotics and hadn't actually done so well after all. I'd not found a doctor or a pharmacy.

But I had found the journal marked, "The Well of…?" Which

I thought was a pretty stupid title, but then most of Frank's work was stupid, I thought, as I opened the book and found it completely empty.

'Damn it!' My hand stabbed me again.

Ignoring it, I spread the papers and my charts out across the table, other charts and other papers still being on the wall, now encroaching onto the mirror as well.

I found some clean sheets of paper and started to write the main numbers down again, hoping to find a connection in the cold light of day.

1909, four.

'Pots of gold at ends of rainbows,' I muttered as I scrawled out some of Frank's other dates once more. 'It all adds up, does it? It all adds up to your being Looney Tunes.' I think that's what I said. To be honest, writing this out now is the only way of trying to get a grasp on what I was saying and doing earlier on. It's almost all lost in a cloud of misty half-remembering. I am not even sure my painful hand is letting me write this out correctly in order, as it happened. There's so much going on in my head that I need to slow down, get it clear. What was I doing?

I wrote out more notes, all the time muttering about him and getting more and more frustrated with what he had left me to sort out.

'1909, the date on the plaque. What does it mean, Frank?' I was angry with him.

Then, 'four boys, who were they, Frank? Why the costume? When was the photo taken? Why four boys?' And something else struck me. 'One was not good enough for you,' I spat the words out, finding a photo of my father in his clerical garb and sticking that to the wall. I drew a line across all the papers from him to the note about 'the four boys.' A note that I must have made during the night.

'I was not enough for you. Why four?' I was angry at him for not being there, for blaming me, for letting my mother do what she did, for teaching me, beating all that stuff into me that I didn't want beaten into me. God. Heaven. Hell. Eternal life. 'Four boys, 1909, where does it all lead and why, Frank?'

But it wasn't about his searching, his notes, his clues and puzzles. It was about me and him and how he had cut me out, left me alone, sent me away, cut himself off. How he had blamed me for things that were not my fault. How he had let me down, promised me things and then not delivered. How he was always more important, him and his blessed beliefs, afterlife, souls, death, and his search for the truth.

'What was more important, Frank?' I was shouting now. 'Who was more important? The father or the son?'

I realised I was crying, but not for him, not from sadness. I was frustrated. And a cold tear dripped from my face and landed on the laptop.

Something, the sight of the laptop perhaps, brought me back to earth. 'Father and son,' I said to myself, and switched on the computer.

Distraction; my photos, I'd still not been through them. Take my mind off the collage of paper and pictures, dates and drawings now scattered across the desk and spreading their madness out and up the walls, rippling out from a photo of Frank right in the middle.

The machine's battery was fast fading and there was no way of plugging it in. I could not for the life of me find the adapter Sarah had packed for me.

'You'll need this,' she had said as she had thrown it across the room towards my bags. I am pretty sure she wanted to throw it directly at me but Ben had been watching.

Ben.

Father and son, some photos of us, and the characters out there, to bring me back to earth. Some of my work for a change.

I found the photos I'd taken, some good, some needed work, others needed throwing out. The lanes, light on stones, features, strange symbols on walls, letters, protecting the property, claiming their ownership, the numbers, registration numbers from a previous occupation. Which one? I wondered. Who wrote these numbers on and what exactly did they mean? More to the point, why did they have to register property? Were the authorities trying to find something? Trying to pinpoint something? Why had Frank mentioned these numbers?

'Keep your mind on the photos,' I said to myself. I was in danger of drifting back into Frank's world.

More images: dead plants, litter in streets, deserted lanes, crumbling buildings, empty window frames like eye sockets, burned out wooden frames, graffiti. The square. The side of the lopsided house. (Why did it ring such a loud bell? What was I missing? No, stay in focus.)

The 1909 square and the father and son, that was what I was looking for. Father and son, and Stavroula had said something about fathers and sons. There was the photo I'd taken of them when they were playing restaurants, or whatever they were doing.

Except they were not there. I flicked forward a couple of images assuming I had the wrong one, but no, the order was correct. I went back. There was no table, no father and son, just the ruins behind them, the iron bars across the windows of some bricked up ruin behind where they had sat, the millstone, the square, the light, and that man Petros standing in the shadows with his cigarette. I checked the time sequence on the data, and the details; all correct.

'What the hell?'

Then I remembered that the images had taken an unusually long time to download. Perhaps there had been a connection error.

I grabbed the camera. The card was back in it and I had not yet deleted the images. I raced through them wondering what on earth had gone wrong with it and also very worried in case I'd lost any shots. 'Bloody thing,' I think I muttered as I came to the same image, the raw image, the original one.

No father, no son, to table.

'They were in that shot.' They were. I say it now as I said it then. They were in that shot. Why else take a photo from that angle? I clicked on:

The boy in costume, yes, the lanes, yes, good. I came to the long shot of the lane, with the light exploding at the end of it as the father and son walked away from me. Except once again they were missing. Perhaps I'd just missed them, but then I thought back and, no. They were in that shot.

'This is…' I started to say, but a voice behind me cut me off.

'The camera that never lies?'

Seventeen

I hadn't heard her come in. I'd been engrossed in Frank's ramblings and mad stories, I suppose.

'Can you see it now?' she said, and nodded towards the table and books.

'What is the number of the well?'

That faint smiled passed her lips as she surveyed the pile of papers. Her eyes fell on Ben's drawing taped to the wall and her brow knitted up slightly. I could see she was thinking and then realised that she was somehow asking me to follow her gaze. I did, and also looked on Ben's drawing. It meant nothing to me, though the eccentric angle of the lines of the building were now starting to make some kind of strange sense. The story was starting to come from the image, the three men standing in a row. Generations.

But what was that story? What did it mean? And how on earth had it got anything to do with Ben?

She was looking at me now. I felt her stare before I turned my eyes to meet it. She was waiting for me to accept that I had to sit down and listen to what she had to tell me.

'Are you ready to listen?'

'Okay,' I conceded. 'Let's say I am willing to listen to more stories. What can you tell me about this?'

I clicked the laptop on to a photo of the 1909 plaque in the millstone square. (I don't know if this is what it is called locally. I call it the millstone square as that seems like a pretty obvious name for it.)

'Dates are important,' she began. 'Your father thought them clues to what happens now, and I believe he was right. We walk and I will tell you about George Stavrou and his four sons.'

'Who?'

'The writing on the plaque,' she explained, 'is the name of the owner of the kafeneion, the café, that this once was. And there is also the date it was opened and blessed. It says, George Stavrou, April the first, 1909.'

'1909. Four sons?' I reached for the photo album and showed her the image.

She smiled, the kind of smile reserved for meeting old friends or young relatives not often met.

'Yes,' she said in a whisper, and then, 'come.'

5

<u>Stavroula's story of The Well of Thirteen. (My recollection.)</u>

The year is 1909. Today is the first day of April and a boy is playing outside of the village with his friends. He has been sent there by his parents and his older brothers. He was in the way. But here he can hardly concentrate on his game. Partly because of what is happening back in the village but mainly, because of what he has just seen glinting in the sun only a few paces away from where he crouches. His eyes open wide. He can't believe his luck.

Today, in the village square, his father is opening a new business. A new kafeneion for the village men to come to and drink their thick, black, Turkish coffee. A place where business can be done, contracts discussed, trade between business arranged and where politics can be talked about. The talk at the moment is of the Turks, and their rule, and their tensions with Italy over somewhere far away called Libya. Far away but important to the island's trade and diving industry, so the men say. Some say another war is coming, others say not to be so stupid. George Stavrou says it has nothing to do with him. All he is interested in now is his new business. Manolis has a thriving taverna on the square, Sotiris has recently opened another one opposite, there are two around the corner, and still there is never enough room for all the customers.

George stands on the step of his new business and looks at his tables and chairs set out in front of it, new, the paint shining, the metal tables ready for his first customers. And they won't be long in coming. As soon as the day's work is over his new business will start.

There has been some talk of where he came by the money needed to open such a large and impressive business. He had, after all, run the building as a simple storeroom for so many years, renting out space to others who needed it. He didn't need to do anything with his building so why now, suddenly, was he opening a kafeneion where he would have to work, to wait on tables? George's answer was simple enough: he had come into some money (he never satisfactorily said from where) and had decided he needed something to leave to his sons. He had four boys and no inheritance. He didn't need to build them houses; wives would come along one day and their houses would be provided, but two of them needed work. The eldest had work on a boat, the second was studying for the priesthood, the third was a bit of a layabout and had not yet decided what he was going to do, so he would be working in the business for sure, and the youngest, Lukas, well, he was still at school but this new venture would secure him a good future.

George was happy, content that he had put his new found

wealth into good use, satisfied that his kafeneion would be the biggest and best, the most prosperous, in the main square. He stood, watching the men coming up the steps into the square. The priest was already there, standing on the millstone and looking up at the newly installed plaque admiringly, getting ready to bless the business. George heard his third son busy in the back, clattering coffee cups and glasses.

He smiled. He had assured his sons' prosperity for many years to come.

Lukas, meanwhile, was out in the fields looking at the thing on the ground in wonder.

He had been sent away so as not to get under his father's feet and was content in a game of stalking with friends from school. On the way down into the valley they had asked him how his father had managed to afford the new kafeneion. After all, they reasoned, there was all the furniture, the things for inside like the coffee cups, the new heaters for the winter, the decoration. It looked stunning inside, but also expensive. People were saying that he had stolen some money from someone whose possessions he used to store there. But Lukas argued against this. Yes, his father did rent out storage space in his building, and he had saved that money for all these years until he was ready to put it into something new. That's what he had done. Simple. And his friends were more or less happy to accept that.

But Lukas knew different. He had an idea of where papa had found the cash, and knew that it had started when they were over Nimborio way.

He had been walking with his father one Sunday afternoon. They had come by the old underground earthworks, the catacombs, as papa had called them. At first Lukas was scared to go down there but his father told him they were very old and very empty and held nothing to be scared of. No one exactly knew what they were for but they were now just cold, damp rooms underground. Then Lukas became excited to go in and wanted to see under the earth, so Lukas and his father went in for a look.

They were just cold, dark spaces underground and Lukas realised that he wasn't afraid. In fact, now he was thrilled to be down there. His father set a small fire and the flames lit the low ceiling, the rocks embedded into the walls, the short passage with the archways, and something small and metallic that glinted in the far corner.

'What's that?' Lukas said, pointing to the shining thing.

His father never answered but instead rushed straight to the far corner and started digging. He instructed Lukas to bring a flaming branch from the fire and, over his father's shoulder, Lukas saw him lift some kind of dirty, small, box from the muddy floor.

'What is it?'

But his papa never answered him, not until they were nearly home. On the way George had cleared the mud from the box and Lukas saw it was in fact a metal chest. He asked again what it was.

'This,' his father said, hurrying and clutching the chest tightly, 'is our future.'

All Lukas knew about the chest from then on was that it was now in his bedroom, under his new bed. He had no idea why, but his father made him swear that he would never talk about what they had found, in case, he said, they had taken someone else's treasure. His father reasoned that if it did belong to someone else then they should have looked after it more closely and he was perfectly justified in taking it for his own. For all he knew it had been there hundreds of years and so no one owned it.

But he would speak no more about it. Instead, he took its contents, a small leather pouch, and gave the actual chest to Lukas to play with. It was valueless, he said, but what had been inside was not. And that was when his father started putting together plans to convert his storage area into a kafeneion. And that was what led to today; with Lukas hiding under a bush as his school friends stalked him out in the fields.

But something was not right. Ever since they had found the chest Lukas had not been happy. It wasn't that he had been sad, but more that he had not felt very much like playing. He had felt guilty. And he knew why.

His father had banned him from looking in the chest right up until the day he had handed it to the boy empty. But Lukas had once snuck into his father's office and seen it on his desk. Being alone in the house he had opened the lid and looked inside, and he still had an absolutely clear and vivid image of what he had seen.

A few days later his father had everything he needed for the new business. It was an uncle who had been paid to do the work and supply the furniture, everything from the chairs to the stove, from floor to ceiling. As was usual, the work was all kept within the family.

A few days after the work was finished, his uncle died. Fell from a roof they said. Lukas only knew something bad had happened because he heard the church bells ringing sadly and he did not have to go to school that day. Gossip in the busy village was that the man had slipped on purpose from the roof. Some said he had overcharged George and was guilt-ridden.

Others said he had lost all his money and was ashamed. Some even said he was so worried about the situation with the Ottomans and the Italians that he feared bad things were coming and didn't want to live in such a world.

And now Lukas thought he knew how the man felt. He too felt sad. More than sad, he felt hopeless. Here, on a sunny day with a fresh breeze and the flowers of spring starting to push through, the trees coming into bloom and a holiday from school, here, with his father opening a new business that will one day be his, a young boy with so much to live for in a thriving village on a rich and beautiful island, he felt sad.

Sad, and now scared as he looked down at the ground and the thing he had been staring at, wondering.

He heard his name being called, but he ignored the game and blinked.

'How did you get here?' he asked the coin that lay at his feet. It was just like the ones he had seen in the pouch within the chest.

Today was going to be a special day after all. He made sure no one was watching him and then did as his father had done with the metal chest; he took the coin for himself.

As he did so he thought he heard something in the undergrowth behind him. He felt the hairs on the back of his neck tingle and rise, and thought he heard something growl close by. A dog, perhaps. But when he turned to look, there was nothing there.

The trouble started from that moment.

The kafeneion opened and life went on, though trade was not as good as George had hoped. The death of his brother, who had fitted out the building, had a resounding effect on the villagers. There were several thousand people living in the area, there were plenty of places to eat and drink, why should they go to this cursed place that had been built on a man's death? George pleaded with his friends and even his family, and a few came to support him. But things soon started to look bad for the Stavrou family.

During this time the business had gone from bad to worse, and not just their family's business, either. Manolis' taverna was all but deserted, there were fewer and fewer people eating out, less money, fewer men came for coffee and more people started to leave the island. Lethargy settled in.

And then someone else died. Deaths happened, that was that, but this man had definitely killed himself, and there was great anxiety in the village as to what to do with him. The church would not bury him, the doors were closed to the family, and so they made their own plot outside the graveyard and buried him there, quickly.

Lukas saw his father with a small, leather pouch, the thing that had been in the metal chest, and he wondered how it had come back to him. He was sure his father had used it to pay his uncle for the work. But then, maybe he had, and maybe now his uncle was gone the thing would just stay in the family. It wasn't important to him anyway. He was just curious.

And then his eldest brother died, suddenly. Coming home from his time on the boat he walked up to the village, but didn't stop at the house. He carried on walking. Those that saw him said it was like he was in a daze; he ignored them all and just walked, up and out of the village. They found him a few days later, his head split open on the rocks high up on the top grazing, under the mountain. He had left a sad note which Lukas had not been allowed to see.

Lukas started to feel bad then. He knew that he was somehow

to blame and he also began feeling remorseful. He had found a coin and kept it. He had not given it up and that was a bad thing to do.

His second brother took his own life by cutting his arm deeply with a knife. He did this in the church when he was learning to be a cantor. He was singing the service and the first anyone knew was when they saw his blood running from the stall and onto the polished floor. The priest ordered the dying man from the church and he was carried out into the lane where he bled to death on his back, looking up at the church tower.

More deaths and closer to home, his family and his friends, and then news came that some in the harbour had died as well. Experts came in from the mainland and declared there was no medical reason for it. People were doing this willingly. And Lukas knew it was to do with him, his greed, his theft. His and his father's. He talked to his father but he was not listening. He was struck down with grief and buried his head in books. He was blocking out the tragedy unfolding around him by reading old books, looking at old maps and searching. At least, that is what it looked like to Lukas.

His last remaining brother took his own life. The business closed. News came that the Italians were going to go to war with Turkey. There was no hope for the business now and more people were talking of leaving, going to Athens or further to find a new life.

Until, on the last day, Lukas knew it was his turn. He hid the metal chest under his bed and went to his uncle's house and a place he knew well, the basement, with its cistern that was covered by old wood. The family well.

He was so filled with remorse at what he had done that there was only one way out. Only one solution.

In the cellar he removed the well cover and stood looking down into the icy black pit beneath him. And then, without saying a word or leaving a note, he simply let himself fall.

5

'Then, as now, suicides spread through the village like a cancer,' she said, gazing ahead. We were sitting on a wall looking out towards the hills, the old fortification and its blue and white church behind us, the village spread out below. Stavroula was still talking. 'The Italians came and the island started to die, until the father found the chest and buried it once more. No one knew why, but from then the deaths eased off. But the island never recovered. Not until fifty years later when the chest was buried long enough for the power of its evil to sink back into the ground. Then we had tourists, and then we had prosperity for a while. The island started to build once more, hotels, shops, people came for holidays and we prospered, though we never saw the same number of people; the wars saw to that. Until recently things were good. And then your father came. He found the chest again, and, well, here you see the results.'

I was speechless for a moment. She actually believed all this, and worse, she was expecting me to believe it too.

'And what happened to this chest?' I asked, hardly believing that I was playing along.

'All I know is that your father found it. He came to realise what he had found and then, like the boy's father, tried to put things right. But he also was unable to finish the task.'

'So he killed himself out of guilt?'

'Who knows why they kill themselves. Who knows what goes through their minds. All I know is that for years, through history, our island has come to prosper and then only to fall, and each time something has caused the decline.'

I looked at her quizzically. 'This is going to turn into a history lesson now?'

She gave a short laugh.

'Romans, then others, all empires rise to fall,' she said. 'The only sure thing about tyrants is that they do not last. The Knights, the Turks, Italians, Germans, all came and did well here, and then something changed all that.'

'Whatever was in that chest? Some kind of evil?' I had a grin on my face as wide as a clown's and just as sincere. 'Why didn't they just leave it buried, or, I don't know, throw it in the sea?'

'You heard the story. It gets found, it draws men to it. It returns. Maybe they tried, in history, to burn it, to bury it, to drown it, perhaps, and yet it comes back. It belongs in one place, and one place only, and until it is there…' She left that hanging.

'And what has this to do with me?' I asked.

'You are your father's son. He has left you the task to finish his work.'

'Why should I?' I felt as if I could be blunt with her then. I felt close enough to her to even start fighting about this if I needed to. But I also felt that the best way to stay in her company was to play along with her stories and see where they led. I could, of course, have just walked away, said goodbye and waited out my time until the next boat came along. But there was something about her that made me want to stay. Not only to spend more time with her where I felt right, but to find out more about what Frank was up to. She had, after all, been talking about 'treasure' and I had, after all, come here to claim my inheritance. All said and done, I need the money.

'Why should you finish your father's work?' she said, without looking at me. She didn't answer herself, just shrugged. 'You need to hear more stories. There are many ways into hell from our earth. Many ways to get down to his kingdom below.'

'What?' Where was this going, I wondered. In fact, where had this come from?

'We believe that something was brought here to be taken to a place, a place it never reached.'

'Sorry? If you're going to be a tour guide you will need to be clearer than that.' I laughed. 'That sounds like one of Frank's riddles.'

'It is,' she said, simply. 'The father was searching for a well of history when his last son died. The well was in his own brother's house and it is now known as "The Well of Thirteen."'

'Don't tell me, unlucky for some?'

'No,' she replied, and in that one short word I could hear her disapproval. This clearly was not a subject to make light of. 'Thirteen members of that one family eventually all killed themselves in that one house, at that one well. The father of that family failed them all, and your father said that no man had the strength to take the curse to where it should be.'

'Whoa! Slow down a moment,' I said, and whichever way I tried I could not hide the smirk on my face. 'So, let me get this right: my father thought that an entrance to Hades, to hell, right, he thought that there was one here? On his island?'

She nodded.

'And that's why people are dying? Because hell wants to drag them down there or something?'

And now she was shaking her head.

'Well, what, then? Tell me.'

'This is all I know,' she said, and she had the air of a teacher explaining for the very last time. 'Frank believed he had found the chest. He thought it held something that caused the curse of suicide on our island. It spreads and will spread wider until what it holds is taken to hell. This was his work and this is what he could not finish.'

'So he left me some books and his clues so I could find this thing and chuck it away? Sounds pretty daft to me, but if that's all he needs…' I shrugged it all off. Happy to go along with her so I could sit with her, not happy to believe any of these stories.

Until a thought struck me and I all but slapped my forehead.

'But if it's old, it's valuable. And if it's valuable I will want to find it.'

She turned quickly to me then and her eyes fired up. 'No!' she said, and reached to grab my arm. But she stopped herself and withdrew it. 'No,' she said more quietly, less urgently. 'This is not to be taken lightly. It is there, out there, stalking the village. It will grow in strength. But hell wants it, and only the one who truly understands, truly cares, can take it back.'

'Throw away my inheritance? What was in this chest? Was it valuable?'

'This is not the point.'

'It is valuable, isn't it? Well, where is it?'

'This is not about money.'

'Where did he hide it?' I stood up, faced her. I was suddenly excited at the thought of seeing this thing that Frank had obviously left me.

'This is his point; he told no one. You must find out.'

'So he left me a treasure hunt?'

That is so like the old man, so twisted. Hey, son, I've got something for you but you have to deserve it. Fail and I flail. Well, maybe that's a bit extreme, but, failure, giving in, suicide even, were not Frank's way. Obscure clues and playing games with my hopes and expectations were.

'This is all one big game, isn't it?'

'Death is no game,' she said, but I wasn't really listening to her now.

I had so many questions in my head. Suddenly, I was feeling light-headed with it all. It suddenly became clear to me that I'd been left something tangible and all I had to do was find it.

My hand stung me like hell right then. But I didn't care. All I cared about was finding this metal chest, the one that had been buried off and on since, what did she say? Romans? That means money, that means value and the chance to sell it, and there's everything sorted right there. Sarah's demands (new kitchen included, how would that slay her, eh?), Ben's private educational psychologist or whatever is needed to rid him of his bad dreams, new equipment for me, a decent start-over for all of us. All I had to do was play along with Frank's game and I'd be home and dry. Simple.

'So...' I turned back to ask her if she knew anything else, but she was walking away from me. 'Wait,' I called, and she did. She slowly looked over her shoulder. She looked sad, I thought, and my enthusiasm dropped like a stone in my guts leaving me deflated and down.

'I go to mourn now with my friends,' she said, and walked on. I was aware of a bell softly tolling from somewhere in the village below.

Eighteen

I followed her, ran after her and persuaded her to give me a chance. This was difficult for me, I explained as we walked down into the village. The day was turning towards evening now and the shadows were cold. I explained something about Frank, about how he and I didn't get on (I put it very mildly and didn't go into detail). I told her how he had been, when I first remembered him, in the Church, and how he had given all that up after my mother died (again, not the full detail), and how he had, for a reason never explained, blamed me for her death. I tried to plead the case of a sceptic against all things 'afterlife' and 'not of this world' in order that she might more understand where I was coming from.

She listened until I had run out of things to say and my words, even to me, were starting to sound like excuses. We had arrived at a wooden bench, me slightly out of breath, she not showing any sign of difficulty with the steps.

We sat facing west, the sun heading towards the hills in the distance, a long, crumbling path of steps and cobbles leading down towards the sea. We sat, a respectable distance between us, on the bench, and all she said was, 'Things that are hidden don't stay hidden from those who believe.'

I looked at her. The pink glow of the dying sun lit her face and warmed her eyes as she stared out ahead. My heart skipped a beat as it seemed to be doing every time I looked at her.

'I believe,' I said, and she looked at me keenly. 'I mean, I believe there is a story,' I clarified. 'And that my father found some kind of valuable object and that the people here believe that this led to their problems. But the link with all the suicides?'

I shook my head. My eyes stayed firmly on hers. 'Not on an island so beautiful, surely?'

Something made me reach out to her then. I wanted to touch her, to feel her hand in mine, but as I reached towards her she pulled back from me.

'I distract you from your work,' she said.

There was something very sad in the way she said that.

'But in a very welcome way,' I said.

She looked away to the hills again trying hard to ignore what was behind my words, but her eyes did flash back to me, as if she was checking that I was still watching her. She was flattered by my words, but keeping up her pretence. She was giving me some kind of cause to hope that...

'Frank spoke about clues,' she said, cutting into my thoughts. 'Did you find something like this?'

'I suppose. I mean there are loads of things that could be thought of as clues.'

I reached for her again even though she'd made it clear she did not want to be touched. I couldn't help myself. There was (is!) something about her that draws me, every time, towards her, to want to touch her, to want to be with her. If there is any kind of magic here, I thought to myself, it comes from her. She has charmed me, bewitched me. And then I pulled myself up short for even thinking such things; after all, who was the sceptic here?

But my hand, moving gently along the bench to where hers was resting, came too close and she stood up.

'Not yet,' she said, and started to walk away.

Not yet? What did that mean? It meant hope.

'Wait!' I rose to follow.

She turned to me, serious, sad, bewitching. 'Please,' she said, 'go and finish Frank's work. For me?'

I would have done anything for her then. But:

A huge, dull explosion rocked the ground I stood on and echoed away slowly, bouncing from hill to hill. I felt it in my chest as I instinctively grabbed the back of the bench for support and turned to face the sound.

'What the…?'

'It is Easter,' she said, her eyes still fixed on me, her expression unchanged, unmoved. 'Tonight, they burn Judas. They are desperate. It is a tradition and the dynamite scares away the evil. But…' She looked over her shoulder and up to the mountain where I could now see a plume of grey smoke rising. 'But, this we usually do on Sunday. They fear that by Sunday it will be too late.'

I could feel all that scepticism coming back to me. I could feel the shadows creep up on me as the sun set, all warmth draining from her face and my body.

'Please,' she said. 'For me.' And then she was gone.

I am at the house. I have his work set out before me. I am going to give this one last look. For her. I am going to read through his madness and see what else is in this box, see what he was doing. If I can find out what he was trying to do, then, maybe, I can persuade these people that there is nothing for them to worry about. If I can in some way cure their superstition then perhaps they will see sense.

And then, perhaps, Stavroula will let me get closer to her.

Perhaps.

5

He sits at the table surrounded by his father's mess. The walls now plastered with notes and papers, drawings and research, the books open across the table, spread out before him. Photographs of buildings, numbers, dates, images of the past, text in so many different languages, history. A jumble.

He sits and reads, looks, searches, all driven by the new aim of finding an answer. Whether he believes or not is a different matter for him now. He knows there is something here, and he knows that in finding the answer he may win the attentions of the woman, but he still does not believe in the same way as she does.

His eyes are drawn to the tape again, but he doesn't want to hear his father's words, possibly his last words. He doesn't need to hear that and he has chosen to blank out and forget the demonic voice that he heard on the tape. Beside it is the silver pillbox, and, once again, he picks this up and shakes it. There is something inside. The thing has a near invisible line around its oval shape marking the lid, but he cannot get his nail in there to prise it open. He reaches for his glass. It is, once again, empty.

He suddenly shivers; someone has walked over his grave and he stops for a moment to think. What did she say? And when was that? Two days ago now? That when you get that feeling you will come to money? He laughs and gets up to leave the room, still trying to free the lid of the box as he goes. He is searching for another drink and there is some in the kitchen.

As he leaves he throws the pillbox back onto the table where it comes to rest on an open journal.

The room waits for him. There is the faintest whisper of chatter from the shadows now creeping in fast as the sun dies behind the hills. A gentle babble fills the air as the dust settles and time waits.

A harsh, metallic slice of a whispered command cuts through

the stillness. The pill box lid pops open. The clue inside waits. And he returns with a fresh bottle and a new determination, and sits once again. Where he notices the open box. It must have happened when he threw it down, he rationalises, and then he sees what is inside and carefully takes it out. He holds it up to the dying light and a smile breaks across his face.

A small, dull and weathered, silver coin. An artefact? An inheritance? A valuable object? The coin from the story?

The answer, he knows, will be in these books. He turns the coin over in his fingers. He can't read the worn, Latin inscription. He can't see the face on the one side, but he knows he is closer to something valuable. He looks back at the pile of books and papers, and sighs. The coin slips into his pocket and the glass slips into his hand.

He starts to read.

One of the interesting things was the "discovery" of the Gospel of Judas and the way it was secretly translated by National Geographic in order to preserve their scoop. To preserve secrecy, they relied on a very small team of experts and did not consult widely with the leading scholars. When they broke the story, they did so claiming that the Gospel of Judas represented the beliefs of a group of Judas supporters who thought Judas had been maligned and that he was only doing Jesus' bidding, aiding and abetting him to get crucified according to God's plan; that it had all been cooked up between them and that one day the world would realise that Judas was in fact a hero and would have an honoured place in heaven. That idea had been around long before the discovery of the Gospel, but it was thought the Gospel was a very early expression of that idea. And that was the news angle that broke the story: Judas was wrongly accused.

But when the leading Coptic scholars finally got to see the text, they took a quite different line on translating key passages. Their view was that the Gospel was very much anti-Judas. This often comes down to the fine nuance of certain Greek words (the Greek words that would have been behind the Coptic translation), and what emphasis they would have been given at that time. Whether, for example, a certain word was understood as a nice word like "spirit" or whether it was understood more as "demon".

While outside shutters are closed tight against the night. A thick shadow slides up the lanes as if the sun is setting unusually quickly and night is in a hurry to arrive.

In the little square, Petros and some village youths have put together the effigy. A pile of wood stands on the millstone, a circle of a fire, a pole supporting the figure of a man, ready to burn. Judas, who betrayed Christ, is to be put to death, by fire. By the fires of hell. The flames he should have felt two thousand years ago will be brought on him tonight. He will be banished.

Stavroula stands in the corner of the ruined square and watches. She has her arms wrapped around herself, for warmth and for security.

They are trying everything, their charms, their talismans, but none are working. It is too strong for them.

She looks up to the strangely lopsided house and its back balcony and her eyes become wider. She puts a hand to her mouth, gasps, and then, scared, she runs away.

Petros looks up to where she was standing as he and his friends throw the last pieces of wood onto the fire, smiling grimly.

A dull, distant explosion rocks the ground.

But the contrary view runs along the lines that Judas was in fact a demon from the 13th realm above the earth. This 13th realm was understood to be where the most powerful demons of all lived. So, while Jesus was God made man, Judas was in a sense being cast as the anti-Christ, the most powerful demon made man. And far from saying that Judas would one day have the most honoured place in heaven, the contrary view says the Gospel claims Judas would never get a place in heaven.

What I'm not sure about was whether (in this 'circles of demons' belief-structure) this meant that Judas was in effect Satan himself, or whether he was Satan's chief demon, a kind of Son-of-Satan. The Jewish belief was that there was a God with lots of different ranks of angels (cherubim, seraphim, archangels, and so on), and then there was Satan (a fallen angel) and his supporters (other fallen angels). And the Christian demonology is developed from the Jewish view.

But the Gospel of Judas seems to come from a rather different "other world" view with these 13 realms of ever increasingly powerful demons. And it has ties to the Gnostics who also had a view about spirits in the stars and special secrets that were "out there". So I'm not quite sure where Judas fits into all this in the contrary view.

In the small house along the lane it wakes the dozing man. Chris sits upright in the chair, the wound on his hand suddenly throbbing, and realises he had drifted off. He reaches instinctively for his drink, his unsteady arm moving out in a sideways direction before coming back on track and finding the glass.

He takes a long swig and slams the glass down, his head cloudy, his thoughts muddled. The only thing that he is certain of now is that his hand is starting to swell so much that his finger is throbbing. In the morning he must insist that she find him a doctor.

He hears the dynamite echo away and thinks that in its dying vibrations he can hear voices; excited whisperings of children shushed by adults, like a chorus waiting in the wings as the show goes on, hushed but bubbling, barely under the surface of release.

And then the room is silent and he shakes his head to clear his thoughts.

The candle has burned down and he watches the flame as he comes to. As he wakes up, he sees it flutter and then fade away. Darkness covers him and he grumbles as he feels around the desk for another candle.

He finds one and is about to light it when he realises there is already a light in the room. It comes from behind him. Another candle he lit earlier?

He turns in his chair and his eyes adjust to the gloom. There is only the very faintest of distant light from a moon outside, but not enough to see by. But there, over by the wall, he can see a long, thin sliver of yellow light. Where is that coming from? What it is? Some kind of flickering candlelight coming from the wall. How is that possible?

He slowly leaves the chair and walks towards it, a few paces across the room, his hands outstretched before him. His hand touches something cold. The cupboard.

There is a light coming from behind its cupboard doors. How is that possible? He reaches back for the candles and lights one, bringing it close to the cupboard. He's tried looking in here before but it is locked. His mind starts to tumble as he tries to rationalise. How come there's a light? On a timer, perhaps? Some kind of night light? But there is no power tonight. Batteries? He's not noticed it before. He crouches down and looks closer, but the gap between door and surround is too thin to see inside.

He looks about the room, throwing the candle at the darkness to light the corners. He needs a knife and heads to the kitchen. The chatter starts up immediately, the voices quick to discuss what will happen next. What will he find? Will he…?

He returns to silence, quickly, and goes straight to the cupboard. Kneeling down he starts to play at the lock with the sharp blade, but nothing is giving. He changes his position to give himself more leverage and moves the candle in closer, hunches his shoulders, cramps himself up to the cupboard, his attention completely focused on the lock.

He finds that if he puts the blade in and levers the door slightly he can just get the tips of his fingers into the gap, maybe enough to force the lock.

The knife slips and he tries again, this time using his wrist as a fulcrum for the blade, being careful not to let it slip the wrong way. His fingertips dig in, quickly becoming hot with pain as he pulls back on the door.

The blade lies flat across his wrist and the only way to force the lock now is to twist the blade. He slowly turns it. It scrapes across the metal of the lock and the delicate skin of his wrist.

The knife bends with the strain, ready to snap and slice.

With a yell, he forces the door and it springs open. The knife clatters to the floor.

He sits back, catching only a glimpse of what was inside before the light goes out. A breeze, caused by the fast opening of the door, blew out the candle that was alight in there.

How was that possible? A candle alight behind a locked door?

It can only be a trick of the light, surely. He moves his own candle towards the dark void of the open cupboard, aware now of the acute silence in the room, only his own heartbeat in his head, the thumping in his ears and the heavy pump of his blood through his infected hand. He holds his light into the cupboard and sees only a crumpled piece of paper.

Taking it back to the table, and filling his glass, he spreads it out, flattens it down with his hand, lights another candle, and stares at what he has in front of him. He sips his drink.

The room on the edge of the candle-spill seems to creep closer until it envelops him with its papers and its images. Words written on pages from books, highlights from printed text ripped from their bindings and now stuck up on the walls like random thoughts from a scattered mind.

Judas. Shall be the thirteenth. Disciples. Romans. Gospel… Chapter? Verse? Meanings? Knights. Italians? 1909. Well? Location? Maps. Drawings. Guts spilled out. Potter's Field? Question mark after question mark. Red circles around words: 13th realm above the earth. Bible. History. Island? More question marks. And a photograph of Frank staring at him, watching, judging, laughing at him.

And now what looks like a map. A jumbled scribble of lines and lanes and numbers, and all written in a dark pencil, drawn roughly, quickly, and screwed up. It twists and turns, an arrow pointing to the millstone square and the word 'Well?', but more arrows, and all leading to nowhere.

Nowhere. A dead end.

And he realises.

'You bastard!' he shouts out, and sweeps everything from the table. The papers, the books, the box, everything apart from the light and his drink. He is shouting at the stuff, kicking it around the room, laughing and drinking, and yelling at his father.

'That is what this is all about!'

He laughs, and drinks some more, and then, wiping tears from his eyes but not caring if they are tears of joy or anger, he starts throwing things into the box.

'This is what it is all about,' he repeats as he randomly throws what he can reach into the box. Papers, books, anything that is to hand that was his father's.

But there are things he misses through his watery eyes.

He comes to the photo of his father on the wall. This he takes down slowly, and then, deliberately, sticks it into the woodwork of the cupboard with a pin through each eye.

The box is packed, apart from some things still stuck to the walls and littering the floor. He sees the small photo album that now lies open, discarded like he was. The image of the four boys looking up woefully at him.

He shakes his head and through his tears he simply says, 'No,' as he picks up the box and leaves the house.

5

Beneath the debris and clutter of domestic life, in the cellar, not far away, a well is covered with a simple wooden cover. It stirred in anticipation once, a few days back when Frank was in the room. No one has been close since. The dust has settled here, the moonlight shines in with untroubled silvery beams. But the light is swallowed by the darkness before it reaches the floor because, in this room, darkness always wins.

But between the stone wall of the large, round well and its wooden cover, a rim of dark red light can be seen, glowing faintly from deep inside.

And now, as the moon fades and the darkness thickens, something stirs inside the walls. Across the large, dusty room, behind a child's baseball cap that hangs from a nail and covers a worn, loose stone, a black, viscous mist starts to finger its way into life as something trapped inside tries to force its way out.

Nineteen

He is stumbling through the lanes, the box of his father's life clutched in his arms, his face wet with tears. He doesn't know where this is coming from, this hate, this sadness, this confusion. He only knows that the only way to lay this ghost to rest is to get it *far away from him*. This teasing, this torture, this planned humiliation. Leading him on, inheritance, suggestions of property, of value, of something to atone for his treatment, his bullying. It's all pouring through him and out of him as he sniffs, draws his breath in hard and stumbles into the kafeneion square.

She is there, the Dutch woman. She is writing feverishly in a book. She has been coldly, calmly, looking for things which may help him.

Since realising that what she has been told, what she has heard and what she saw in that book might actually be possible, she has started to see threads. She too can't explain why she feels this. If she didn't know better she would say a darker force, something beyond her, is starting to disturb her rational thinking and her feelings.

She can see the tunnel ahead and there is no light at the end. But along the way there may be answers that will help him understand his own demons.

She sees him now, stumbling into the square as she sits at the café and writes by the dim light outside. She stands as he lurches up to her and she can smell the drink on his breath. But that is not what worries her. The first word she says is, 'Frank?' And he glares at her.

'Christopher?' She corrects herself, but before she can ask

what the problem is he is bumping into the table and leaning in too close to her.

'I got it,' he slurs. 'I figured it out.'

She is used to dealing with desperate people, but she fights for words now.

'Yes?' she asks.

'It's his one last dig,' he says to her, and wipes his eyes. His face falls suddenly serious. 'His one last... kick in the nuts. One last try at completely screwing me up.'

'You might think this, Christopher.' Her experience kicks in. 'But...'

'He was sick, Helen.' He gives her no chance to rationalise or discuss. He knows his mind. 'He was sick. It's all some kind of psycho-game. He was sick!'

'No,' she says, and picks up her book. 'I have been reading. There are things...'

But he has gone. He has lurched away across the square and up the steps, away from her and into the lanes.

He stumbles on through the twists and turns of his father's map, heading for the drop. That big high drop he saw when he arrived. That will do, that's far enough down. Throw it. Chuck it. He trips on a step, grabs at the wall for support and gives himself just a brief moment to slow and calm.

It doesn't help.

But it gives him time to see a light up ahead and to hear voices. Something is flickering through the darkness. The stones of a wall are turning from black to grey to red to orange, and he can hear crackling. A fire.

He pushes himself away from the wall and sways, walks, runs towards the light.

A church bell tolls loud and profound close by and a deep

rumble of gunpowder rolls through the darkness as he approaches a turn in the lane.

He can see sparks now, rising up amid smoke from up ahead. He climbs some steps, pressing down on his knees, his chest sore, his head pounding, his hand burning as he carries the box up and into the millstone square.

A group of villagers stand looking at the fire in the middle. At the front of them is the long-haired man. Petros is just moving back, away from the flames he has just been fanning. Around him the other villagers stand talking, smiling at the flames, some crossing themselves as the bell clangs on.

The flames start to reach the feet of a figure that is tied to the pole and he recognises the dark trousers. He understands what Petros was doing now, making a guy for the bonfire. He approaches, calming, not wanting to draw attention to himself and sees a young man throw something into the flames. A second later the fire crackles and spits as a cracker explodes inside the mass of glowing wood and rubbish. Another young man throws another red stick and then someone throws one on the ground. It explodes near Chris' feet and he leaps back, out of the way.

He has been seen.

Petros is looking at him now. He looks mean and angry as he strikes a red stick against a box of matches and throws it. Not at Chris, but near him. The firework cracks open with an ear-splitting gunshot of a noise; contained within the ruined walls of the square, it amplifies and hurts.

The flames of the fire strengthen and grow. They are up to the figure's waist, now. The villagers turn their attentions to each other. The talk grows louder, more confident and more excited as the flames reach up the body and towards the head. Some people start clapping, others laugh and jeer, more bangers are thrown, and Chris looks at the face on the guy.

He drops the box and sees his father looking back at him.

It is a mask, a photograph like the one he found and stuck to the cupboard. Frank. They are burning an effigy of Frank.

He has a flashback. He is young. His mother stands on the edge of a cliff high above them. They are on the edge of some woods. They have left the car and walked. It's a sunny day, there was the promise of Coke and a picnic when they found the right spot. They had been to church. He had done everthing right and now they were about to eat. But she went away.

He can hear his father calling for her and shouting. Then he looks up. The sky is white and the cliff is high, higher than he can climb and almost too high to see the tiny figure on the top, looking down, feet on the edge. He feels himself sway. He knows it is his mother.

And then his father's face comes into his view. Close up, angry, white, panicked.

'Stay here,' he orders. 'Have faith. I will talk her down.'

He doesn't know what's gone wrong, what changed. What happened here? But, as he looks up, he sees the tiny figure high up and now it is falling through the air and he hears his father's voice scream out, 'No!'

In the square, he opens his eyes and sees the flames lick around the photograph of Frank's face. The paper doesn't burn, or even blacken or twist. It just stares back at him, mocking, grinning, defying him to take that next step. Dare you boy?

He kneels down, his eyes on the face as the flames rise around it, and Frank's cold dead eyes glare back at him, and he picks up a journal. Defiantly he throws it into the flames. The face just stares back. He throws another, and then a third, all the time staring back into that face and waiting for the flames to burn it away. They don't. It carries on laughing at him.

The bells ring louder, the dynamite booms out and the villagers throw more crackers, and some start to turn their attention towards Chris. The flames explode and leap. The heat is on his face as he screws up papers, throws in fistfuls of photographs. The whole lot goes into the flames.

'No!'

He hears her voice and it is enough to spin his head away from the flames and towards the people. There, standing just beyond the line of villagers, is Stavroula, and she is calling out 'No!' But it is too late. The clues, the papers, the books, they are all going to burn.

He looks back to the flames. The image is still there. Frank has not burned yet. He picks up the last journal and looks back to Stavroula. But she has gone.

The last book. 'The Judas Curse.' He throws it into the flames. Takes the silver coin from his pocket and throws that. All of it. Gone.

But still his father's face grins down it him impossibly untouched by the roaring flames. He feels the intense heat on his face and in his lungs and he feels a hand on his shoulder, pulling him back, a woman shouting.

'This is madness!'

Helen is with him, dragging him away from the fire, and then he hears her scream.

'No! Please, no!'

He looks across from the nightmare vision of his father

refusing to burn in hell to the sight of a youth from the village stepping towards the flames. He holds a petrol can over his head and is pouring its contents over himself, Chris can smell it.

'Someone do something!' Helen screams, but no one is moving. The villagers are all now watching Chris. It is as if they can't see the boy. As if they don't want to.

To his right, Chris sees the boy drop the can and walk steadily, purposefully towards the fire.

And then he hears a voice close in his ear whispering his name. A man's voice. He looks back at the effigy and sees his father lift up his head and open his mouth and say the words, 'You betrayed me.'

A sharp hiss, a deafening roar and a blinding flash of light to his right.

He staggers to his feet and runs.

And, in the dark cellar, not far away, the wall trembles and something inhuman starts to breathe again.

Twenty

The outside wall of the house drips, wet with washed paint and water. A broken bottle lies on the path, a discarded bucket, his father's initials wiped to a smear in the midnight frenzy as the last lung-tremble boom of dynamite growls away into a darker night. The wreath of flowers, once hung on the door to protect, lies ripped and trampled on the cold damp stones protecting nothing, and the metal gates stand firmly slammed against the hopes of the village.

The long-haired man squats against the opposite wall, his tear-stained face screwed up with anger and hopelessness. His narrow eyes stare coldly at the house as his heart beats faster with fear and anger.

'What have you done?' he whispers.

A shadow to his left, a shape moving, a shifting form of deeper black against the cold stone turn in the narrow lane. He suddenly realises how alone he is, how vulnerable, how unprotected they now are. He stands on unsteady feet and wipes his face with the back of his hand.

'What have you done?' he repeats, and spits towards the house.

The shadow moves closer and he turns and walks quickly away.

§

Inside the house, a solitary candle burns down towards a spreading pool of soft wax on the table. Discarded papers litter the room like cast-off thoughts. The laptop sits useless, its battery dead, the camera still attached, the mobile phone beside it. The solitary chair, the small table, a bottle, a glass, his jacket thrown into a corner, the open cupboard, empty, the dusty, wooden floor, the peeling paint around the shuttered window, the overhead wire and fragile bulb, and the last melancholy whispers of the once hopeful.

Nothing moves, nothing breathes in here as the night creeps through the room, an invisible presence that brings the rich velvet comfort of silence. It settles its peace on the walls, drapes them with the indigo-crush of mourning for those now abandoned, settles the wailing voices to silent acceptance of fate, hushes the hopeful whispers of the lost and wandering.

The damp, cold inevitability of night silences the whispers and calms the excited expectation as it moves into the small hallway, weaves and rolls, tumbles stealthily over itself across the floor, up towards the painted ceiling, down across the front doors, sealing all within.

It fingers its way towards the soft candlelight beyond the bedroom door, creeps in, around the door jamb, under the bed, over the covers where he lies sleeping.

It slides across the bedside table, dirtying the stream-clear liquid in a water glass, coating its companion bottle, choking the candle, threatening the light.

It paints the dark walls blacker and creeps closer to his half open mouth as he lies stupefied in monochrome dreams of burning fathers and falling mothers. He turns his head, eyes moving behind screwed down lids, furrowed brow, pained mouth.

It covers him, smothers him in its heavy cloak and slowly, insidiously, starts to seep into his skin.

A flicker of light in the room, the hum of the fridge in the kitchen, a distant drone of a power plant and the overhead lights glow into life. The quiet beep of the mobile phone, the dull green glow of its face. A message.

Asleep, he clutches the sheet and screws it tight in his hand as his breathing becomes lighter, faster, and his brow leaks sweat and alcohol. Tears from his screwed up eyes, a fast draw-in of breath and a gasp as his eyes flash open. They stare up towards the ceiling and the eye-splitting light of the glowing overhead bulb.

He sits upright, takes a moment to realise where he is, his head clouded with the alcohol, his heart in his throat, and the image of his falling mother fast scurrying back to the depths of his mind.

He gets his breath as he instinctively backs up and huddles against the head of the bed, drawing his legs towards him.

He listens. No sound.

He waits. No movement.

But there is something in the room with him. Something has changed, either inside him or within the room, something is different.

Something is there.

And slowly he realises what it is. His eyes pull him from the safe vision of the end of the bed and towards the bedside table, drawing his attention to what now stands there. The glass, the candle, the bottle, and now a photograph.

Frank, his face looking back accusingly from the yellowed paper. The same photograph that they had used on the effigy.

And it stands on a book, 'The Judas Curse.'

The same journal that he had thrown last into the fire.

5

In a brightly painted, toy-strewn room, the small boy clutches his bear, lost in innocent and adventurous dreams. But his dreams are disturbed as a dark shadow crosses up and over his bed. Unaware of what stands beside him, the boy finds his dreams receding, the adventure is fading and sleep is no longer there to save him.

As he opens his eyes and looks up, he is not scared. It is as if someone told him to expect this, as if he knew this is what he has to do.

He feels something heavy land at the foot of his bed and he holds out his bear to the presence beside him. But it has not come for the bear.

The boy swings himself from the bed and looks towards the window. Dawn is coming, the room is starting to glow silver and cold as the first light from a grey clouded sun sneaks in. But he doesn't feel cold. He simply stands up, clutches his bear in one hand and looks towards the door where the dark presence is now receding, leading him.

He nods, happily enough, and walks towards the door. He reaches the end of his bed. There he stops for a second to collect the noose which has been left for him. He trails the rope in one hand and his bear in the other as he leaves his room. He follows the presence and walks calmly towards his death.

Twenty-one

I don't know how to start on this. This could well be the last thing I write for you, Ben. This could be my last imitation of your grandfather's journal-keeping. Ironic, eh? Someone will explain it all to you one day. I hope that someone is me. No, I know that that someone will be me. But this may be the last time I can write these things down, thanks to the pain in my hand. I just changed the dressing, putting a new and clean handkerchief over the cut and it actually looks like it's not infected now. I don't think I will need a doctor. The hand is just so painful and the main pain has spread from the cut on my finger towards the centre of my palm, making it hard to hold a pen.

But this is all an attempt to avoid writing down what I remember of last night, and what happened this morning.

I don't remember much of last night, to be honest. I know I drank a lot, the empty bottles show me that. I've now been through everything I bought the other day and can't get any more, so that won't happen again. I can't get any more to drink, or even eat, possibly, because there is now no more shop up here and no way, so I am told by Helen, of getting any more provisions until the next boat comes in. That may be tomorrow.

Last night.

I remember taking Frank's books and stuff from the house. At least, I seem to have taken most of it as some of it is still here. And I remember finding the locals burning an effigy, doing their 'Burning of Judas' ceremony. I remember bells tolling for funerals and thinking nothing of it as that happens a lot around here. But then someone had also told me (who, and was it in a dream?) that there are always death bells in Easter week; they call it Great Week here. But, whatever, it's all a mess and a blur and all I need to remember is that I'd had enough of Frank's mad ramblings and these mad locals, and that beautiful girl who speaks in riddles and promises me all while giving me nothing. (Note: edit some of this out in case Sarah reads it. Note to that note: no, leave it in, she cheated on me, and I am not even considering cheating on her, not yet, so let her read it. Who am I writing this for?)

I'd had enough of Frank's lunacy and chucked it out. There you go, done and dusted. I must have also washed Frank's initials from the house wall, and thrown away his wreath of anti-evil flowers that was on the front gates. It's done. I had made my case and firmly discarded any thoughts of superstitions and evil and all that stuff.

All that is left for me to do now is pack up my gear and wait for the boat.

Who am I kidding? This is what I would like to feel, but I can't. I can't help but think that there is actually something more happening here. Whether it is to do with the chest, or box, that Frank found, if it has got anything to do with some ancient well, some superstitious writings and rambles from the past, the Gospel of Judas and those myths, well, who knows? But today I do feel something.

This is hard to figure out because this is not how I work. There's a photo on my camera showing the father and boy sitting at a table in the old 1909 square. I was there. I took the photo. When I checked the camera this morning, as I worked all this through, there is no father and son, only the table. I know, it is only a fault in the camera. It has to be. That is the only explanation. I know this, and yet...

But I can't check it on the laptop because that has died on me. The second battery is also drained and there is no way to charge it.

I woke to find one of Frank's journals by the bed with a photo of him that I must have left behind. I was pretty sure I'd thrown that particular journal away but I'd obviously left it here. It's here on the desk now and I need to make some notes about what's in it, in light of what we talked about today. But more of that later.

So, last night was a blur, but they burned their effigy and I made my point and they threw bangers at me, if I remember right, and it was all pretty mad and drunken. And today, well, today I went to make sure I'd not dreamed it all.

I was standing in the square. The millstone was covered with ash and some half-burned logs. There was no sign of anyone, no bells, nothing going on. It was a cold, grey day (and it still is) and there's a wind that's pretty biting, I have to say. And there's no heating in this house.

Anyway, I was standing there looking at the ashes and kicking around some discarded, red cardboard tubes from the crackers, when she appeared on the far side of the square. She was wrapped up in a shawl of some sort. It slashed a flash of red across her shoulders, brightening her customary black outfit. I remember thinking she always wears black.

Stavroula stood and looked at me for a long time, and me at her. I wished then that I'd cleaned my teeth better. My mouth was still very stuck with the left-over smell of last night's drink.

It wasn't until I saw her, the first living person I'd seen since waking up, that I remembered what had happened. It came back to me with a sickening slap across my stomach and I looked at the burn marks on the flag stones. It was there, last night, that someone had poured petrol over themselves and set themselves alight. Wasn't it? I saw the red petrol can in the corner of the square and felt sick.

'What was that madness?' I asked her across the remnants of the fire, pointing to the can.

She, as has become her custom, answered my question with something of a riddle.

'You see,' she said, stepping closer, 'it has been around us for many days, waiting. And now it comes closer. Now it starts its descent like a hawk falling to its prey. Now it is with us.'

'Oh, please,' I said. Although I admit to finding her the most attractive person I've seen, probably ever, I must also admit that she drives me crazy when she speaks like this. Unfortunately, this seems to be the only way she does speak.

'This is your curse?' I laughed, and shook my head.

'This is what your Father set upon us,' she said, calmly. 'This is what visits our island each time the chest comes to the surface, each time it is found. This is what your father promised to end.'

'This needs specialist help,' I said, kicking at some of the half-burned logs. 'You need someone from the mainland to come and put an end to this hysteria. I'm not qualified for that.'

'He thought you were. He had faith in you.'

'What?' This was not to be believed. 'My father had no faith in me. He hated me.'

'That is a strong assumption.' She walked around the remnants of the fire towards me and stood with her back to the tall, askew house as she spoke.

'Maybe you misjudge him. Your father promised us that he would find an end to this. He let us down. Then, he promised that you would kill this once and for all. And you arrived here.'

'And you've been blaming me ever since'

'Guiding you, not blaming.'

'Not you, I mean… They were throwing sticks of dynamite at me last night!'

'They were not. That's only a custom. Small fire crackers to ward off evil.'

'Yes, me! I am evil. Or, so they think. Anyway, what good did it do? That young man still…'

I had a flash of a man falling to his knees, on fire, and the crowd watching me, doing nothing.

'They don't know what to do,' she said. 'They only know that he promised that you would do what he could not. They, we, know that it is here now.'

'What?'

She didn't answer. 'That it is growing stronger with every word you say against the truth…'

'Oh, don't start on truth. You will sound just like Frank.'

This wasn't turning out how I intended but there was something growing inside me, some kind of anger, or possibly even hate, something festering that had been in here a long time and now I felt it was time for it to come out.

I can't explain it, not even now, but something within me had changed. And it started when I woke up in the morning and saw that photo of Frank by the bed, looking at me, close.

'What you did last night,' she said, 'was wrong. You have given him the upper hand now.'

'Who?' I demanded. What was she talking about now? 'No, on second thoughts, I don't want to know. This is, and has always been, ludicrous.'

'You do not feel it?'

She took a step towards me, her intense eyes penetrating.

'You do not feel this new presence in the village?'

'I feel a thumping headache and an empty stomach,' I said, rather churlishly. 'And cold. Nothing else.'

'When you burned Frank's work, you also burned our hopes,' she said.

I shook my head and folded my arms. 'When is the next boat?'

'If you go to his grave, then you will understand that this is not the end of it.'

I looked towards the general direction of where I remembered the suicides' graves to be; up and above the village.

'No point,' I said. 'He's dead. That's that. That is the end.'

'There is life after we die,' she said. 'There has to be.'

I saw in her face then some kind of desperation. Okay, so she has been trying her hardest to get me to fall in with her ideas about this thing, whatever it was that Frank had been meddling with: old superstitions, talked about, written about, and his work on it coinciding with a spate of suicides brought about by the decline in the Greek economy and country. She'd done her best to put her... what would you call it? Her ethereal view on this? Her supernatural slant? And she had tried every tack from being beguiling, which I quite liked, to being gloomy, which bored me, to being sad and vulnerable, which also appealed, to being harsh and determined, which simply reminded me of Frank. Now, though, now she genuinely looked desperate, as if she had just realised that she had failed at something.

'I care about you,' she said, simply.

That caught me off guard. I paused for a deep breath.

'You do?'

I don't know how she did it but she got right under my skin

then, under my skin and into my heart. I'm sure my face broke into a grin. I took a step towards her without thinking and held out my hand to take hers. But she pulled away.

'No. Not yet,' she said.

I wasn't hurt or annoyed this time. 'Okay.' I backed away, still smiling.

'I am sorry,' she said, 'but I am in mourning.'

She looked over her shoulder, towards the large house and the lane beyond as if she was expecting someone to come around the corner and catch her out.

'There's no one there,' I said.

And realised.

It suddenly struck me that she too has lost someone, or more than one person. She too has suffered loss and the only way she could get through it was to believe that she would see these lost loved ones again when it was her turn to join them. I suddenly had this vision of Stavroula also taking her own life, and that thought left me feeling hollow inside. I thought of her being buried in a suicide's grave marked only with a roughly hewn cross like the others, when she would have been brought up to believe that she would be laid to rest under marble, and watched over forever. Something had changed in me this morning and I was able to understand this about her.

But I didn't know what to say.

'My island is dying,' she said, and took another step towards me, eyes fixed. 'Help it while it still lives.'

I was right. She was giving in to this depression, the hysteria that had clearly affected everyone else who had recently killed themselves. Their belief in this superstition, like hers, was strong enough for them to take their own lives, and here I had the chance to help her. How?

No, not how. Why? There it was, the deal, the negotiation. Help her (somehow) and she would… what?

My mind was starting to race and tumble and I was having trouble putting clear thoughts together. She made it worse:

'Love starts with trust,' she said.

'What?' Strong words. Strong words that I am sure my father once used.

'That is what Frank used to shout.'

'He betrayed us, but you have the strength. He knew this.'

'He knew nothing about me.'

'He knew you could finish what he could not. He believed in you.'

I backed away. 'He believed in me? He actually said that?' This was too much to throw at me.

'He told me you would have the strength,' she said. 'Now all you need is the faith.'

I needed some time to process this, to take the data in and weigh it all up. I needed someone rational to talk to.

'I have to… I'll just…'

I was flustered. Frank believed in me? What kind of twist of the knife was that? My mind clouded up. I turned and walked away, waving vaguely over my shoulder. She would be there, somewhere, later, she would be around. I would come back to her. Later.

'I'll be waiting for you,' she called after me, as if she had just read my thoughts.

I was heading towards the kafeneion square in search of Helen. I passed the closed supermarket and heard the wailing and weeping of distress coming from inside.

Apparently I had the strength to do something about this.

Twenty-two

I found her in her usual place at the café in the square, dressed in a coat and scarf, a woollen hat covering her mess of flame red hair. Only this time she was not being served. The place was closed. She was drinking from a flask and flicking through a notepad. She saw me looking hopefully towards the closed door. I pressed my face up against the glass but inside was dull and looked as cold as it was outside.

'They have gone,' she said. 'Left.'

'Left? There's a boat?'

I sat at the table with her, wishing I'd brought my jacket out with me. The day was colder than the day before and the grey sky was doing nothing to warm me.

She pushed her small flask-cup of coffee towards me and I sipped some gratefully as she talked.

'The fishermen from the bay,' she said. 'But they only take family and messages. They have no room for us foreigners. So, we stay and wait for the ferry. There is one coming in tomorrow, they say. Meanwhile, I send word with a fisherman, a letter to pass on to the authorities. Maybe they send someone tomorrow. But to do what? These people need their priests. But no; also gone. Soon there will be nothing left here, only us two and their ghosts, yes?'

I looked at her expecting to see her smile, some kind of hint of sarcasm, but she just looked grim.

'You did not sleep so well,' she stated. 'Too much to drink, perhaps?'

'It was a bit rough,' I said. 'Bad dreams.'

'You remember what you did? What you saw?'

I nodded. 'He just set himself on fire.'

'Yes. I was there. It is like they want to find more and more bad ways. They want to find worse ways to end their lives, that is it. Punishment in death.'

'It's beyond superstition,' I said, thinking of Stavroula. 'These people actually believe that something is coming for them.'

She nodded. 'That boy last night, and then this morning, at the shop. Did you hear?'

'I heard noise from inside just now, but, no, what happened there?'

'The man at the shop, he, how do you call it? He took out his own eyes with a knife. Yes, he gouged out his eyes and then pushed the blade of the knife into the hole. This he did on purpose.'

Just the thought made me feel sick. But then her news got worse.

'And then another,' she went on. 'This one a child.'

She looked me directly in the eye as she mimed pulling something over her head. Suffocation, I wondered. But then she made a circle from both her hands, thumbs and fingers, and tightened it around her neck, sticking her tongue out and tipping her head to one side in a kind of grotesque parody of a hanging.

'Young boy. From a tree, with a rope. Did it himself.'

'Oh, God,' I groaned. 'What is wrong with these people?'

'And so young. The age, it makes no difference.' She took the coffee back and poured more for herself. 'Adults we can understand more easily, they know what they do, they know their problems and they make their decisions about their choices. They find their solutions. But children? And so young. Five, six he was, maybe. And how to tie a rope like this. Who does this for him? His parents? Himself? There is no sense here no more, only the questions. Yes?'

I said nothing.

She continued, 'This is so rare. Young children do not do this.'

She looked at me and put her hand on mine. Its coldness gave me a jolt. 'Soon,' she said, 'the dead will have to bury themselves.'

'Maybe help will come tomorrow,' I said, and I was aware how flat my voice sounded.

'Yes, maybe. I have sent word with a fisherman,' she repeated herself, and I wondered if her resolve, like mine, was also being worn away. It was as if her thoughts were never quite on what she was doing or saying. Always somewhere else. 'People out there need to know what happens here, what happens in this country.'

'You think they care?' I asked, looking across at the empty square. A ruin stood on the far side, abandoned long ago by the looks of it. Abandoned for a reason. A war, an economic decline, a recession, a depression. If so, it was a countrywide depression, not a personal one. Not a wretchedness that led the owners to die at their own hands. 'If they cared,' I said, 'they would have been here by now, surely.'

'Who is they?' she asked. 'Who is this mythical "they" of our blaming and our hopes? They will come and save us, will they? I mean, save them. Who will? Their leaders? Where are they? Their priests? They have all gone. They fear the "Evil" as much as their people. There is no *they*. No, there is only *you*.'

I looked back at her sharply.

'Not you as well,' I said, astounded that this sensible woman should be agreeing with them.

Okay, I'd only known her a few days but she was speaking

187

with such conviction that she was suddenly sounding like Stavroula, not Helen.

I expected her to be smiling cheekily or winking at me, but no. She was deadly serious this time.

'There is only you,' she repeated. 'If you will not help them then who is "they"? To the people here there is only you.'

'To do what?' I said, exasperated.

She held up a finger for me to wait and flipped open her notepad.

'I have here,' she said, 'something I found in the book. You remember this? We were at your house and I find this book and see your son's drawing and it gives me an idea. A thought. I worry as I walk home because of what Frank once said to me. It was to do with fathers and sons and passing down. I don't remember so good. We were sat here, sitting here, at this same table and...'

She stopped dead, mid-sentence, and looked away to the ground a little way off, thinking, remembering perhaps. I am sure she looked sad then, regretful, as if something had passed between them and she was actually missing my father.

'Were you close?' I dared to ask.

She looked back at me and searched my face with her eyes, practically frisked me with them.

'I am a scientist,' she said quietly. 'Like you, I believe in facts. What facts have you?'

'How do you mean?'

'Work it through. Your father said that it would all make sense, yes? I think this is what he said. This was not so long ago when he was starting to become ill. Oh, I say ill, but I mean an illness of the mind that even I could not help with. He says it will all make sense if we look at the facts. And if we have faith in them.' She looked at her notes, flipped over a page. 'Here I discover something strange. It was in the museum book. And that is a fact.'

'The fact is,' I said, looking over her shoulder at the door again, 'I want a drink.'

'Ah, yes, the drink that cures all ills?'

'You talk of solutions. It's a solution.'

She shook her head, not impressed. 'We talk of facts. So...' She started to count off on her fingers while glancing at her notes. 'Your father discovered a box, a metal chest he calls it. Fact. He was researching about Judas who may or may not have been fact, but he was researching, and we know this. Fact. He learned stories, some of them you now know, I think. He talked of a well? You know this story?'

'Entrance to hell, legendary, not fact, but it's in Greece, according to some myths. Yes, I read that part of his journal. He thought it was here on this island.'

'Yes, and why not? If it is anywhere it might as well be here.'

'It is a myth.'

'Yes, and that is a fact. So, he finds the chest. What is in it? He hears of a well. He learns the story of the four brothers, and you have their photograph. He sends you some things, that image and a link to the square where he writes 1909, the year the father of the boys opened his kafeneion. And in this square the local people they burn their Judas each year. And he writes it all down and he searches for answers, and he finds an answer.'

'He does? How do you know?'

She held up her finger again.

'He finds what the people on the island think is the answer. But the question now is, are you ready to hear it?'

That's the point isn't it? I ask myself.

Am I ready to hear what she, the only really rational person I've met in the past few days, has to say about my father's work and the clues he left behind? All of it has something to do with the gruesome deaths that are happening around me.

What can I say? Nothing. I shrug, and leave the decision up to her. After all, she is the professional.

'Yes,' she said, and nods. 'Yes, you are not ready to hear this. But I tell you all the same as it might help you out of our depression.'

'I'm not depressed,' I said, defensively.

'Depression, confusion… Yes? So,' a look back at her notes, 'we are looking for an answer and here we have the facts and they tell us what? That your father came to believe that he had discovered and unearthed something bad. Something that had been on the island for many, many years.'

I wondered if she was talking to herself now. She had become more and more engrossed in the notes and was hardly looking up at me.

'Each time it was discovered it brought the end of the island, well, it brought the island down. He talked about the Romans being here and falling, and then others taking the island, the Knights of Saint John were here and then they were defeated, and then the Turks were here and they were wonderfully successful, until…'

'That's just history,' I said. 'It has nothing to do with Frank.'

Again the warning finger, her head still in her notes.

'History that repeated itself all the way until 1912 when the Italians took the island, when it was a place that was at its zenith, with success and trade and business and was thriving. And then? Clang! Death bell. Then it started to die. Yes, this is history and this is fact. As is also the opening of the kafeneion in 1909.'

'So?' Where was she going with this?

'And the story of the boy and his father who found the chest in the catacombs? The date?'

'1909.'

'So, I think about this, as did Frank, and I looked in the museum books, as did Frank, and I find the same story.'

'Would this be the museum of local folklore mentioned in that leaflet on the ferry?' I asked, with a slight smile. She nodded as she scanned her notes again. 'Yes, quite.' She looked up at me. 'The museum of folklore,' I emphasised. 'Lore. Not fact.'

She waved her hand at me, on something of a roll. 'Here,' she said, 'I make notes. The books tell legends and stories, yes, I agree, but each one has the same theme. That something is missing…' She thumbed through pages and I wondered if she and Frank had had similar discussions about these subjects. I could imagine her dismissing his arguments as I would have done. But not now. Now, as she rifled through her notes, she seemed quite passionate about telling me whatever it was she had found, and it looked to me as if she actually believed it.

'Ah, yes,' she said, when she finally found what she was looking for. 'Hell is missing a soul.'

'I'm sorry?' I'd heard this before from Stavroula.

'It is the common theme here. Each of the island stories deals with the same theme. They say that hell is missing a soul and that the soul is found in the chest that was brought here many years ago. The Romans, remember? And that each time the chest is brought to light the soul, which of course is evil, walks among the people. It grows stronger as it feeds on the desperate lives of the poor people who succumb to it. It fills them with remorse, it brings them down, it drags them to hell in its place. Only, they don't get there. Suicides wait in this religion. They cannot enter heaven and they do not go to hell. They will only be free when this soul is led to where it belongs. In hell. A place, if you are believing their stories, where it never rested yet, but where it belongs. And so, they bury the chest and all is well. Until time passes and history repeats.'

She looked at me. I looked at her.

'This is what they say,' she said, as if defending herself and passing the blame.

'And no one thought to throw it out to sea, or take it somewhere else? Burn it, melt it down, crush it?'

'Ah, but yes.' She flicked through more pages, didn't find what she was looking for and then delved into a bag that was under the table. She pulled out another notepad and flipped pages until she found what she was after. While she was doing this I was wrapping my arms around myself and wishing I'd brought warmer clothes with me.

'Here,' she said, looking at her notes. 'Frank and I discussed this. They were trying to do this many times. Each time the decline of the island happened they discovered the same cause. The chest, or what was inside it. And each time they tried to be rid of it, until the only way was to bury it.' She looked up at me. 'And the final answer, of course, is not to bury it again. It will only be found. No, the final solution is to put it where it belongs, and that is in hell. And the entrance to hell is on Earth.'

I said nothing.

'This is Frank's theory not mine, of course,' she said. 'He argued that wherever the thing came from, it was brought here with the purpose of being thrown to hell, maybe through this well that the boy killed himself in. Who knows? It is sounding like the way legends grow, no? A well, deep, someone dies in it, water is made bad, disease comes from it, so this is hell down there, you see? But whatever. Frank was certain that is why the chest came here. He found it, but its power became too strong before the well could be found. This is straight from your father. You do not read it in his books?'

'Why didn't you tell me this the other day?' I asked, flatly.

'Would you have listened?'

'Good point.'

'They tried to burn it, it would not melt. In fifteen hundred and... something, they took it away and tried to use it against the Turks, in the fighting on Rhodes, and in one day over fifteen thousand men died in one battle. The next day it was here, back again. When the Turks took the island they buried it in the catacombs where it stayed, deep and silent until the boy and his father found it. Then, as we know, tragedy took the boys and then their friends, and the evil thing spread outwards across the village until the father found the hidden chest and buried it again.'

'But the island continued to decline,' I pointed out. 'So the leaflet in the boat said.'

'And so the book says, and so Frank believed, that this is because the thing was not buried deep enough. It is simple, he said to me, and he said a song, you call it a hymn, yes? Yes. Nearer my God to Thee.'

'You're losing me now.'

'Your father, he said the evil, he would not call it a curse to my face because I laughed, he said that the evil worked in the same was as Nearer my God to Thee. The closer to God, the closer to heaven, therefore the nearer the chest to mankind, the closer to hell mankind would become. And then he said it was here, he was sure of it.'

'What was?'

'The only way to kill the evil. The way into hell. You see now?'

'I see that you and he had more in common than you told me. You both came to believe this?'

'I believe that these people believe all this, and this is why they do what they do. But the real question is, how do you stop it?'

'I don't,' I said, pointedly.

'It is not your problem?'

'Is it yours?'

She sat back and studied me. 'I do not know these people,' she said, at length. 'They owe me as little as I owe them. But all the same they are people. And they cared for your father, and so did I. And yes, I want to understand what is happening here. For me it is fascination. But it is also for work, and this for me is a study. Else I would have left when there were more regular boats. Else I would not stay among such death and tragedy. No, I do not believe in curses, but I do see clues and facts.'

I saw her eyes become glassy then and I wondered if her mind was drifting off into thoughts of her husband. I wondered if she stayed on the island to try and make sense of whatever had happened to him, or to be near him.

'And what exactly did you see the other day?' I asked, also being defensive, as I felt she was now being. 'What was in that book that made you run the other day? You looked, then, like you believed what Frank was believing.'

And by the look that passed across her face I could see that she did and that I had just caught her out. Scientist, I thought. She is as spooked as the rest of them.

'Whatever got a hold of him,' I said, 'has a hold of you too, now.'

She actually turned pale, and reached for her coffee. The little beaker trembled as she took a sip.

'It is cold,' she said, and put it down. 'I stay to learn what happens. I do not fear this curse. How can I? But I fear for these people and I am sad that I cannot help them. And so you should be also. Your father did what he could to help. He took their side, he believed for them and tried to find the answer to what he had started.'

'He felt guilty for discovering the chest and letting lose their evil curse, you mean?' I laughed out loud. 'I think we've covered this.'

'Yes, he did, exactly,' she said. 'And so he worked and he found the answer.'

'Which was?'

'Which was written in the books you burned.' She sat back in her seat and folded her arms. 'The well. But he could not finish the task. The evil was too strong for him too, and took him like the others.'

I wasn't buying much of this. 'All this is, it's just…'

'Pappekak?' She leant forward again. 'Can you honestly say that now? Think. There are easier ways to kill yourself than to take out your eyes and push a knife into your brain.'

'Yes, okay!' I said, and stood up. 'But it's mass hysteria. You must understand that? You honestly can't believe that this is all possible, what they believe in, I mean. Can you?'

'It takes more strength to believe it than it takes to dismiss it,' she said.

I stood and looked at her, aware of the cold silence around me. This woman had been closer to my father than I had ever been. She had spent more time with him in the last few weeks of his life than I had in the last twelve years. She knew him, and she talked about him, and now, I realised, she believed him. For whatever reasons she had, she now believed in Frank and what he had discovered as much as the villagers did.

But I still did not.

'You are right,' I said. 'It does take a hell of a lot more to believe than to dismiss it.'

'And,' she said, 'it takes so much more to act.'

Something caught the corner of my vision, and I looked towards the glass door of the café.

'Oh, so there is someone...' I started to say, but then realised my mistake.

Helen turned to look behind, towards the door. 'What?' she said.

'Sorry, I thought I saw someone inside,' I said, convinced that I had. I looked behind, over my shoulder. But there was no one there. 'A reflection, perhaps.'

'They have all left,' she said, and I saw her pull her coat closer around her shoulders.

'I could have sworn someone was looking out.' But, checking the door again and then looking through the window, I could see quite clearly that the café was empty.

'Trick of the light' she said.

'But a strange one,' I replied as I nodded. 'Whatever it was, it was looking directly at you.'

Twenty-three

He's walking back towards the house. He knows his way now, so much so that he is hardly looking at where he is going. His head is down, his mind is a swirling whirlpool of superstitious ideas and beliefs. It is madness. Almost.

He has voices in his mind. Some telling him that this whole trip has been complete nonsense and that he will be away from it soon, and others telling him that there is something real in all that's been taking place; that somehow his father was right, there is something here and these people are suffering because of it.

And in that chatter of competing voices there's another one; the clear voice of reason, Helen's voice, and it is saying that all these superstitions and beliefs are rubbish and are not to be believed. But on the other side there's Stavroula and her pleading eyes, her helpless face and her strength of commitment, her belief that it is real; that Chris' father did what others had done before him and awoke the thing that kills the island.

But then, there is something in his mind that's more than voices, the visualisation of thoughts, like a dream showing feelings in real forms, tricking his mind into believing that each stone he puts his foot down on as he walks is a new idea, a new thought. He sees the sounds as images, as colours, anything but what they really are. Inside his head he is standing on the edge of a fast moving ever-downward spiral of events and stories that is now the whirlpool that he is precariously on the edge of and yet drowning in.

Opposite is Stavroula, calling him to her, telling him to

believe and let it go, understand, let it in, believe her and help her. Then, there to his right, is Helen, wavering on the edge now, telling him to look for the rational explanation while at the same time her own feet inch towards the edge of the vortex as she uncovers more history, wavers, starts to believe the person standing opposite her, Frank.

And he has known all along that this is true. It is here, it is killing the village, killing the island again.

But what is it?

And why leave it to Chris to not only understand it, accept it, believe in it, but deal with it.

Why him?

It takes more to believe than to dismiss; he remembers her words. He doubts his own strength. If he could understand what it has got to do with him then maybe he would understand more.

'It's hopeless,' he says, as he looks up.

He has seen something from the corner of his eye. A shadow, a quick dart of a black shape sliding from a doorway, a coat-tail whipped up as someone turns a corner, perhaps a priest? But they have all left the island.

He knows this house now. It is the house by the shop where Petros lives, but he didn't just see a man. It was only a shape, a trick of the light.

And yet there was something about it...

He looks down at his feet again and kicks a stone from the path. It clicks against a rock and the sound... that sound of stone on rock...

A flashback to the day in his childhood. He was looking at the ground then as well. He was obeying an order from his father. 'Stay here.' His voice had been stern, as always, but also tainted with something else; not fear, he was calm, he was in control, but something had happened and his father was... What was that sound? A stone falling, a click of stone against rock.

Accusing. That had been the tone of his voice. 'It is your fault. You have let me down badly, son.' He hadn't. 'I told you not to let her walk away.' How could he? He was too young. But he was blamed. 'Stay here. I will talk her down.'

He stayed there, wondering what he had done or said that would make his mother run off. He doesn't remember. But he remembers the small flower growing just beyond his feet as he stands holding the edges of his coat, afraid. The flower was yellow, or was it blue? He has been back to this memory so many times he has started to reinvent it, to add details and colours. A small, innocent flower growing from a bed of rocks, he remembers that much. The breeze rustles the plant in the silence. Silence that is broken by the sharp click of a stone against rock. And then another. Stones falling from above.

He remains, head down, looking at the ground, and distantly hears his mother's name called.

Her body hits the ground at his feet, crushing the flower and splattering blood into his face.

He looks up sharply, one hand reaching out to the stone wall for support as his heart suddenly races and his head pounds. He sees the tails of the man's coat flick around the corner.

He runs. It can't be. Frank is dead. He turns the corner. No one there. Of course it wasn't. Just a trick? No, no trick. The door to the next house is open. He went in there.

He stops, holds his head, breathes deeply and knows that the only way out of this is to try and understand it. He doesn't have to believe. He will never believe in anything that has anything to do with his father, but he can try and understand.

Calmer, he makes his way back to the house, prepared now to give a little.

5

He passes the open door not seeing the scene that unfolds inside this house.

The father and his son stand in a doorway looking into a room. It is a cold room with high windows at one end, a large dining table in the centre beside which is a chair. Some other furniture stands abandoned in the darker corners. The window's shutters are open and the cold, spring light rasps in like shimmering steel. The father and son stand looking towards the light and seeing only white sky through the window as, between them and it, a man sits with his back to them at the head of the table. Slowly he reaches out and picks up a meat cleaver.

The father and son just watch.

The man raises the cleaver in his right hand and holds it out to the side forming a shadow-puppet image against the dazzle of the white day beyond the glass. He holds it there for a moment and the father grips the son's hand more tightly.

The son's eyes don't move. They stay, transfixed on the cleaver. It glints once as it descends.

The man brings it down sharply, silently hacking at the top of his leg.

Over and over again.

Twenty-four

Frank's Notes from 'the Judas Curse' journal:

My assumption was that what the Gospel of Judas was really saying was that when Satan learned what God was up to with Jesus, he did the mirror thing of sending his most powerful demon into the world as Judas, to sabotage God's plan, and that Judas, by bringing about the crucifixion, thought he was scuppering Jesus' mission, only to discover that he had in fact fulfilled it. And he had therefore failed. Some kind of "Judas in limbo" situation, perhaps? Where he was too scared to go back to hell having failed. And this gives us the "historic" background as to why Judas was active on the island. And it also seemed logical to me that since Judas had become the "icon" of betrayal and guilt-ridden suicide, that his "curse" would be to make others the same.

Leaving the Gospel of Judas aside, there is a quite separate early Christian view that Judas (back to the usual view of Judas) was so guilt-ridden about having betrayed Christ that he knew he was condemned to go to hell. And that he believed that if he got to hell (i.e. killed himself) before Jesus was crucified, then, when Jesus came to free everyone from hell (known in Christian doctrine as "The Harrowing of Hell"), Judas would already be there and would be sprung along with all the rest. The Harrowing of Hell is an official church doctrine, but the idea of Judas getting there first in order to be free is not. But it's nonetheless an idea that circulated. I don't know what the official Church view is on where Judas stands in relation to the Harrowing of Hell. There is probably some very clever Jesuitical exception somewhere explaining why he didn't benefit.

Transcript of Chris' tape recording:

No more books, no more pens. Hand is too painful for that and yet there is no sign of infection at all. It's like a deep-rooted stinging that stretches from the cut at the base of my finger to the palm of my hand. No idea why, the cut is all but healed, but, hell, it's like my hand doesn't want to hold a pen. I've got the Dictaphone and I am recording over my father's voice, erasing it. Among the things I've got that were not thrown on the fire is his book. This journal I forgot to throw away. So, why the hell am I doing this? I mean why am I recording this? No, no, no... [*Something mumbled. Tape off, on again.*]

Hi, Ben, this is your dad here. Look, I wanted you to know what went on, why your granddad died and why I didn't want you to come here. I intend to wrap all this up and let you have it when you are older. I don't know why. It was like something grabbed me when I left you, and in order to keep you close I decided to write my adventure down. Seems like the adventure has turned a bit strange, and now, well... No! [*Something mumbled. Tape off, on again.*]

This is my forth day on the island and I've decided to go along with it. Even if I think it's crap, the people here believe that there is something dark at work that is causing them to kill themselves. Stavroula is convinced of it, Helen is starting to believe it too. I can't get off the island until the next boat and there is a rumour that there may be one tomorrow. That gives me the rest of today and tonight to try and sort out what Frank was on about and put these people's minds at rest.

A bit embarrassed about how I went last night after a few drinks, but that's over and done with. Stuff got thrown away but I left some things intact. His journal and Ben's drawing. I've still got it, little soldier. And my notes.

[*Tape clicks off and then on again. The sound of a bell tolling outside, distant.*]

I got back from seeing Helen, my mind awash with all kinds of stuff. But let's not go over all that. Let's go slowly and clearly. I came in and took the photo of Frank that had been put, or I'd put, rather, by the bed, and stuck it on the wall next to Ben's drawing, like the other. I took a bit of delight in putting the pins through his eyes. Then I sat down with the journal 'The Judas Curse' and started to read his and my notes.

Just as I did that I got that feeling that something was walking over my grave again. I laughed and held out my hand expecting money to fall into it like Stavroula told me will happen when you get that feeling. Load of rubbish, of course, but then again, maybe it isn't. I'd run out of anything to drink apart from water, and, after last night's performance, that's probably not a bad thing. Anyway, I'm killing time.

As far as I can make it out, Frank was on a trail that went something like: There was a gospel of Judas, written by him or about him, or completely made up, I don't know or care. There were stories about a potter's field and blood money, and how, after the death of Christ, something was brought to the island by the Romans and buried here for some reason. After the decline, I think it said. Father's journal outlines some of these stories but only in sentences. Snippets of information. Hang on.

[*A shuffle of papers, turning of pages.*]

"Other ancient legends include the idea of the thirty pieces of silver being cursed. And this legend goes back to the fact that the man who used the money to buy the potter's field burst open and spilled his guts, after which it became known as the Field of Blood. But again, there is a mistranslation argument with some saying this was Judas himself and others saying it was another person. This also brings in the debate on "hanging". The popular assumption is that Judas hanged himself by a rope from a tree. But some scholars point out that "hanging" could also be interpreted as impaling yourself on a sharp stake in the ground (the poor man's way of falling on your sword) in which your guts spilled out and you were left "hanging" there in an upright position. They believe this is how Judas killed himself. Which ties in with the story of the man spilling his guts in Acts of the Apostles."

Then he goes on about the history of the island, just as Stavroula has outlined it to me. And then, towards the end, his writing starts to get jumbled up, like he was drunk or going crazy, which undoubtedly he was. Example:

"Another quite different (but old) belief is that Judas became the first vampire, spawning all subsequent vampires. It's the concept of the dead-undead. Vampires are "stateless" as far as the real and the spiritual worlds are concerned."

Okay, I thought to myself, so I've got the history up to speed. Now what?

Frank's clues, as I call them. He sent me his old photo album but with some images taken out and others left in. Some I'd not seen before. There's him and my mother, only she's been ripped out of the image for letting him down. Letting him down! She was mentally ill. Sorry. Er... there's the four boys who I suspect are the boys in the story about the well; the kid finding the chest with his dad, the café and all that. And then there's his cryptic note that it 'all adds up'.

It certainly doesn't.

Hang on.

[*Tape off, then on again.*]

I remember I actually said that out loud because a church bell started to clang outside somewhere and I wondered who was doing it, if all the priests had actually left the island. And I also wondered why they would do that. But then I remembered that the bells are attached by a rope that hangs out into the street so anyone could be ringing a bell. I was thinking about Frank at the time and it broke my thoughts. It rang and rang and a rhythm was set up. One and two, one and two...

Numbers. I was counting in my head, subconsciously.

One and two and three and…

Numbers.

It played its monotone tune, its limping rhythm, short-long, short-long, until it stopped, paused and started again. One-two, three-four, five-six, all short-long, and on until the end. And then a final long clang, a pause and again.

I counted the rings: six sets of one-two and a final long clang left held to echo away.

Thirteen rings each time.

A breakthrough.

Numbers.

Specifically the number thirteen.

I lurched back to the book and flipped pages. There were numbers all the way through it, dates and times and so on, so what was it that was playing at the back of my mind?

Specific numbers.

Nineteen-o-nine. The Well of Thirteen. Four brothers. These numbers kept being repeated by Frank in his books, and these were the numbers he had sent me in the photo album. The four boys, the well, the plaque on the wall, it all added up.

Literally added up.

I scrawled the calculation out in the book as the bell clanged on incessantly outside. One thousand nine hundred and nine plus thirteen, plus four, it comes to one, nine, two, six. Nineteen twenty six.

The bells rung outside and now inside my head as well. The laptop had died on me but the camera still worked and I was able to flick back through the photos I took a few days ago. And as I did, I remembered what Stavroula had said. The registration numbers. Left over from a previous occupation. The Italians had registered the houses when they took the island. They had each been given a number and I had photographed some.

I found the image I was looking for. There it was, on a grey stone wall: the number 1926. Was this just a coincidence? Had I manipulated the numbers to add up to something I knew was already there? If this was a clue, or a marker, why hadn't Frank just written down: Go to house number 1926?

Why? That made me laugh aloud then. Also, I think I was starting to go a little bit crazy myself, if I am honest. I was stupid. I mean, I know Frank didn't want me, didn't even like me. He blamed me for my mother's death, said that I had said something to her in the car that day, upset her, tipped her, and she had run off. She'd climbed to the top of that cliff and he'd told me to wait at the bottom while he went and talked her down. But she jumped anyway, and since then I've been scared of falling too.

But I didn't make her do it.

He did. He nearly drove me to it as well later as I grew up. He promised me so much, this and that and gifts and Christmas, and then none of it came through, none of his promises ever fulfilled. He led me on and let me down repeatedly through my life. 'Betrayal will make you stronger,' he would say, like he was preparing me for some future ordeal. Like something out of a film. Rubbish the whole lot of it. He just liked winding me up and here he was doing it again.

[*His voice is very loud at this point and the sound on the tape distorts as he screams into the machine. Eventually it clicks off. The next is much calmer.*]

I went to the square, 1909, where the millstone was still covered in black from the fire. The debris had been swept away, over the edge and into the deep empty shell of a ruined building, more like a pit. A long black trail of soot and ash could still be seen from the round stone heading towards the pit and I stood with my back to it as I looked up at the plaque.

I was here. I'd been here before, one day before, or two, I can't remember, but I knew that I'd been taking the images here. The 1926 number was a close up. The images around it didn't help, but it was near here somewhere.

And then I knew that I was dealing with something that even the perfectly rational Helen would not be able to explain. I looked across the square and towards the strangely lopsided house with the high walls, the back balcony, and I knew I had seen this before.

I'd seen it before leaving home.

It was the house in Ben's drawing.

But how did he…?

I was looking at the side of a high house that stood tall behind a ruined building. In fact, there were buildings all around the base of its façade facing onto the square. The entrance had to be somewhere else and I felt drawn to find it. I can put it no other way. I knew I had to see inside that house.

I walked towards this house from the square, slowly trailing the wall with my hand and it was like I was having some kind of dream. As my fingers bumped over the rough stone walls, the graffitied metal sheets guarding boarded up doorways and windows, it was as if I could hear the ridges and furrows left by the stonemasons, or by the metalworkers who'd made the sheets, or the brushstrokes left by the painters. The mortar between the rocks crumbled and fell to the floor in a cascade of soft whispers, the rise in a stone was the rise of a hushed voice, the metal seemed to sing out a high pitched laugh as I touched it, and then I came to a gap in the ruin. Silence, as I walked past it touching nothing. Then more sounds felt rough on the tips of my fingers as I brushed along the next wall.

And the really strange thing is that I could swear the sounds got louder the closer I came to the set of metal gates, the old, orange rusty ones beside which was the stencilled number I was looking for. 1926. I touched the number and the sounds stopped, all but a deep, resonant rumble kind of noise which I put down to blood pressure in my ears. I was still angry, still confused, and the church had only just stopped ringing its bell.

The metal doors were half open, unlocked for sure, but all the same, I lifted the hand of Fatima, the Khamsa, and let it fall. It clanged loud, ringing any imagined sounds from my ears, and I called out, 'Hello?' But no one answered.

So, after knocking again, I pushed the gate slightly and it opened with a loud creak. If anyone was around they would have heard me. I was convinced then that the house was empty. It felt cold and abandoned.

I found myself in a vaulted lobby. A set of stone steps curved up to the right, I assume to the floor above my head, and to my left was a long flat wall. And at the end of this a dark, shadowed archway, open to the lobby, and I knew that was where I was meant to go. It was like it was calling me in.

Beyond the arch was some kind of storeroom, like a cellar though on the same level as the ground, a high ceilinged storeroom, completely dark apart from a shaft of light coming in from a misplaced window high up on one wall. My eyes slowly adjusted to the darkness and I fumbled for a switch. There was something about this house that I knew already, something I recognised even though I knew full well I'd not been there before.

A cellar. The very word rang a bell.

The room was full of family clutter. That's the best way to describe it. Shelves with paint pots, and tools along one wall, a great pile of old chairs, furniture and broken toys lying on top of a raised, stone wall, planks of wood, ladders, a washing machine, bags of toys and damp newspapers. The usual things any family might discard and store for no reason.

Reason. What reason? Why had I come in here? What was it that had drawn me in? The answer seems obvious now as I sit and recall what happened. All is simple now. But then?

It was a feeling of coming home, of inevitability, of having been here before. I looked around. Frank wanted me to come to this place to find something. What? Another clue? Maybe, I thought, he just wanted me to spend a wasted few hours looking around someone else's rubbish, a taunt from beyond the grave. That's more in his line.

I let my eyes scan around the room and its walls once, a full three-sixty turn, thinking all the time that if I didn't see something meaningful then I would go. Give up on the whole thing. I still couldn't believe I was going along with it all.

I was just turning back to the arch through which I'd come, almost at the end of full circle, when I saw something on the wall, just hanging there, meant for me.

A baseball cap like Ben's.

Ben's birthday. The note on Frank's calendar came back to me. How had he known? Sarah must have told him.

That made sense to me. It all started to make sense to me then. Of course! Sarah had not only gone behind my back with... well, she'd not only cheated on me with another guy, she'd also gone behind my back about Ben. She'd told Frank about him. Maybe they'd spoken on the phone. I tried to imagine it. Me out at a photo shoot, Sarah at home calling my father behind my back, knowing I would not want Ben to have anything to do with him. Her believing it was her Christian duty, letting him speak to Ben. How did he know when Ben's birthday was? How did he know this was his favourite baseball cap? How come Ben had drawn a picture showing granddad? And...

The picture!

The lopsided house. This house. How had Ben known it? Had Frank sent him pictures? If so, why? If not, then how did he know of the place? It is distinctive, certainly, when seen from the other side, and it has something to do with Frank's trail of mystery, but what? And why did he draw three generations of stick men, him, me and Frank, outside it? What is the significance?

It could only mean one thing and I walked to the cap on the wall knowing that I was going to find something. Again, it was like I was being drawn to the place, and I couldn't stop wondering why I'd not felt like this before? I mean, I'd walked by this house, I'd seen it from the square, I'd even photographed the outside of it and never felt pulled towards it like this. I can't explain it. I'm not a poet or a writer, I just knew that I was in the right place. This was where Frank had wanted me to come all along. So the last question was, why hadn't he just told me to go there and find whatever was hidden there?

And, as I took that little baseball cap from the wall and saw the crumbled mortar behind it, I knew why.

I wouldn't have come straight here if he'd told me to. Frank knew I wouldn't do what he wanted, he knew I had to work it out for myself. I knew that I had to believe what he was writing about in order to be in this place. It was all worked out in steps, in stages, a progress, and all manipulated by him. He knew me better than I realised, and this was his way of showing it.

Half of me was shouting 'nonsense' in my head, the other half was pumping with excitement. Frank had found something here, something valuable, and he had left me a trail of clues to find it. To prove myself worthy. And I had. And right here, behind this stone, was my reward.

The stone had clearly been tampered with, and recently, too. The mortar around it had been scratched away while the other rocks in the wall were untouched and in place. The stone itself was easy to move. I clawed at the mortar for a while and then started moving the rock back and forth, left to right, until more mortar fell away, again with that imagined tinkle of laughter sound, and the rock started to inch towards me.

Finally it came away and I let it drop by my feet. It left a dark recess, deep and showing me nothing as I squinted inside. I reached in, hardly daring to wonder what I might find, let my fingers creep in further, then my wrist, then my forearm.

A sudden screech from behind me, close in my ear. I leapt back.

I shouted, turned on my heels and fell flat against the wall.

Something had been there. I had felt a breath on my shoulder, heard the sound in my ear. I could hear nothing now but the crash of my heart in my head. But across the room I could see that large mound of broken furniture and rubbish had fallen away. It was a flatter pile now, disturbed by something, a rat, a cat, a bird, I don't know, but it had scared the living daylights out of me.

I recovered, smiling and then laughing as I got my breath back.

'All done now?' I asked the room generally. There was no reply, of course. After all, rats don't talk back. Still, letting out a long breath I turned back to the wall.

To see a man's face only inches away from mine. Dark black eyes, foul breath.

Watching me.

'What the...?' I immediately cowered away and then stopped, and realised. There was no way there could be anyone there. I was close up against the wall. Rocks and dust were inches from my face, not a person.

This room, the something in it that I could feel and yet pretended wasn't with me, it was that that was playing me up. I reached into the dark recess again and stretched in further, keen to take whatever was there and then run.

Perhaps there was nothing there after all.

No! There was. My fingers touched against something cold and hard. I grappled for it as best I could and got a hold and then slowly dragged it back towards me.

And here it is. On the table before me. It fits the scratch

marks in the wood perfectly. This is what my father saw moments before he died, when he recorded onto this tape. He must have pulled it from the desk, making the scratches, and then taken it to hide it. I wondered, was it then that he left me that mocking note in the book? I didn't care. I'd found it. I'd allowed him his last game, his last taunt. I'd followed his clues, I'd come here, seen that he'd left me an old property on a dying island. I'd had my final belly laugh from dad. I'd learned that he and Sarah had both betrayed me. I had discovered that he had turned on everything he preached, hypocrite, and killed himself. I'd been all through it, heard the stories, done as he'd wanted, given in, and got my reward.

It is a small chest, like in his notes, like in his drawings, like in Stavroula's story. It is the same. The one found in 1909, the one that was then buried, dulling but not quite taking away the evil it harboured. The one that contained the curse that is now stalking this village.

But why left there? Why not bury it completely? What was Frank doing? He left it there knowing that the curse would stay living, stay strong. Why? I thought he liked these people?

Think, Chris. [*A pause in the tape though it is still running. The sound of him pacing the room.*] He left it there so that the curse would… stay alive… and I would… I would have to fight to stop it. Left it this way so that… I get it… so that he could control my life from beyond the grave, even after he is dead.

Sounds right.

It is an old metal chest. [*Sound of a handle clank, and a slide-and-thud.*] There's something inside it, I can feel it move. And I am about to open it and find out exactly what he left me. [*Tape clicks off.*]

Twenty-five

He stands in his father's old room and looks around. He has not destroyed it all. There is the book, the papers on the walls, the images of Frank pinned to the wall and the Judas journal. And now beside it on the table is the chest.

Locked.

He is holding the knife again and this time he kneels at the table and starts on the lock with the blade of the knife. His hand pains him. The closer he gets to understanding the truth the more pain the invisible wound inflicts. But now his mind is on other things and he blocks out the pain as he tampers with the small lock. There is no sign of a key and somehow he knows he will never find one. The task cannot be easy or else he will not rise to it. He imagines his father noting this in some book somewhere as he plans his son's challenge. 'Make yourself worthy,' he used to preach to the boy of five, probably younger, from as young as Chris can remember. 'Make yourself worthy.'

The knife probes inside the small opening and manages to get a purchase on something. A tiny, delicate click. But still the lock remains closed. It needs smaller hands than his to open it.

He is just standing up to stretch when he hears a sound from outside the room. Outside, but still within the house.

A slow, deliberate hand-clap.

'Who's there?' he calls. There is no reply. 'Helen? Stavroula?' Nothing.

A trick in the air as his imagination runs on ahead of him. He waits, standing still, expecting... anything. Slowly starting to accept that he is not in a rational place. His mind is not settled and he wonders if it ever shall be again. He looks back to the chest.

And hears another hand-clap from out in the hallway.

He knows now that there is someone else in the house with him and his grip tightens around the knife.

The afternoon is wearing on. The dusk will soon be sliding in, dimming the light and shrouding the village. The house grows colder as he stands looking at the door to the hall. Whoever it is waits out there.

'Hello?' he calls again, but his voice is less assured now.

His anger is leaving him to be replaced by something else. A darkness falls across his face, a shadow from the inside out. He has the feeling that his heart is sinking, but he grips the knife more tightly and steps towards the door.

Another hand-clap. It is taking a slow, measured rhythm now, one after the other, the same volume, the same timing. A very slow, deliberate, round of applause.

He steps into the dimly lit hallway. The double doors to the outside world are closed but ill-fitting. A small crack of light shows him that the courtyard is in daylight. Weak and watery yellow light seeps in to lie helpless on the dusty floor. He hears another clap, this time from the bedroom across the hall. The door is slightly open, the darkness behind it cold. The air smells damp, heavy.

He hears the sound of a man's sneering laugh, mocking as the hand-claps continue from inside the room.

'Who is it?' he says, and there is a crack in his voice. He gets his breath, steadies himself. The laughing stops for a moment. But then continues. 'Who is it?' he calls, louder this time, with frustration, and takes a step towards the door.

He lifts the knife, reaches out and touches the wood, tries to look through the crack between door and frame, but there's nothing behind it but darkness. Only the light from the hall will illuminate the room and he considers returning for a candle, wishing he had left the bedroom shutters open. But the laughing is right here again, and the applause, on the other side of the door only inches away from his hand. Something could reach out from that darkness and grab his arm right here, right now, if he doesn't…

He throws open the door and it crashes back against the wall. Immediately the laughing and the clapping stop. There is no sound, not even an echo. It is as if he never heard a thing.

And the room is empty. Almost.

By the light from the hall now reluctantly stealing into the room behind him, creeping over his shoulder, he can see there is something once again standing on the bedside locker. A frame, and, as he turns it around, he knows what is going to be in it. The photo of his father, within the frame, replaced on the table, but now the eyes are missing.

'Impossible,' he whispers to himself. The photo is pinned to the cupboard in the other room. He reaches out to take the photo. 'This is not…'

He doesn't finish the sentence. His hand explodes with a sudden flash of pain as if a firecracker had gone off in his clenched fist. And he hears a voice. His father's voice:

It has me now. I am caught. I know what it wants to do. I know what I have started and what has to be done. But I can't do it. I can't do this! Who can do this? When it comes to it, who can actually do it? Oh, God, why did you set me this task? The price is so high.

The tape. But this cannot be. He has recorded over the tape.

He is suddenly completely consumed with grief. He stumbles to his knees, clutches the photo frame to his chest, falls back against the door, tears pouring from his eyes in torrents that he didn't ask for and cannot stop.

I think I have found out where it is. I am sure. It's unbelievable, but yes, this is the only explanation. Leave me alone! Voices. Is it madness? Are they real? Am I worthy? I need help.

Not possible!

He howls like an injured animal as, through his streaming eyes, he looks at his father's eyeless face. His chest heaves and sobs and he bangs his head back against the door, over and over again, numb to any pain now that he is consumed by inexplicable sadness.

They have rested so close to the place where they must be taken, but can he do it? It is in the numbers. It all adds up. I am sure of it, but a better man than me must take this on. I am sorry. Maria, Christopher, little Ben. I am sorry. But I know what must be done.

He feels like his heart is being eaten from the inside out as he crawls his way back across the hall, back to the lighter room, to the desk, to the chest, pulled towards it as if he knows that the answer lies inside. But, in reality, he knows nothing. He doesn't understand what has suddenly gripped him, what is taking over. He doesn't know why he feels like this. It is as if everything he has ever known to be sad about in his life is bubbling up to the surface all at once. But it is never quite breaking through. It is always just beneath, always there, in his chest. He is unable to swallow it, unable to spit it out. Every moment of sadness from his life is inside him now; his mother's death, the nights after his beatings, his father's cruel hands, his lonely nights at school, the bullying, the endless, long walks across open fields that should have been beautiful, the longing for friends, the teenage years alone, discovering Sarah's betrayal, everything, all there, and no hope of anything good being let in to calm the pain.

The sounds of his father's last few moments before death.

The dull thump of heavy things landing one on top of the other. Breathing in short, sharp gasps. Static noise, something in the air. Frank crying, writing, books moved. Inaudible muttering. 'Christopher.' A scream.

He pulls himself to his feet as he throws the framed image into the room and hears the glass shatter. The sound encourages him. A positive act. Fight back. He walks into the room on unsteady feet, holding the walls for support, picks up the frame, rips out the image and takes it back to the wall. The pins are still there.

'Not possible.' He says it with more conviction this time and starts to drag himself upright. He looks at the table. The tape machine sits there, the tape turning.

I can't do it!

'Not possible.' He pins the image into the plaster and then stumbles backwards into the armchair, where he collapses. The tears dry on his face as he takes deep, long gasps of air and tries to control his emotions as the tape rolls on.

Frank's sobs. Fading. Footsteps leaving the room. The front door slams. Only the sound of the dust in the air. The tape runs on recording the silence of the room.

And then he hears that sound and knows it is not a stretched tape, not a battery slowing down the recording. It is a low, bestial growl of a voice and it is demanding him to:

Bring it back.

5

Across the village, Helen stands in the room she has occupied for the previous months and looks around at her own pile of books, notes and things collected during her stay. She has had news that the boat will be coming in tomorrow morning and leaving again in the afternoon. She will be going with it. Whatever is happening here is beyond her. She is no longer comfortable here. But there is one last thing she needs to know before she leaves.

She picks up her book, the one she took from the museum, and heads out into the afternoon. This confused young man with the sad eyes and quiet manner needs her help and she has had an idea.

As she closes her courtyard doors she has a thought. She usually leaves them open, unlocked. They are always safe. But today she feels uneasy. Perhaps it is the Englishman who has made her feel this way. Perhaps it is because she, too, is starting to believe that there is something stranger than reality taking place, that the villagers might be correct. But whatever it is, she is not happy at leaving her house unlocked.

For the first time since she came to stay on the island she locks her doors and makes sure they are locked tight.

She wonders if she should not perhaps paint her initials on the walls or collect some flowers for protection.

'Now you are just being stupid,' she says to herself, and touches the Khamsa on her door. 'She will protect you. Oh, God!' She manages a laugh to herself. 'Now listen to me.' And hurries off through the village.

As she walks, fast and with a purpose, she passes a house that now hangs two white sheets from an upstairs window. Another, opposite, has one hanging from its balcony. Surrender, perhaps? "We give in." Or traditional signs that a death has occurred in the house. She doesn't want to think about it. It might be someone she knows.

She follows the path past more and more white-sheeted houses where once families sat outside chatting with neighbours as children played harmlessly and free from threat. She sees discarded toys, a small bicycle, an empty shopping basket, a small enclosure with a sheep bleating, a dead lamb at its feet, abandoned. There is washing on a line, filthy again and faded by the sun. The street is empty. Any sounds are coming only from inside the buildings and from the overhead cables.

She stops and looks up.

'This is not right,' she says.

There is no power. There was last night for a while, but not today. So why are the cables humming and hissing. Is that hissing? It is. No, it is not. She listens harder, turns her head. Not hissing. It is like whispering. The kinds of whispering you hear children make at night when they are talking in bed and they should be sleeping. Voices in the cables.

Now she knows she is making things up. She moves off, quickening her pace and shaking her head. Such things cannot be. The rot here goes back a long way but it stays all the time with people, with governments and laws, and decisions from far away. It has nothing to do with voices in the sky, nothing to do with superstitions. And yet...

She reaches Frank's house. What was Frank's house. Now it is Chris' house, or will be when he finds another solicitor to deal with the paperwork. She looks at it and speaks to herself.

'Such thoughts are good,' she says out loud. 'Rational thoughts. He must find a solicitor, but not yet. He must get away on the boat tomorrow and come back when things here have improved.' But then she sees that he has tried to wash the letters from the walls and there are no more flowers guarding his door. 'Oh, my,' she says, concerned. 'What has he done?'

As she enters the courtyard she realises that she can't stop herself from believing the villagers' superstitions, and she chides herself. 'It is all pappekak,' she says, and taps on the double doors to the house. 'There is no evil here.'

She feels an icy draft come from around the doors. It plays around her ankles and her hair and then leaves her. It feels as if someone has just left the house as she has arrived and she opens the door with a feeling of unease.

Something is wrong, she thinks. There is something wrong inside this house. She steps into the hall calling for Chris.

She finds him in the sitting room in the chair. A feeble shaft of low light penetrates the dust that swirls around him as he sits, stock still, his eyes red and puffy, a knife in one hand and the bare wrist of the other held up.

She watches, helpless for a second, as the knife comes closer to the wrist, and then realises she must act.

Dropping the book, she runs forward, grabs the knife and pulls it away from him. He gives it up without a fight. It is like he is too weak to care. She throws it across to the table and hears it clatter there. Kneeling to him she takes his arm, lowers it, and he, trancelike, turns to face her.

'There is no point,' he says, and his voice is weak. 'It is him. Laying traps. Bringing me down.'

'You drink too much this time,' she says, but there is no smell of it, no bottles litter the floor. But it must be the only rational explanation. She draws up a chair and sits, holding his hands as he looks beyond her to the papers on the wall.

'Listen.' She starts in a calm, reassuring voice. 'Too much talk of dead things and not enough doing, yes?' She looks to the window. It is getting dark outside. 'Tomorrow you go to his grave. You see he is dead.'

'I know he is dead.' His voice is measured now, flat. 'That's the point. He is dead, and yet I've still got to prove him wrong about me.'

'You carry much anger,' she says. 'Leave it at the grave.'

'That's what he left me. Anger. That's his legacy.' He turns his head to look at her and realises that she is there with him. 'He blamed me, made me believe it was my fault, but it wasn't. She wasn't my responsibility.'

'And this makes you bitter, of course. You feel very alone, sure. You say these things because there is no closure. You know this also, I think.'

He suddenly gets up from the chair and takes one stride to the desk where he picks up the journal. 'I can feel his evil, right here,' he says as he shows her the book.

'There is no evil, only anger.' She stands too, and steps towards him. 'You need to say farewell to your father. It is the first stage. I work with you, yes?'

He stares at her for a moment and there is something deep within his eyes that unnerves her. She feels them grip her, feels him looking behind her eyes and into her mind. She can almost feel him fingering through her secrets, discovering her own sadness, searching out places where no one is allowed to search.

'What is it?' she asks, trying to get him out of her mind and back to the room. 'Christopher?'

His eyes focus back on her face and she feels released.

He smiles. 'I give in,' he says, simply.

'So, this is good.' She takes his hands. 'This is good. This is what you need. You start from here. You accept what he did now, and later you will see that you are correct. First, you must work through the process. Tomorrow, when there is daylight, you see his grave, you take the boat, go. There it is ended. This is so.'

But she has misunderstood. Her abilities, her words, her reasoning, are all shot to pieces in this place, and he knows she is heading towards the wrong path. He pulls his hands from hers and turns to the desk where he picks up the metal chest.

She gasps. 'You found it? Is this it?'

He turns to face her with it, still smiling now, but it is somehow not a smile.

'There is no point in talking to his grave,' he says, and his eyes dart to the photo of Frank that is pinned to the wall.

She sees that someone has cut out the eyes and her heart pumps a little faster. This is not good.

'You must,' she says, nervously. 'It is the face of him, now. It is all you have.'

Something grips her from inside, in her chest. Not a physical pain, but something else.

'He let us down,' Chris is saying, and she is listening, but she is suddenly aware of the feeling inside her. It is sadness. 'My mother, me, he let us both down and he knew it. That's where his anger came from. He turned away from us, from me, sent me away, was never there at holidays, always absent. Love was never home.'

She feels a tear on her cheek but it is not a tear for him. She doesn't want to cry. She doesn't cry. That is not her. That is not Helen. But she can't stop herself.

Something around her is gripping her and crushing her in melancholy, like a too tightly held fist of flowers. And she can't throw the feeling away. More tears pour from her eyes.

'Okay,' he is saying.

She has not taken her eyes off him but she didn't see him change. He has determination now, his eyes are alive with something else.

'Okay. I will play his game.' He steps towards her and puts the chest down on the table.

She wants to speak but cannot. The grief is too intense.

She watches him step towards the museum book, bend down and pick it up from the floor where she dropped it. She wants to scream out and bellow with grief.

'I'll find his well. I'll finish it for him, to show him I can. I'll throw it all back.' He is shouting like a madman as he slams the book onto the table and starts turning pages. 'I will find it and I'll throw it all away.'

And his voice, his determination, suddenly lifts the despair from her. She feels it rise up through her body and burst out through her skin, from her bones to her flesh and then out to evaporate into the air in the room.

Sadness is gone. Lifted.

For now.

She knows that, inside, something has touched her and taken hold. She senses that it will not go away again.

'So,' she says, and she hardly believes how calm her voice is. 'You take his cup of poison?'

Where did those words come from?

He does not answer. He pours over the book. She moves back to the chair feeling cold now and wraps her jacket more tightly around herself. She thinks. Rationally.

'Soon it will be dark. I will find candles,' she says, but stays in her chair watching him. 'And I stay here with you. We watch each other tonight. You can read the book, we can both search for the clues.' She looks at the drawing on the wall, the chart of numbers, the chest on the desk. 'You found the chest. Next is what we do with it.'

She knows he is close to finding his answer and she is concerned for what he might do when he does find it.

5

In another part of the village a woman enters her kitchen and looks around. She has a job to do and she needs to do it now before it gets dark. First she takes a chair, a wooden, upright chair with a rush seat that will become very uncomfortable after only a few minutes as she is too big for the seat. But that's how the chairs are, that's how her life is. She sets this down facing the door. The door leads to the lane outside and is made of wood. It has a thumb-latch on it and when her husband sneaks back in the morning, usually around dawn, she will hear him try and lift the latch silently. It always betrays him with a click as he presses it from outside. The small metal bar will rise and the door will open inwards.

She looks to the plate rack built into the wall to the right of the door, strips of batten holding the best china in place. The plates lean forward slightly, kept safe by the strips of wood. Her gaze rises from the rack to the ceiling and then over to the back wall behind the chair, opposite the door, where she sees the embroidery hanging. This she takes from the wall and puts safely to one side. She then looks at the table in the centre of the small room, sees that it is clear of clutter, that the plastic covered linen is straight and clean. She is happy that everything there is just so. Next she checks the pots and pans over the arching fireplace. Here she gives a wry smile. This is her dowry, the copper gleaming, the pewter still undented after all the hand-downs and years. But what use is a dowry when your husband prefers another woman's fire?

But no, she will not dwell on that. It is all neat and tidy, that is what counts. The fire has not been lit for some days and it has been cleaned out. Everything looks smart and neat, and in order and presentable. She is ready.

She looks back to the door again and takes a length of twine from her apron pocket. She attaches one end to the latch and then feeds the twine across the gap to the plate rack, through and around the battens and up to the ceiling. She wishes her husband were here to do this. He is so much more practical than she is. But then, if her husband were here she would not be doing this in the first place.

Still smiling and humming gently to herself she measures out the twine and then stands up on the chair. She can just reach the old iron eye on the ceiling that has been there for over one hundred years. She once used it for hauling water up from the cistern under the floor. The pump does that now. She feeds the end of the twine through the eye and lets the rest of it fall. There is just enough.

She steps down from the chair and takes a copper pan from above the fireplace. This she attaches to the end of the twine to form a weight, leaving only what remaining thread is needed for its purpose. Ironically her dowry will now serve a more useful purpose.

Finally, she sits in the chair directly facing the door and tests the angle. All is as she wants it to be. She gets up, opens the door and checks the height of the copper pan. Everything is in place. Everything will work. The length is right, the weight is right, the chair is in the right place. She closes the door.

Still humming, she opens a cupboard and takes out a radio. There is nothing much playing these days. It's mainly static, but there is a faint sound of music coming from a Turkish station, its airwaves straying across the waters and across the island when the breeze is right. But, whatever is on, it will keep her company through the night. She places the radio on the table beside the chair and returns to the cupboard.

She takes out his shotgun and cracks it to make sure it is loaded. It is. Good.

Back at the chair she calmly sits, attaches the twine to the trigger and very carefully sits with the gun in her lap. She adjusts her hair. It feels right. She smoothes down her apron, has one last look around and satisfies herself that all is just so. When the door opens, the copper pan will drag the twine down and the last thread of it will pull back on the trigger.

So, making sure that the tension on the twine is exactly as she wants it, she gently angles the gun towards her throat and waits for him to come home.

Twenty-six

Outside in the night it grows stronger. The closer he comes to discovering the truth of what he must do the more determined it becomes to stop him. This is how it has always been. This is how it lives on. It knows that it will win again, it always does, but it needs to be stronger, and so it takes lives, each life giving it more strength, more power, and a more solid form as it draws its life from the lives of those who give in to it, until it is complete and able to fight, until it is physical. Its presence is out there, growing more powerful by the day, and none of the charms or prayers or superstitious acts can stop it now.

It is almost with them. It has seeped in from the impossibly deep black nowhere, through time and legend towards life. It has leached its clawing-fingered way over the wet ground, between the dank, mouldy rocks of beneath, towards the dry, grey stone of above. Like before, it has found its way out from its hiding place and been drawn closer and closer to the surface, to the chest that keeps its secret. And now, drawn from the dark places of its hiding, it creeps closer to the things it craves, the things it needs.

The souls of the living.

The more souls it takes and keeps in the dark limbo of nowhere the more it thrives and will go on thriving until it is the most powerful, until it alone walks above the ground, until it is free and there is no one left to unlock the riddle of the silver chest and destroy it.

♪

In the dim, silent room she sits in a chair, her head down over the old book that smells of damp pages and age. He is at the table with his father's work. He is starting to understand, and each time he lets another defence crumble, so it out there senses and grows a little more wary. He came here with a solid defence around him, protection against all he chooses not to believe in, and now, each time someone helps him knock a small stone from that defence, so it outside grows more protective. It can feel the potential in this man, but he, even while reading his father's work, is not yet ready to accept it all. It keeps the advantage.

And yet he chips away, and she helps him. It turns its attention towards her as she sits in the chair, the night ticking past in long minutes of deep thought, the air thick with the unheard chatter of lost and wandering souls.

She reads, her scientific mind turning over legends and tales from the past. She smiles at the old superstitions and yet feels a pang of doubt in herself. These things cannot be and yet she has seen them. She cannot account for what she has seen in any other way. But still, she, like him, refuses to believe what she reads, what she knows to be true.

She uses the blade of the sharp kitchen knife to turn a page and reads aloud.

'There is something here about suicides,' she says, not even aware if he is listening. 'This is from many years back, the Ottoman times. It is an account by Cavus Bekir, a guard in the invading army, translated later.'

Dates and times, numbers, real things are important to her. This is fact, this is evidence. This is a truth that she can cling to. This was written and this was believed. Knowing this means she doesn't have to believe it herself.

'This is from just after the Ottomans took the island over from the Knights of Saint John,' she says. 'Listen. "The enemy, the Knights, fought bravely as they had done before, here and on other islands. They held aloft their great wealth and their treasures and yet from within that treasure came their downfall." This is written by someone who was there at the time,' she points out again, as if to underscore the fact that this is not her believing, only repeating. '"As we came to their fortification high above the settlement we found them all dead, but not dead by our machines or arrows. They were dead by their own hands. We walked onto the island from our ships and expected their last defence, but none came; no blood shed by us, no fighting. We knew we had not defeated them, but we rejoiced that something had."'

She looks up. He is still at his journal under the flickering candle, making notes, sticking more pages to the wall, starting again, drawing charts.

'Are you listening?' she asks, and he nods. She reads on. 'So, "Those left on the island had run from the village calling 'great plague' and abandoning their masters to their fate. They gathered… at Emborios and sheltered there. Their leaders spoke of the great evil that took their lives…some were cut down for abusing us so."'

She starts to run the tip of the knife across her cheek, like a cold finger gently stroking her flesh and sending a pleasant tingle to remind her of someone from the past.

'"But soon we learned the truth of what had happened. Such strange religion they have, such strange beliefs. That something should rise up to save them and yet cut them all down, that something should be here that they think they can use against us. We came to the fortification, swords drawn, weapons ready and found only the broken shells of armour on bodies with red slits for throats. Someone had done the work for us. They had done the work for us themselves.'"

The blade plays from her cheek to her throat. The corners of the room grow dimmer and the darkness senses that her guard is dropping. She reads some more in silence as her fingers turn the handle and direct the blade back up, gently caressing her skin like a lover's finger, under her chin, across her soft lips. She rests it, blade flat, against her bottom teeth and lets her tongue probe the needle-sharp tip as the darkness encroaches and slips unseen, up from behind her chair.

'Here!' She flicks the knife away from her lips and turns a page quickly. 'Here, Chris. "We came by their legends from some at Emborios who swore that the Knights had been digging at the Kastro. They had believed they had built their great wall around an ancient power and from here they took their strength. I was dispatched to search the fortification looking for what I know not, but the people on the island knew. There was, they said, a silver chest brought here from long ago and it houses all evils of the world. It keeps the souls of all suicides. They also believed that no soul could rest until hell's missing soul was delivered. My men and I laughed. But then, Kepci, and later Salih, were found dead, and not by any hand of enemy, but by their own.

"'This, the island leaders said, was the curse of the Knight's treasure, the chest. The thing they had sought to bring them power had turned on them. None of us believed, of course, but still, a casket was discovered and taken to Emborios to show the islanders how wrong they were.

"'No sooner had the chest been taken there than they started to walk into the sea to drown themselves, or to climb the cliffs and jump. We thought we had found some great weapon but my leaders saw the same effect on our own men, and so I was charged with destroying the chest." It is the same chest I think,' she says, looks up and then reads more.

"'I obeyed, of course, but the closer I brought it to the fire the greater the feeling came over me. Such sadness, then hopelessness, then despair. I could not do this thing. It was as if the chest would not let me.'"

The chest is sitting right there on the table. She can see it and yet she feels no sadness, no remorse or despair. She looks back down to the book and draws the candle closer. The knife returns absentmindedly to its playground and she runs it softly down her cheek, softly up again.

And from the unseen corners of the room it starts towards her silently once more.

"'I took a hammer and brought it to bear, but the thing remained unmoved, untouched. I took heavy rocks and stones and built a pile to crush it and still to no end. I was to be held to account for this thing and so I buried it in the animal shelter where only the goatherds go. Deep beneath rotting layers of dung in the soggy mud floor, I dug a hole and buried the thing. From then on, sanity returned to the island.'"

She turns another page and sees another island legend is told, but this bears no relevance to what she is trying to understand.

As she turns more pages the knife blade slips to her lips once more and then into her mouth. But this time it does not stop. Her vision becomes blurred, she squints as the candle dims further and the page becomes dark. There is something uncomfortable in her mouth and something drawing her hand closer to her face. She can't think what that feeling might be but there is something inevitable about it. Something feels right as she tastes cold steel against her tongue and her teeth touch on something solid.

'Helen!'

The shadows scuttle back and she throws the knife from her mouth and across the room.

'What in God!' She exclaims, and stands up staring at the knife in disbelief.

'Are you okay?' he asks, and she nods, silently.

'I am, fine, yes.'

She recovers, realises she has been lost in thoughts and remembers his condition from a few hours ago.

'How are you feeling now? Are you feeling better?'

He nods.

'I think I have found something,' he says, and returns to his book.

She picks up the knife, touching her tongue to her lips to make sure they are not bleeding, and takes the knife to the window. There she throws it out into the night and hears it clatter onto the rocks of the ruin next door. Out of harm's way. She closes the window firmly and makes sure it is secure. She is feeling less confident now.

'What did you find?' she asks as she approaches the table.

'Just some notes. But, look,' he says, 'something about suicides. How they do not make it to heaven or to hell. They remain with us.'

She looks over his shoulder. 'Ah, that old story. Yes, he had beliefs about life after death,' she says, remembering Frank, but now not so fondly.

'I vaguely remember his sermons at the dinner table,' Chris says. 'Different religions think different things, suicides get buried at crossroads, their souls go to purgatory, it's a sin to take your own life, you won't get into heaven, the spirit lives on, all that stuff.'

'And hell is missing one soul in particular,' she says. 'But whose?'

'You know, Helen?' he says, sitting back. 'I can't say I care much. A few more hours and I can get out of here. Leave these people to their own mess.'

'But why?' She looks at him. 'You have started to accept what your father was doing, what he was trying to do. Why stop?'

'Come on, you don't believe all this?'

'We have discussed this before,' she says. 'What I believe is not important. It is what they believe that matters. You are coming close to finding something that might help them see this as simple superstition, or not.'

'Or not? You do believe it, then? This myth, this curse?'

'I don't know what I feel now.'

'Not feel, believe. You believe that hell is missing a soul because someone from five hundred years ago wrote it? You think that all these people's souls actually exist and because they took their own lives their souls are, where? Out there somewhere? Doing what? No, Helen, I'm not close to finding anything. I am not even looking.'

'Then what are you doing now? Look at the wall.'

There before him is evidence that he is changing his mind, or losing it. It is like he sees it for the first time. The wall is now covered with pieces of paper, taped there by him.

He has charts: "1909 + 13 + 4 = 1925 = Ben's cap = chest, locked, no key." He has dates and names: "480 BC, Athenian League, Christians? 1261 Byzantine. 1282. 1309 Knights. 1522…" There are titles and numbers, references from books, "You shall be called 13th", "Gospel of Judas", "Potter's field",

"The four brothers?" And there, in the centre of it all, is Ben's drawing.

'How did he know?' He says this very quietly and mostly to himself.

'There is something else,' she whispers, and pulls up a chair to sit beside him. 'There is something here we are not yet seeing.'

'What is it?'

Outside, the night has settled in. Out there it is growing more aware, more on guard. In the cellar, the stones in the corner that surround the well start to tremble as deep below, through the cold rocks and slivers of cracks, a red glow of flame opens its clawed hand and senses the first chance of success.

'A reference we are missing,' Helen says as she looks at the photograph of the four brothers on the wall.

She looks, too, at the image of Frank and then to the drawing.

'Your son has never been to this island?'

'I had never been to this island!' he replies.

'And yet he drew this. In a dream?'

'From a dream, maybe, I can't remember now.'

It is true. He can't remember what Ben said. He cannot even remember what Ben looks like. He shakes his head and realises that he doesn't even have a photo with him.

'You do not remember?'

'No, I don't,' he replies, bitterly. 'I didn't pay any attention.'

'Ah,' she says with a slight sound of triumph in her voice. 'You acted like your father! Like father, like son, eh?'

'I was in a hurry to leave, that's all. I was going to tear it up and...'

'Yes?'

'Something Sarah said about Ben needing closure. He drew it because he found out his grandfather had died and so this was his way of expressing… Look, I don't know. You're the psychiatrist. You figure it out.'

'Psychologist,' she corrects. 'But even so. Closure, yes, this is good, but you said he didn't know his grandfather. Your son never met Frank? Why, you yourself had not seen him since you were young. So how did he know to draw this place?'

'No idea. I expect Sarah showed him a photo or something. I mean, she and Frank were obviously in touch with each other behind my back.'

'I am sure that if she was, then she thought she was only doing what was right for the boy.'

'What she thought was right? Yeah, sneaking off with someone else while I was working? Keeping Frank up to date with my life, things that I didn't want him to know, without asking me? Probably even letting Ben talk to Frank by phone? I mean, why else would he want closure? Then teaching my boy that it's all okay 'cos we all go to heaven when we die and Frank will be happy?'

She can tell he is starting to become agitated again and she feels her own sadness for his problems, but she cannot let them cloud their task. If only she knew what that task was.

'So,' she says, 'you do not approve of that? Of your wife telling your son about heaven?'

'No,' he spits back. 'And I am surprised you entertain the idea. When you're dead, that's it. End of story, right?'

'How can I say? I have not experienced that. People believe what they need to.'

'Well, I don't need to believe that there's a place we go to after we die,' he says. 'I don't believe in anything.'

'But you are starting to.'

He looks at her intently, and right inside, right down inside, he knows that she is right. All that is happening, all he has seen and felt, he can't dismiss it all as coincidence, as 'just one of those things.' If he can be honest with himself he can say that, yes, he believes there is something supernatural at work here. He just needs to hear himself say it in order for him to get over his embarrassment at believing it.

'Maybe.'

But she is not listening. She is looking at the chest on the table.

'Like father, like son,' she whispers. 'There is another story that we are missing. There is more you need to know and we have not discovered it yet. And what was in this?' she asks herself.

She touches the chest gently but it is enough for her to know that she has done wrong. There is something in that metal, something inside, that sends out a sharp stab of pain that races through her fingers, along her arms, and grabs at her heart.

5

The first glow of dawn starts to break across the mountains of Turkey that surround and shelter the small island in a curve of thin, rocky fingers of land. Today the sky is a deep red, the colour of summer heat, but it brings no warmth. Instead, it brings a dull crimson glow that turns the sea to blood, a huge, calm, pool of blood that surrounds this forgotten island. No one comes to help. Those in power leave those below to survive as best they can against the odds that have been dealt to them. All the island can do is wait, abandoned, ignored, betrayed.

High up in the village Stavroula stands watching the sun come up in its angry, blood-soaked sunrise. All around her is silence, no bells, no birds, no chatter, no breeze, a silence that seems to last an eternity.

Until footsteps on the lower path draw her eyes downwards. A male form, weaving slightly, making his way home in the dawn. She hears keys fumbled at a lock. A catch lifts, a door opens. A gunshot cracks out into the daylight.

She closes her eyes.

Twenty-seven

For him the dawn of his last day on the island wakes through bleary eyes ringed red and stinging with lack of sleep. His books lie around him, his papers and scribbles, drawings and charts, numbers and ideas all spread out across the desk that he lays his head on.

He looks across the table top, the journal in close-up, the wall out of focus. There's the tape recorder but he is no longer inclined to relate his story. His hand will not let him write for long, his body will not let him move towards the journal to leave his thoughts for his son.

All he wants to do is sleep.

Dawn breaks, its light exhausted from doing battle with the determined army of night. The light creeps wearily into the house and around the chairs, across the table, along the floor. It brings with it the whispers and chatter of those waiting for him to move.

Outside, the evil presence grows stronger as another victim takes her life. Her husband stands at the doorway, motionless, looking at the scene but taking nothing in.

In another part of the village, a small boy, dressed in his best parade costume, searches the shelves of an outhouse for just the right tools.

In the cellar, the force beneath the well waits in anticipation, feeling that this one might finish the task, feeling that this time the right pieces are in play. It waits, hopeful that it will, at last, be brought its missing soul.

A soul which wanders the lanes, taking more of a physical form, swirling like black fog into a house, taking its victims like fuel to its fire, stalking, circling, growing stronger and feeling victory within its grasp.

While far out across the blood red sea, the small ferry glides reluctantly towards the island on its last voyage to this forsaken place. And it brings with it the last pieces of the puzzle.

Everything is in place now. On this stage set of ruins and secrets, mysteries and clues, everything is ready.

5

Chris' eyes are just about to come together in a wonderful final release of sleep when he hears a sound from outside. He drags himself upright in the chair, twisting his neck to relieve tension in his upper back.

He turns to see Helen asleep in the chair. The big, old book lies open at her feet, showing an illustration. But his mind is not yet on that. It is on that sound he just heard. What was it?

It has stopped now. A dull thud, he thought, and from outside. He didn't imagine it because Helen is now stirring as well. She yawns and looks around, and then, as if suddenly sensing danger, she sits upright.

'Are you good?' she asks, concerned.

He nods his head. He is not. He feels uneasy. He senses that something has changed and something new has arrived with the dawn. And he is listening.

A muffled cry? A whimper?

Thud.

'What was that?' Helen voices his thoughts, and stands. She stretches herself out and bones crack.

Thud.

He moves to the window and looks out, but can see nothing.

Helen, on the other hand, is looking at the book at her feet. She bends, picks it up and takes it to the table to lay it flat.

Thud.

'Is that someone building something?' he asks. He feels the sound in the wall. 'Someone banging on the house?'

'Look,' she says. 'Look at this.'

He comes back to the table and realises that he can smell himself. He has not washed in days. He has not shaved. He wonders how he looks but cannot face his reflection. Instead, he looks at the wall and feels foolish, too many notes and thoughts, dates and ideas, too much rubbish. He can't look in the mirror. He has covered it, too. Instead, he looks at the book.

A large, full-page illustration in black and white, old, maybe very old. A strange scene of a man holding a small casket in his hands on one side of a round, open pit, while on the other a woman, her face looking down, hidden by a cowl, holds a candle. Between them, from the black hole of the pit, a winged demon is rising up amid smoke. The illustration has a title: 'Bring it back.'

'The Well of Thirteen?' he asks.

'But where?' she replies. 'I feel that the answer is staring us in the face.'

Their thoughts are interrupted by a scream from outside the house. He rushes from the room into the hall and to the double doors. He pulls one open and crosses the courtyard in a second, throwing back the clanging metal gates and stepping out into the lane.

He sees a woman running away, still screaming as she staggers and trips around the corner. And looking down at his feet he sees blood.

Lots of blood, a river of it streaming from the steps and into the street. And then he sees where it is coming from. The boy he had photographed a few days ago, the one wearing his traditional costume, crouches at the door, clearly injured in some way. An attack, perhaps? He wonders who would do this to a child. Then he becomes aware that something is not right. The boy has an arm raised. The arm is the source of the blood and he is holding it against the window frame.

Chris isn't sure what to do at first. He is no doctor, but keeping the arm raised seems like a good idea. He crouches down to tell the boy this, and then realises that the boy is staring straight ahead, his eyes dull. He senses Helen arrive at the gate, and gasp. He wonders how the boy can hold his arm aloft while…

Then he sees the nails that have been driven through the wrist and into the woodwork. As he watches, the blood stops flowing from the wound, the boy's head flops forward and the hammer drops from his hand.

A small black cap with a tassel falls from the boy's head as Helen and Chris stand, shocked into silence.

'This is madness,' she says.

Her voice jolts Chris into action and he tries to support the child, but the boy is not moving.

'He is dead,' Helen says.

Chris lets it all go. He falls back against the wall distraught, the broken child in his arms, and starts to cry. But Helen bends to him and grabs him by the shoulders, shakes him.

'We must do something to help,' she says.

He is about to scream at her when he sees a sudden change in her eyes. He stops crying. He felt something. Something unseen moved along the lane and between them. It pulled her away from him, and yet she is still there. It walked over his grave, it passed through him, it got through his protective wall of scepticism, and it was evil.

Helen stands upright again and her face falls to a dull, exhausted expression.

'I go now,' she says, simply, and starts to back away. She treads on the small black cap and that sends a pang through Chris' heart. He reaches for it, grabs it as she backs away. 'I go now,' she repeats, and turns. Slowly, sadly, she simply walks away.

Chris, confused, angry, upset, not knowing what he feels or what he is doing, looks at the blood now on his hands. All kinds of images pass through his mind, all manner of ideas, words and meanings. He ignores them all and puts the cap back on the boy's head, pulls it down with a sharp little tug and draws his fingers down the boy's face, closing the eyes.

At that moment, he hears the ferry in the distance, its klaxon blaring as it approaches the island, and with a huge roar he pulls himself to his feet.

His mind is made up.

§

Although Helens' house was firmly locked when she left, the darkly clad figure that has just approached her door has no trouble gaining entry. It swirls up the step, its coat-tails following in a swish, obedient spirits sewn together in a train of black. The figure, calmly, almost cheerfully, opens the door and lets itself in to wait.

§

In the house, Chris storms back into his room with newly found determination. But this is not determination to look once more at the notes, the drawings and the clues. He grabs anything which is his, anything he came with, and throws it into a pile in the chair. He takes his bags from the bedroom and starts filling them with his equipment; his deceitful camera, his lifeless laptop, his haphazard notes and the tape recorder, throws them all in the bag angrily, but with a finality that feels good.

He checks the desk, passes his eyes quickly over the wall and its madness, over the books, the illustration, and finally to Ben's drawing. He rips it from the wall and tears it up. There. Done. He throws the pieces to the floor and sees the image of the four brothers, the photo from the album. Hadn't he thrown that on the fire? Had that gone, too? No, it had stayed here. Hadn't it? At some point during the night he must have found the image and put it on the wall. So why is that important? George Stavrou and his four sons?

Sons.

A moment of hesitation. Maybe he should speak to Stavroula again before he goes? The boat, Helen said, would stay some hours before finally leaving the island, probably never to return. He has some time. What about Stavroula? Hadn't he felt something for her? Doesn't he still? Maybe he should just wait a while, calm down, find her, go to the boat together for help and if no help comes then leave. Together. That would give him time to study these notes just a little longer.

'No,' he yells out to whatever force he thinks is in the room with him. 'No! I am not staying. You've had your fun.'

He takes the photo of the four boys, intending to tear it in half, but as soon as he holds it he stops. He wants to cry.

He hears a voice. Is that in his head? Is it Stavroula's voice? Was it something she said? Fathers and sons. Helen said it too. Sarah had said it. Just what Frank would have done. Just what Frank... his father. Our father.

'Shut up,' he yells out, and turns around.

The room is empty.

He looks at the photo and sees his bloody fingerprints now on it, covering the face of one of the older boys. But the angelic, innocent face of the youngest looks back at him and it seems to be asking one question. 'Won't you help us?'

The boys' father found the chest. The boy killed himself. The curse spread from father to son.

'It spreads...' he says, and he remembers.

Notes in his father's journal, and in the stories, about how the suicides spread out from the father, who found the chest, to the son, to the other boys, and then out into the village.

'It starts with whoever finds it, and then...' He knows he is close to some kind of answer. 'It kills those closest, first, those we care for most. Father, then the sons, then the family around, and then all others. Anyone that Frank cared about has died, the islanders... Anyone close.' He rationalises as he looks at the photo and then the drawing. 'And now it comes for me, me last because Frank cared least of all for me.' He laughs a mad, short laugh of hate and throws the photo to the floor.

He doesn't realise that he at last understands. He has what is needed, now. And he hasn't noticed that there is no longer any pain in his hand.

He returns to the table for the mobile phones. His is still dead, but Helen's...

Shows that there is a message.

He presses the button, sees the date, realises he has been so absorbed in Frank's trail of deceit and game-playing that he missed the call, missed the message, and now he reads it.

And his heart all but stops.

5

Sarah stands holding Ben's hand, a small suitcase in the other hand. She is faced with the sight of an abandoned lane, cobbled and majestic, the stones bathed in warm morning light. A tree of some kind grows from a ruined building ahead of her, branches twisting through windows that are no longer there, a pile of old wood, a broken door, perhaps, lying just inside the gaping doorway.

She is hot and tired from the walk up the hill. The few people on the boat, the crew only, had stayed on board but had directed her to the village with gestures and reluctance. She had walked up, climbed the slow hill, followed the road until it narrowed, and then narrowed again, and finally reached this junction. And she had seen no-one.

She had tried to warn him, tried to ring back, but there was never a tone. She had sent a message and thought it had got through but could not be sure. All enquiries she had made had led to the same answer, anyway; that this was to be the last boat to the island for the foreseeable future. It would wait a few hours and then leave. So, she is sure Chris would still be here.

Wherever and whatever here is.

'Granddad is near here,' Ben announces, and looks up at his mother.

'Yes, Ben,' she says down to him. 'We will find someone who can show us the way. We'll say goodbye. We will find daddy and then we're off, okay? Maybe we can buy some flowers.'

A woman comes around the corner and walks towards them. She is dressed in wild colours, her flame-red hair is out of control and needs brushing. Her arms seem weighted down by bangles and bracelets.

'Excuse me.' Sarah attracts her attention and lets go of Ben's hand. She fishes a photo from her pocket as the woman stops. Her eyes are unnerving, seemingly looking through Sarah and beyond. 'Do you know where he is?'

She shows the photo of Chris to the woman who looks at the image. She nods, points behind her, signals, up, right, up and then walks away.

'Thank you...' But she has gone.

And so has Ben.

'Ben?' Sarah feels an icy brush of panic on her skin and hurries on, up some high steps and into a small ruined square.

Ben is there, standing on a blackened, round stone and looking up at the side of a strangely lopsided house that seems familiar. She ignores it for now, grabs his hand and continues on her way.

Twenty-eight

Chris hoists his bag onto his shoulder and looks around the room. Nothing but the mess he has been living in. All his possessions are in his bag, everything else is left over from Frank. They can keep the house. The Tzandakis firm can deal with it, give it away, let it rot to ruins like so many others. He is done here, it's time to get home to his son.

He is only slightly remorseful that he tore up that drawing. He can see the pieces of paper by the table where they fell. Strangely, the three stick men that Ben drew all occupy the one scrap, all three characters un-torn, and looking back up at him.

He takes only one thing from Frank. The silver chest. The only thing of tangible value that his father left him. Chris leaves the room, out through the front doors, and heads across the courtyard. He hesitates at the door, reminding himself not to look at where the small boy lies. The same boy he photographed, the one who did show up on the photo, the boy who wore his Greek costume right until the end, right until the madness caught him. He shakes the thoughts from his mind and opens the gates.

To find Sarah and Ben standing on the blood-washed step.

There is a moment's stand-off. Both adults look at each other. Ben stares at the blood on the ground and Sarah pulls his arm, making him look up to his father. This sight is not much better.

'Why?' Chris asks, and it takes Sarah a moment to recognise his voice.

This is not the same person that left them a few days ago. His face is gaunt, much thinner than before, and she immediately wonders how much drinking he has done. His hair is matted down, there are dark bags under his eyes which themselves are rimmed with red and bloodshot. He has been drinking all night, for sure. His clothes hang from him, untidy and wild, and she has a flash vision of the flame-haired woman passing her in the street. Her mind races to drugs and parties and she has to squeeze Ben's hand hard to stop the thoughts from getting out of control.

'I messaged you,' she says. 'I told you we were coming. Why is your phone off?'

But he is looking down at Ben now.

'Ben?

ʃ

Across the village, doing its work in yet another house, the black-coated figure somehow hears the name, and its head, now recognisably human, turns fast towards the sound.

Ben.

And it knows that this is the final challenge. But it has taken enough. It is strong now, it can protect itself, and it knows that this one is going to be as weak as the last. A grin breaks out across the white face like a weeping sore, and the figure begins slowly to turn towards the door.

ʃ

Sarah cannot believe the mess she sees within the house.

'What has been going on here?' she demands, as they march back into the building and she sees the main room. Papers on the floor, maps, pages torn from books stuck to the walls, open journals on the table, empty coffee cups, dirty plates and glasses. And that smell.

'What died in here?'

She goes immediately to the window, telling Ben to sit at the table out of the way.

As she turns back from opening the window she sees Chris put down a small metal casket on the table. Then he throws his bags into the armchair and turns on her, his pink eyes aflame with anger.

'Yes, I changed my mind,' she says, before he can start. 'He needs to pay his respects.'

'No, he doesn't. Not to him.'

'He wants to say goodbye.'

'Go, back to the boat. Go now.'

'No, Chris. Look, I don't know what you've been doing, or taking, or drinking, and I don't want to. But we came here to do one thing, and that's what we are going to do. We have a few hours. So, where is the grave?'

She watches as Chris shakes his head. He's got a hand up to the back of his neck and that means only one thing. He is thinking up a lie.

'You don't know, do you?' she realises. 'You've not been. You have not even been to your own father's grave.'

He is mumbling and the fingers of his right hand are twisting and curling as he looks at the floor.

Suddenly he is down on his knees and is heaping up papers and books onto the table. He stands over the table and starts flicking through pages fast, all the time mumbling.

'Fathers and sons,' he says, and keeps his back to her.

'He was your only father. I can't believe you would be so pig-headed, so selfish as to… For heaven's sake, Chris, look at me!'

He does not. His mind is deep in the mad search for the last few answers. He voices his thoughts.

'Fathers and sons,' he says. 'It comes for those most loved. He didn't love me. He knew it would not come for me until right at the end, but he was talking to Ben.'

He rounds on Sarah suddenly, pointing accusingly at her. 'You put them in touch. You found him, let Ben talk to him. They knew each other. Oh, God, Sarah, don't you see what you've done?'

And then he is back to the desk and the papers. 'And now, it's going to come for him, you see? And you brought him here right to it. He knew. How did he know? No, no. Not that, that's not how it was.' He is sifting through papers, searching for something. 'He cared about Ben. He drew me here, played me along, but he thought Ben would be safe over there. He knew I wouldn't bring him. He wanted me to finish what he started so that Ben would be safe. He didn't care what might happen to me in the meantime.'

'Chris, you are making no sense,' she says, and now she is starting to worry. She is in a strange place, she knows no local language, she is alone, and Chris is having some kind of breakdown right before her eyes.

'It's here and getting closer,' he says, and then bangs the table. 'Where is it?' he shouts. 'What have I got to do?'

'You need to take this back.'

The soft, quiet voice of the small boy brings him up short and he looks down.

Sarah sees that Ben is holding the silver casket. 'What is that?' she asks.

'Don't touch it,' Chris says, but the boy won't give it up.

'If you don't take it back, then I will. Granddad says I have to.'

251

'Ben, stop it,' Sarah says.

Chris takes a step back. 'Say that again. How… What else did granddad say?'

'His nightmares have been getting worse since you left,' Sarah says. She is still too scared to come too close to Chris but she is edging towards Ben, ready to grab him should this man get too close.

'Tell me, Ben, what else did he say?'

'Just that,' the boy says, and smiles. He tilts his head to one side as if listening. 'If you don't do it then I will. That's the way he wants it to happen.'

'Who, granddad?'

'No, the other one. The darker one. He is further away. He is the one who wants it back.'

'I don't understand, Ben,' Chris says. His mind is teaming. He might not understand but he knows that this is not the right place for Ben to be.

'Take him away,' he says to Sarah, who is now nearly at the table.

'He came to say goodbye to Frank.'

'Don't fight me on this.'

'On what? You're raving, Chris. What's gone on?' She too is confused and now more than a little scared. She sees him reach out to Ben and she is in there like a shot, pulling her son away from him.

But Chris only wants to take the chest. He grips the handle tight, now, and thinks.

'Right,' he says, and she thinks she sees him change slightly. He looks more alert all of a sudden. 'You stay here. Don't leave the house. Don't let anyone in.'

'Just tell me what is going on?' she demands.

'I can't explain. It's all so jumbled. It's dates and numbers, and everything added up. You… No, I can't… Just stay here. I need to find Stavroula.'

'Where is the grave, Chris? We'll see it, he can say his goodbyes and the nightmares will be over. We can go home and Ben will be happy. You want that for your son? To be happy?'

'Sarah, just be quiet.' He's moving towards the door, one hand palm out to her to keep her at bay. 'Stay here with Ben. I have to find it. I have to do this. Don't let anyone come near you.'

And with that he backs out of the room and she hears him leave the house.

Sarah is exasperated, at a loss. She throws herself into a chair and puts her elbows on the table, her head in her hands.

'Elbows off the table,' Ben says, cheerfully, and smiles at her. He scans the room and his face becomes serious. He sees the pieces of the drawing scattered on the floor by the table. He slips from the chair and drops to his knees.

5

Chris runs through the lanes, past the houses draped with white sheets, past the initials painted on walls, past the closed doors. He shouts for Stavroula. He calls for help. No one answers and no one hears. He runs into the millstone square. It is empty; no villagers, no help. He looks up at the strange tall house; no-one on the balcony, no help there. He looks at the remains of his burnt journals and books; no help here.

He runs on and his mind races along with him. He doesn't know what he is up against, but now that he has started to take down his thick stone wall of disbelief the ideas are flooding in, and, as he races towards the kafeneion square, his thoughts start to come together.

The chest must go to the well, to the pit, back to the demon that wants it. He recalls the illustration in the book.

The chest contains the missing soul.

The chest came here thousands of years ago but whoever owned it was taken in by its value. Greed took hold. They sold it. Used the money for their own gain and then let loose the curse that killed. That made them kill themselves. They buried it time and again through history, and each time greed came back to find it and dig it up.

The closer to the surface, the more it kills. It must go back to the well or else it will take first him and then his son.

But where is this well? This 'Well of Thirteen,' the pit he must throw this casket into? Stavroula must know. At least, she will know more stories and now he is ready to listen.

He only hopes that he is not too late.

And then he sees her up ahead.

'Stavroula,' he calls out, but she is walking, passing from right to left across the end of the alleyway. He runs. He reaches the place where she was and sees her at a distance, moving quickly. 'Stavroula!'

She turns and sees him, stops and smiles.

'Wait,' he calls, and starts towards her.

'I cannot,' she calls back. 'I am sorry. I have to hurry.'

'I need to speak to you. Hey!'

But she has turned another corner.

'Please, wait!'

He races after her and finds himself in the village square. The kafeneion is closed, the tables and chairs stand idle. The place is deserted, apart from Stavroula who is crossing the square.

'I get it now,' he says as he reaches her. 'I understand it all.'

'Do you?' she asks, cryptically, the faintest hint of a smile on her face.

'I get the story, the legend, okay? I understand that people feel there is something here making them do this and I'm willing to play along, to do what they need me to do so that they will see it's over. But I need to know where the well is. Look, here's the chest. I just need to find the well.'

'You understand, perhaps,' she says, and the crystal clarity of her voice not only stops him, it calms him too. She stops walking. 'But do you believe?'

'In what?'

She looks down at the chest and then back up at him. She seems amused.

'This has always been the trouble, I think,' she says. 'Your father had no trouble in believing, but you? Will you let it in?'

'I don't understand,' he says. 'What do you mean?'

'You said you did understand.' She takes a step away from him. 'I think, my Christopher, that you are not quite yet ready. You still do not believe.'

One half of his mind wants to laugh at all these thoughts. What is she saying? What is she thinking? This is madness and he knows it.

But the other half clings on to the fact that everyone around him believes this story and half of these people have already died because of it.

His mind is now firmly made up. Find the well, get rid of the chest. Give everybody what they seem to want.

'I am doing what you wanted,' he protests.

'You need to believe. Only then will you be able to finish your father's work. I must go.'

She walks away, leaving him gaping after her. Then she stops and turns back to him. 'But I will be waiting for you,' she says, and hurries away.

It takes him a second to fathom her meaning and somewhere inside all the madness and confusion of what's going on he feels that spark again, that 'something' between them. He starts after her, but, when he reaches the lane to follow her back in to the village, she is turning the furthest corner. He runs after her, only to find the lanes empty.

But the doors to the house at the end of the lane are open and he recognises the scarf that hangs across the back of a courtyard chair.

'Helen?'

There is no reply.

'Helen,' he calls again as he steps into the small, pebbled, courtyard. There is an open door leading into a kitchen, it looks like, and he steps in. It is dim inside but silent and cold. There is a smell, unpleasant, like the smell of something rotting out of sight, behind a wall, under a stone, and it feels as if the house has not been used in a while. But it has. He sees clothes hanging over the back of a chair in another room, men's clothes. There is a pair of men's boots by the door, and a man's overcoat. Chris makes his way cautiously through to the next room. He sees simple signs of life, an open book, a pair of glasses on a newspaper, washing in a pile, and a pushchair. A child's toy.

He understands what she was keeping back, what she was hiding from him. Not just her husband, but a child too? He realises how little he knows about this woman and he feels desperately sad for her.

'Hello?' he calls louder, but still no reply.

He steps into the room and sees Helen, her back to him, sitting in an armchair.

'Helen.' He says it one last time, but he knows she is not going to hear him.

He approaches slowly. He doesn't want to see but he knows he has no choice. He has to be sure.

She is sitting with a large book open in her lap and it shows the same illustration, the pit, the woman with the candle, the demon. But lying on top of it is a photo of Helen with a good-looking man around her age. They are a handsome couple. It is a recent photo and it was taken on the island. He recognises the scenery but not the man or the child, a daughter, held tight in his arms.

He is grateful to her for the way she has done it. The empty pill bottles are beside her. There is no blood, no fuss. Just sadness.

He feels the first icy touch of despair start to grip around the base of his skull, its grip starting to tighten as everything ahead of him now seems pointless.

He leaves the house feeling alone and knows that the only one who can help him now is Stavroula.

He retraces his steps back to the millstone square where he now sees the father and son up on the balcony looking down at him.

'Hey,' he calls up, and they continue to look down. 'Stavroula? Where is she?' But they do not reply, they just watch.

And then he realises they are not watching him. They are looking beyond him to something behind him and he spins around. There is the long-haired guy from the boat, Petros. He may be crazy but at least he is there.

'Hey, Petros,' Chris calls. The man doesn't turn around but

lifts his head to show he has heard. 'Where's Stavroula? Have you seen her?'

Petros stays looking away but raises a hand and points up and beyond, back over Chris' shoulder towards the mountains.

'What? Where?' Chris doesn't understand.

'She is with the dead,' the young man says, and lowers his arm slowly.

Now he understands. 'The graves?' Chris turns towards the higher village and hopes he can remember the way.

He runs from the square.

He leaves Petros staring at the empty ruin and slowly turning around to face the lopsided house. His head tilts up towards the father and son who are still there, silently looking down. But Petros doesn't see them. Where once his eyes looked out, round and alive, now there are only empty sockets, caked with dried blood, and behind them the scrambled mess where his brain had once been.

Twenty-nine

He's pounding on, forcing his legs to take one more step after another, up through the narrower lanes, the mountain above and ahead all the time. He passes the closed churches, the draped white sheets on houses lining his way, the shuttered windows. He hears sounds of crying from inside empty ruins, the wails from behind the walls, and overhead he hears the chatter and hiss of the telegraph cables as a high breeze slices through. And above that, he may be wrong, it may be the lack of oxygen in his searing lungs, but he thinks he sees the skies darken.

The suicides' graves.

He tries to remember the way up to the side of the mountain as he gasps the last step up into an open square. Two large ruined houses stand opposite, a church to his right. Up some more steps, that might have been the way, but he can't remember. He knows he must hurry. Ben is in danger. He turns left and up, certain that he is heading towards the road.

As he forces himself on, he is not just fighting the pain in his lungs and his legs. His heart is sinking, his will is being eroded away. He can feel the force at work, the presence of whatever is out there in the lanes with him. It is following, close, watching him as he turns into a narrower alleyway. He feels the claustrophobia pressing in on him as the way ahead narrows further, the walls grow higher. He turns sideways. This is not the right way. He is lost.

How much easier it would be to stop now, to just sit there in the lane and let it all end, let it win, let himself go. Everyone would understand. Everyone has the same feelings. Utter hopelessness, it's pointless, there is no reason to go on. He can't help anyone. He wasn't cut out for this. Just slow down, stop here. Die.

He clenches his fists, thumps them against the wall and shouts a yell of defiance. It is not getting him that easily. He has to find Stavroula, make her see that he understands, that he believes her. Make her tell him where this well might be so he can throw this damn metal casket into it and be done.

It grows heavier in his hand at that thought, and the handle starts to cut into his fingers. But he tells himself he has to ignore that, just as he must ignore the blackening skies above him. You don't really believe any of this. You are lying to yourself. Sit down, take a rest, let it happen. Just put the thing down and leave it there.

'No!'

Ben needs him. He cares for his son. He is not like his father.

He bursts from the end of the narrowest lane and onto the open path. This is the right way and there, up ahead, clinging to the edge of the mountain, he can see the makeshift graveyard. He runs again, the chest held tighter in his grip. There is only one place this is going and that's to hell where it belongs.

So you do believe?

As soon as he thinks this he sees the graves up ahead with Stavroula looking down at two together, side by side. She looks up at him, smiles regretfully, turns and walks away.

'No! Please,' he shouts as he runs towards her. 'I believe you now.' Hollow words? 'I need to ask you…'

She ignores him and walks on until she is out of sight and he is left gasping for breath by the two wooden crosses where she stood. He's infuriated by this woman for a moment, but then something else takes over.

Then it really hits him and he falls to his knees. A dark melancholy washes over him like a heavy wave crashing on a shore as heavier clouds roll across the sky, leaden grey clouds offering nothing but darkness. He feels beaten. He just wants to give in to it all, curl up and…

'No!' He roars the word out as he slams the chest down on the ground. He has Ben. He has to fight this for Ben's sake.

He wipes tears from his eyes and the grave before him comes into focus.

There it is, at last. A roughly written name on the wooden cross: 'Frank Trelawney, Xenos' and the year. Beside it is a photo of his father and a recently placed wreath of flowers, only just starting to wither. A candle burns inside a lantern and glows brighter in the gathering gloom.

His father's grave.

He feels nothing, and the realisation drags him further into despair. He wants to feel something, but there is nothing there.

Slowly, his eyes are drawn to the grave beside his father's. Another suicide, another victim, another cross and flowers, candle and photo, and another name:

'Stavroula Tzandakis.'

At the base is her photograph, already faded and yellowing with age. Beside it a bunch of long-dead flowers and a candle, the flame long extinguished.

Stavroula.

It's not possible.

His mind races through flashbacks: She moves out of the way when he goes to take a wisp of hair from her face, hears her voice, 'Tzandakis, difficult? No, she is dead.'

Herself, she was talking about herself. That's not possible.

'This is not allowed,' she had said, and, 'I am to be a guide.'

She was telling him the truth. It is not possible for them to touch or be together in this life because she is not in this life. And she is a guide. She has been guiding him. To what? Guiding him to believe that what she has been saying is true. There is life after death. But why does he need to believe that? All he wants is the location of the well.

He can't believe that he is thinking these things. He can't believe what he now has there right before him. His father sent the clues, set the trap, threw out the bait to him. His father instructed him to find her, knowing she was already dead. His father believed in the lost souls, their eternal life after death, wandering, waiting for someone to come and free them. He sent her to meet him when he arrived. She showed him the house, his inheritance. She guided him, manipulated him to open up his mind. 'An open mind is of more value than a closed book.' Was that what she had said? It doesn't matter. All this time she was leading him on. 'I will be waiting for you.' Waiting where? And all this time she was dead?

Not possible.

He remembers trying to take her hand in the square but she pulled away. They have never touched. He has never seen her touch anything. But didn't she pull him back from the edge when they were climbing up, when he first arrived? He thinks, fast. No, she just called his name. He's never seen her drink or eat. Can I take you for a drink? No. And no photographs. She knew she would not appear on them and he would know her secret too early, and if he'd known then he would have run. She moves across the alleyways and lanes as if she is floating. All the clues have always been there but he has never seen them. Not until now.

'Visit your father's grave and you will understand,' she had said. Had he done that he would have seen hers, but then what would he have done? Would he have been able to end this sooner?

'End what?' He shouts it out and hears his voice crack. He is getting worse. He feels lost, helpless. He doesn't understand what she wants.

'Your guardian angel walks with you.' She had said that about that feeling of someone walking over his grave. He'd felt it more than once. She had been with him. He had heard voices in the cables and in the ruins. Her voice, the voices of others. The wandering souls who cannot be free until he returns this silver box to hell.

He believes now. He has seen the evidence. He has his facts.

Chris sees the candle burning in the small tin lantern at Frank's grave and sees Stavroula's candle unlit by her photo. There are matches and he slowly takes one from the box. He has no idea why he is doing this. He doesn't know what he is going to do next, but this feels right. He has tears on his face, he has nothing in his heart, but to light a candle and draw some kind of strength from it seems to be the right thing. He opens the small glass door to the lantern and strikes the match. He sees the flame rage and calm and then lights her candle and watches it for a moment before closing the door to keep it safe.

Then he turns to Frank's lantern and lifts it. As he opens the door he hears a low rumble of thunder high above and far away. The air turns heavy and he blows the candle out.

The sky darkens angrily and from somewhere far below in the village he thinks he hears a voice calling his name. A man's voice, coarse and angry. But it is a trick of the wind. The wind that rushes up the valley and up over the high cliff edge to the side of the graves. It howls across the ground through the cross and markers, blows photos to the ground, extinguishes candles in their lanterns and rushes towards him. Stavroula's candle blows out and Chris senses he is no longer alone. The wind has brought someone to him.

Trembling now, vulnerable, he turns.

And sees his father standing behind him, bearing down. He wears a long, dark coat that writhes and lives around him. His white hair falls straight around his gaunt face, his skin is grey and his long fingers are reaching out towards Chris.

Chris scrambles back on his hands, kicking out with his feet, he crushes Stavroula's photo and his father's flowers. He can't form words, he can only shake his head.

But Frank speaks to him, and his voice is calm. 'You have the strength son,' the apparition says. 'You have the strength.'

'Get away from me!' Chris yells out. He can't believe this. This is too much. 'You are dead.'

Whispers arrive behind the tall dark figure, all chattering, and Chris can hear them clearly. 'We are all waiting, help us, you have the strength.'

'Christopher.' Frank's voice is soft. Living.

In that one word, in the name of his son, he manages to impart to his frightened child all the trust the man needs. His tone says let me guide you, I can help you. It should calm the frightened man. But it doesn't.

Chris shakes his head, his heart pounding his skin crawling with fear as he looks up into the face of the man he once called his father.

'Who are you?'

For a moment the face is that of Frank, but Frank calm and caring, gentle. And then, in a flash and flicker of a candle, it changes. The whispers around him turn to screams, the clouds above pile up heavy and dark and the thunder cracks closer. The face changes, still Frank but what lies behind is evil. It is in there.

'He had no strength,' the voice says, and it grates like twisted metal, pierces through the heavy air, each word made up of a thousand hopeless screams. 'He gave in to me,' the voice says and a skeletal hand grips at the collar of the coat and pulls. It draws back the black material to reveal the scars left by the rope that burnt Frank's flesh as he hung from the tree.

Chris backs away further, grabs the casket, and starts to get to his feet. He holds the chest in his hands. The thing before him sees it and laughs.

'That will do you no good,' it rasps.

The whispers turn to shouts, to desperate yells, pleading voices all around them in the air, in the black clouds above. All imploring Chris to help them, to set them free. The figure, the thing that has Frank's form and yet is not Frank, looks at Chris and a quick burst of lightning changes the expression on the face.

'They have been waiting,' Frank says calmly. 'The restless dead. You have there what they need.'

Chris can only act on some kind of instinct. 'Where is the well?' he asks, now fully on his feet.

In an instant the figure has changed. Evil is back.

'I am here to see you fail,' it spits the words and takes a stride towards Chris.

Chris runs.

5

He is running through the lanes, as the dark skies chase him, the whispers, the screams, the voices of the dead all around him. The thoughts in his head are pushed aside by incomprehensible things: the knowledge that he has just seen his dead father, that his form is possessed by something evil, and that the girl he has been talking to for days has been dead for weeks.

The curse. It kills those closest, the ones that love.

Frank, and Stavroula? Was she the first to die because…? He jumps down three steps at once, crashes into a wall, trips on a step. But where is he going? Thunder crashes above him and the air is thick with the sound. He is getting away from that. From Frank. From whatever his father has become.

He takes a corner, too fast, slides sideways into a metal door. A wreath hangs on it, fresh flowers, a couple of days old, a photo beside it. Chris looks into the face, sees the long hair, the large round eyes. Petros. Another victim. Another soul. He spoke to him only minutes ago.

The images in his photos come back to him as he stumbles into the millstone square. The father and son at the table, there when he took the image, not there when he processed it. They were never there. They were dead, long dead. All around him, ghosts, apparitions. And the closer he came to understanding the more of them he could see?

A huge roar breaks his scattered thoughts and cuts through his mind. He spins and looks back up towards the mountain, the sky is black with evil clouds, crowding in on him. The chattering, whispering voices scurry into the rocks and the walls.

He is alone, but still there is a presence with him.

No. Not with him. It is on the move now, and he knows exactly where it is going.

Thirty

In the room, Sarah is at a loss as to what to do. She paces the room and feels a cold draft blow in from under the door. Looking through the window she can see that the weather is changing. What was just now a clear, blue sky is growing dark with clouds. There is thunder rolling around and the room is dimming. She pulls her light jacket tighter around her shoulders and wishes she'd brought something warmer. Then she realises she is not cold, but frightened. The lights don't work, it's becoming hard to see, but at least the boy is settled as they wait for Chris to return.

Sarah pushes her hair back behind her ears and comes to the table where Ben sits arranging pieces of paper.

'What's that?' she asks, attempting normality. 'What are you doing?'

Ben doesn't answer, but it's clear enough. She recognises the shapes and colours of the drawing the boy did. It has been torn and he is now putting it back together.

'Why did he do that?' she whispers to herself as she wonders what took place in this room. She wonders what has happened to Chris in these last few days.

She has little time to think, though, as suddenly there is the clang of a metal gate outside, the thump of wood on wood, and the door swings open to crash against the wall.

Sarah leaps up. Ben calmly carries on with his puzzle, and Chris looms in the doorway.

'We have to go,' he says. His face is wet with tears, smeared with dirt and dried blood. He clings tight to the metal chest as he leans on the door jamb gasping for breath.

Sarah feels the rise of panic in her stomach. She takes a protective step towards Ben.

'Go back to the harbour,' Chris says. 'Find a boat, ask anyone to take you, beg them. It's here and it's coming for Ben.'

'What's here? Chris? What's the matter?'

Chris has moved to the table and put the chest down. Sarah wraps her arms around Ben, but he fights back against her, the puzzle nearly completed. Chris picks up a book and starts looking through the pages.

'You're scaring Ben,' she says. 'Chris? What are you doing?'

He throws the book down and leans across the table to the wall. He is looking for something, his finger is tracing lines across the pages of illegible notes and numbers. He is muttering 'it all adds up', and shaking his head. 'It will all add up when I believe. Okay, so now I believe. What's the answer?'

The room shakes with the power of a great thunderclap outside and Chris spins away from the table.

'It's close,' he says as he backs towards the wall.

But then he stops. He sees what Ben is doing. His son is holding the last piece of the torn drawing in his fingers. The three stick men standing in front of the house.

Ben looks up to his father. 'You see? You, granddad's ghost and me.'

Chris grabs a chair, pulls it to the table quickly and sits beside Ben. Sarah tightens her grip on her son.

'What else did you see, Ben? What else was in your dream?'

'Leave him alone,' Sarah says, but the power is going from her voice. She no longer feels scared. Now she is starting to feel the first energy sapping pangs of sadness, and she has no idea why.

'What else?' Chris grabs Ben's shoulders and Sarah is

appalled at herself because she doesn't stop him. She lets go and stands back. Her knees are weak and she looks for a chair.

Ben looks at Chris and then draws the casket across the table to put it between them.

'Granddad came and told me about this,' Ben said.

'He was here?' Chris turns to Sarah, sees her sitting in the chair, her face taught and her eyes narrow. 'Sarah? He was here?'

She shakes her head as her lip quivers. 'No. Ben, I told you not to make things up.' Her voice is flat, dull. She speaks in a monotone. 'He is dead.'

'I've seen him, Sarah,' Chris says, and his eyes flash to the window expecting to see that dark figure coming towards them. Where is it now? What is it doing out there? What traps are being laid? What lives are being taken? He tries to focus, but sees the cold face of his father, and yet, not his father. Focus!

'It's him, but it's not. It's… It's someone inside him.' Focus! 'Something inside.'

Ben has pushed the chest towards his hand and Chris feels the jab of cold metal against his skin.

'You have to take them back,' Ben says, and opens the lid.

'How did you…?' Chris is mesmerised. 'That was locked. How did you do it?'

Ben just shrugs. 'It was granddad,' he says. 'He came through the house when you left and told me it was open. It was.'

'He was here? You saw him?'

'No, not saw.'

Chris can't comprehend it, but after what he's just seen and after what he just met he isn't going to waste time on wondering why. Anything is possible now. He knows it and he has no time to wonder. He must follow his instincts.

He grabs the chest and pulls the lid right back revealing the contents at last.

A small leather pouch.

'That's it?'

'Granddad said that you have to take them back. He said that if you don't then I must.'

Chris stares at his son for a second. 'He said that?'

'It's the only way, daddy. What did he mean?'

'It's not up to you, son,' Chris says. 'He left this for me to sort out. It's my responsibility.'

Chris takes the leather. It feels slimy in his hands, like the skin of a snake that has slithered through mud, scaly and old. It has the touch of something that makes him want to go and wash his hands. He wonders what has touched it, who has held it. He imagines all manner of crawling, biting things infesting the leather, insects, bacteria, now transferring to his fingers, and he wants to throw the thing away. But he fights against it, follows his instincts. He pulls the pouch open and tips out the contents.

Dark, blackened coins tumble from it and fall into the chest with a small rush of metallic clatter.

'Granddad says you have to take all thirty.'

Chris' eyes flick across the table and the clutter of notes and books, drawings and papers. The Judas Curse journal. Coins. Suicides. The figure at the graves, the wandering lost souls of the dead. He looks at the wall, the mirror still half covered in torn papers and charts, numbers and writing, and realises that he has become his father. He has taken the same bait, been drawn into his madness. But to what point? How far did Frank get before he gave in to it?

He vividly remembers the tape playing, his father's voice, and the shouts of 'I can't do it', and knows he is at that stage. He can't do whatever needs to be done to save this place because he doesn't know what he has to do. It's not clear. It has not been explained.

He remembers that growling noise at the end of the tape and knows it was a voice, 'Bring it back'. The voice of something unearthly in the room after Frank had run, something that has been watching it all unfold. The voice from the depths that is missing a soul. One soul.

The soul of Judas Iscariot embodied in those coins and now free to inflict his curse of betrayal and suicide on the world again.

Yes, he does know what to do. He feels it inside. He either sees this through or he does what his father did, takes himself outside, ties a rope around his neck, and leaves his son to fight on and die.

'I am not my father,' he says, and feels the first stab of confidence shock him into action. 'Where's the well, Ben?' he asks, and it sounds like someone else saying the words.

Ben points to his drawing, to the house, and the room grows darker still.

'The same place?' Chris looks at the broken image, the crazy paving of a shattered dream, and the pieces of paper start to shift. They rustle in a breeze but he doesn't take in what that means. The same house as the chest? He plays the tape in his mind again. His father leaving him the notes, then running from the house, hysterical, and going… Where? To this place, to that cellar, and there hiding the chest away.

Why did Frank not bury it? Why didn't he put it back under the earth like everyone else through history? Why leave it near the surface, close enough to humanity for it to slowly work its evil, take more lives and bring that thing back from the dead, the thing that wants to keep these coins on earth? Why not bury it?

Because he knew that Chris would succeed where his father could not. Frank knew that Chris was the one who would finally end this curse, destroy this evil. His father knew that he had the strength.

Another stab of confidence wells up inside him, but it doesn't stop the room from growing darker still, and he smells the putrid stench of death approaching.

He looks up from the drawing. He knows where the well is and he knows what is waiting for them outside.

'You need them all daddy,' Ben says, and the sound of his tired, small voice brings Chris to his senses.

'All?'

'There are only twenty nine.'

Ben has counted the coins into piles and is looking up at his father with sagging eyes. He is growing tired.

No, not tired, listless.

'Twenty nine?' Chris remembers the coin in the pillbox, the clue. It was obvious. He should have seen it then. He should have put it all together. Coins. The journal, the names, the suicides, the history, it all adds up, now. But then? He didn't believe then. He didn't want to, but now? His heart skips beats. 'Thirty pieces of silver.' And the other clues fall into place. 'Romans, the Holy Land, trade with other countries, Potter's Field, the coins that Judas used to betray Christ, bought a field, the owner killed himself, the coins went… Where? He knows the answer: Across the sea to here, where they were buried, found, each time bringing the decline of the island, bringing death, so buried again, then surfaced, each time killing.

He knows some of the answers now, but one still eludes him. Why? Why did Frank leave these clues? Why not just write it down in clear, simple instructions? Why put him through all this?

'Granddad said he would try and stop you.'

Chris is suddenly aware that Ben is talking to him. 'What?'

'Granddad said that you needed all thirty, and that he would try and stop you. That's all.'

'Who would, granddad?'

Ben shakes his head and points to the coins.

'Not granddad. He wants to help. He said he doesn't want to be in hell.'

Thirty pieces of silver. That's who.

But the final coin? He threw it away.

'Sarah,' he says, and looks to her, turning cold at the realisation that she has been silent.

'Sarah?'

It's like she is in a trance as she sits in the chair, still and pale, her eyes staring ahead but apparently seeing nothing.

Chris grabs the chest, grabs Ben's hand and lifts him up, carries him to the chair, and takes Sarah by the hand.

'Sarah, we have to go,' he shouts at her, tugs her arm and pulls her to her feet. 'Don't give in to it, don't let it in.'

She follows, a dead weight at the end of his arm, but at least she is moving. He heads out into the courtyard, into the strange glow of the oppressive sky and out into the lane.

It hits them. A great burst of hot air rushes down from the mountain, swirls through the lanes, dragging up papers and rubbish as it goes. The white sheets and emaciated flags fly up after it, set free from houses, buffeted by the wind and falling helplessly to earth like desperate people leaping from a high burning building. The rootless souls of the dead. But these souls are not free. They cannot be free until the coins are laid to rest in hell where they belong, taking the restless soul of Judas with them.

Chris can feel their power in his hands as he stumbles against the wind, the chest held tightly, his son held tighter, and Sarah, now crying and despairing behind him.

'Keep up with me,' he shouts over the growing wail of the wind.

She makes no reply, but he can feel her hand, feel that she is moving.

They move on as fast as he can go, his head down against the dirt and leaves that are blowing up all around him. His eyes focus on the stones of the path, each one a step closer to the last coin. Each step a moment from his life separated by zigzags and jagged lines of cement and weeds, like the torn pieces of Ben's drawing, stepping stones through his past.

The past that plays through his mind as he drags his family up the steps towards the millstone square and the lopsided house.

His mother: brief memories of soft hair and kind words. His father: deeper scarring memories of pain and fear. Each step he forces down erases another memory, focuses his mind that little bit more on what he has to do. He has learned in these last few moments not to question it but simply to accept it is happening and to believe in what he has to do.

They round a corner and the billowing skies crack with the sound of furious thunder high above. The earth beneath their feet seems to shift and move, and yet no rain comes, no lightning hits the earth.

The howling wind brings the voices, the mad, screaming

wails of the dead, now frantic, as somewhere out there among the lanes and ruins Judas stalks in Frank's form, knowing the moves ahead, knowing what this man will try to do and using everything in its power to stop him, just as he has stopped all others before him.

Chris knows this as he feels his son's warm body falling limp in his arms. He knows that his family are giving up, that the curse is eating into them the same as it found its way into Frank. He came close but he could not finish the task. He left it to Chris and there is no way he is going to let it take his son.

To do so would make him the same as his father.

That thought gives him more strength and he forces himself up the last few steps into the square.

'Sarah,' he shouts. 'Sarah!' She looks up from under heavy eyelids, hardly understanding.

'Leave me alone,' she says, wearily. 'I just want to sleep.'

'No. Stay awake. Here.' He thrusts Ben into her hands. Her eyes brighten a little as she feels the child's warmth. She looks around fearfully and grips her son tightly.

Chris is at the edge of the drop into the dead ruin below. Any thoughts of failing are far from his mind now because down there in the blackened and burned remains of his father's work is that small box and that last coin. He slips over the edge and lands among the burnt papers.

The wind whips the ashes and debris up around him and it attacks him like sentinels defending their master. He kicks at the half burned books, the black sheaves, and then falls to his hands and knees.

'Chris!' He hears Sarah call from above and starts searching harder, faster.

He tears at the soil, pulls apart the weeds beneath the ashes, finds pieces of burnt clothing from the effigy, throws them aside. Frantic, scrabbling, dirt under his nails, his skin catching on stones, the burnt out smell of bonfire in his nostrils.

'Chris!' Her voice is more desperate now.

And then he finds it. The small pill box, caked with soot but intact. He picks it up, shakes it, claws at it, gets a nail into the tiny crack of the lid and pulls. The lip opens and he pockets the coin.

At that moment the voices attack him.

'Come with us. Leave it alone.' They have changed. They are spiteful now. 'It is easy. One moment of pain and it is done.' He sees a piece of metal in the ashes of the fire, the rusty, jagged edge of a tin can lid, something sharp enough to cut flesh. 'It is so easy. A moment and it is done. Be free. Come with us.'

This is what his father felt. This is where he got to, and he gave in to it. He came this far and no further.

'No!' Chris shouts and starts to scramble back up and into the square. 'You're not getting me. You can take him, he was weak, but you're not getting me!' He shouts back at the wind and the calling voices as he feels invisible hands pulling at him, dragging him back into the ruin, into the ashes of his father's funeral pyre. 'You're not getting me too!' He screams it out, and in one last effort drags himself up from the pit. He knows where he is going. He knows what he has to to do and nothing can stop him now.

He drags himself to his feet in the square, triumphant, assured, ready for battle.

And sees the figure of his father standing over the prone body of his son.

Thirty-one

It's happening inside a nightmare through clouded vision in slow-motion.

The black, seething figure that is one moment his father and one moment the soul of Judas is drawing Ben and Sarah away from the safety of the millstone and out, across the square towards the lanes. Chris knows that as soon as he loses sight of them they are lost to the evil. Lost in the lanes, lost to despair. He gets to his feet, staggers across the square, fighting the wind, fighting the voices in his head, and lifts Ben into his arms.

The thing rounds on him, somehow rising up to a height above him, and bears down on him, roaring. But he doesn't look. He won't give in. He grabs Sarah's hand and makes for the lopsided house.

'Put them back,' the voice behind him roars. He takes no notice. He gives it no satisfaction. 'They belong in the casket,' it snarls. 'You are no father to him. You're a drunk. You are weak,' and it is his father's voice now, taunting, playing with him.

Chris looks up to the balcony of the house and sees the gaunt father and his innocent son looking down. He can't read their faces but they are watching. He stumbles up the steps, around the corner into the next lane, the metal gates of the 1926 house just ahead. And the black, putrid vision of betrayal swoops above his head and follows.

'Running away, giving in to it, turning away from him?' The voice plays with him, one moment close in to his ear, the next at a distance, lost in the wail of the other voices. He sees shrines along the side of the path now, a body discarded on the way to burial. He sees withered wreaths of flowers blow towards him along the lane on the raging wind, and photographs of the dead, scattered and abandoned.

He reaches the door, the deathly cold grip of the monster behind him, and Sarah's voice moaning and crying.

He turns to look at her. The thing is gone, but in its place is Sarah, giving up, dying, the will to live leaving her, being sucked away. Hopeless. His son is becoming a dead weight in his hands.

'Stay awake,' he calls, desperately, and kicks open the metal gates.

Sarah raises her head and screams.

Standing inside the lobby is Petros, his eyes gouged out, dried blood flaking from the sockets, caked and chipping away, his face white and drawn, his hand, bloody and still holding a knife, outstretched.

'Take it,' he says, and Chris sees Sarah reach for it. He knocks her arm away and moves past the man.

'You can't,' he shouts. 'It's not real. These things are not there.' He knows that the dead can't touch, can't pass things on physically. Stavroula taught him that. She showed him that when she wouldn't let him touch her. That's why this thing cannot take the coins and go. It cannot hold them. It needs the living to do its work.

'I'm sorry, Chris.' He hears Sarah's voice behind him. 'I shouldn't have treated you like I did. You deserve better than me.'

'None of that matters now,' he says, and takes three strides towards the cellar.

'I'm sorry.' She sounds wretched, a woman who has given up everything. 'I let you down.'

He pulls her into the cellar and stops dead in his tracks. He feels Ben in his arms, growing heavy. The chest burns into him as he stands, his heart racing almost as fast as his mind.

He scans the room, a deserted space of discarded family clutter. A washing machine, boxes, unloved pictures in frames, mother's things, father's tools, children's toys. He stands in this graveyard of a family's possessions with his son, his wife, his family. And he stares in disbelief across the room.

Dust swirls in the cluttered room dragged up from the rough floor by the raging wind that finds passage through cracked walls and the broken window high up. Pieces of broken glass glint in shafts of confused light that flicker from candles, and behind those candles are faces. The faces of the dead. Each one holding the burning flame of its shrine, each one standing beyond a round, stone wall, now freed from the pile of debris that covered it. The well, the pit, now waiting, and oozing the red smoking light of somewhere far below.

The illustration: the pit, the demon clawing its way out to grab the contents of the chest being offered, the woman behind with the candle. Hell is ready to receive the coins. Chris is walking to the edge of the pit, ready to deliver them, and on the other side stand the souls of the dead, ready to be freed, to go to their final resting place. He believes. He accepts, and he knows he has nearly won.

Stavroula stands on the other side, lifting her head towards him, her soft skin radiant in the heat from below, her eyes wide and round, encouraging him on, her candle flickering and throwing a glow on her face.

Helen stands beside her, hand in hand with the man from her photograph. He holds their daughter and they are smiling, nodding reassurance at him. Beside her, Petros comes to join the father and the son, the boy in his costume, other villagers, people Chris does not know, and he hears their whispers. It calms. Their chattering begins to die down as the wind finally settles around them.

The room waits. Chris puts Ben down, gives him to Sarah who realises what a precious thing she holds in her arms and pulls Ben tightly to her. She looks across the room and sees the people. She gasps and whimpers. She pulls Ben towards the security of the shelved wall, cradles him there, curls her legs up, and watches through this nightmare as Chris steps towards the well.

He feels the end within his grasp now. He has it all, the coins, the well, the belief. He doesn't question it. He knows. He takes out the coins, drops the chest and pours the first of the money into the palm of his hand.

The dead step forward, eyes on him, silent, still, and he feels a rush of power as he drops the first coin into the well.

'It's not going to work.'

He looks up and sees his father standing with the others, his eyes dead and lifeless, his lips moving slowly.

'Isn't this what you wanted?' Chris replies, dropping another coin into the pit. 'Isn't this what you meant me to do? To do what you were too weak to do?'

Frank shakes his head. 'I knew you would be strong, son. I knew you could do what I wasn't able to do. You are lucky.'

'Lucky!' Another coin. 'Lucky to have you as a father?' More coins into the pit.

'Lucky to have him as a son.'

Frank turns his head towards the wall and Chris follows his gaze. He sees Sarah slumped against the wall, helpless, her eyes staring, her mouth open, and beside her, Ben. He is holding something against his arm, a tool from the shelves, a saw, and he is starting to saw at his wrist with it.

The tall, dark figure of Frank stands over them.

Chris snaps back to the dead beyond the pit. No Frank. He turns back to his son, and Frank has gone, but Ben is starting to draw blood.

'Sarah' he yells, and tries to move towards them, but something has him pinned to the ground. He feels some kind of icy grip around his ankles, his feet held firmly.

Sarah looks at him, and then reaches out to the shelf beside her.

Looking back, Frank is again with the dead, and beside him Stavroula is looking at Chris as he throws a handful of coins into the pit. He pours out more into his hand. But now Stavroula is shaking her head and he doesn't understand. This is what she wanted him to do, isn't it?

Frank's eyes flash, the chattering starts up again, twenty-two, twenty-three, they count the number of coins being sent to their resting place, but still the figure stays there.

'What did you expect?' Frank taunts, but it is not his voice. The father has gone and now the voice is that of those thousands of tormented souls, each syllable made up by screams of agony and hate, betrayal and death all crushed together to form words.

The voice of Judas.

'What do you expect? That I would vanish into the pits of hell, that I would let my soul go willingly?'

Twenty-five.

Frank's eyes move again towards Sarah, and now he is smiling. Chris looks. Sarah is lifting a nail gun from the shelf and Ben is now clawing at his broken flesh with his fingers.

'They are coming with me,' the thing says.

'Twenty-six.' Chris throws another coin into the well. 'And this one is for you, Frank. You can go down there with him. Twenty-seven.'

Frank laughs. 'You don't understand do you?'

'Twenty-eight. If you want his blood money, you can go and get it yourself.' He throws in the twenty-ninth coin, drops the pouch and reaches into his pocket for the last one.

'Why do you think I left you clues?' It's Frank's voice now, back again, and soft, reassuring. The voice of a father.

'What?'

The voices fall silent. Something shifts.

Chris is aware of the sobbing sounds from behind. He sees Ben scratching at his arm, tears falling from his eyes. He sees Sarah lift the heavy power tool to the side of her head. He screams out.

'Sarah, no! Look at Ben. Sarah, look at Ben.'

Her dull eyes turn towards him.

'She doesn't love you.' It's Judas' voice, taunting. 'And you don't love him.'

'Sarah!'

Something connects and she drops the nail gun. It's a weak effort but she manages to pull Ben's fingers away from his wrist. He fights back and she pulls again.

'Christopher.'

The voice stops him and he looks back to see his father standing before him, calm, kind, his hand outstretched. 'Trust me, Christopher. I left you the clues so that you would understand, so that you would come to believe me. I realised too late that only you had the strength to do this. You could succeed where I could only fail. I wrote it in that note, Chris, and I knew it would make you stop and think. I would have done anything for you, if I had the strength. And despite what you might think, I do love you.'

Chris holds up the coin. 'Thirty.'

'What did it say in the book, Chris?'

'I'm doing it! I'm giving them back to hell. And you can rot there with them.'

He throws the coin and expects something to happen. But nothing does happen. The thing before him is not Frank, and now it is laughing, the sound filling the room as the dead shrink back, cower away from the black figure that now writhes and growls, filling the room with its hate and its scorn, laughing as Ben digs deeper into his arm. More blood flows, and Sarah lifts the gun to her head once more.

'Weak,' the thing laughs. 'Hell doesn't want my money. It wants me. Look.'

Chris feels a weight in his hand and looks down. The leather pouch is back in his palm, and it is heavy with the weight of thirty pieces of silver.

Chris knows he is losing.

'The books, Chris.'

He is confused at the sound of the voice. Looking across the pit, through smoke that rises up from it, he sees Helen's face smiling back at him. 'What did it say in the book? Think.'

He has thought. He has remembered.

'Give them back.'

'No, Chris,' she says, and her calm reassuring voice cuts through all the madness around him. 'Look at the facts. *It said bring them back.*'

It hits him.

He hears Stavroula's voice and looks up. 'You have the

strength,' she says, 'now you only need the faith.' She is holding out her hand to him, smiling.

He looks across to Sarah, and Ben in her arms. He is clawing at his flesh with his nails, she is lifting the gun to the side of her head once more.

Frank, that thing, continues to float over him like some angel of death, scornful and triumphant.

'You don't have the guts,' it spits, right in his ear, inside his head. 'You can't finish this. None of you can. You are all too weak.'

On the other side of the well, Chris watches as Stavroula takes the hand of the small boy in his parade costume, blood on his wrist. She grips it tightly, giving him support and comfort, and Chris understands.

He knows what has to be done.

He knows now that he has somewhere to go.

Looking across at Ben he sees the dusty old baseball cap on the ground beside him, the hole in the wall where the money had been. So near and yet so far. If he'd believed, then, maybe, he would have just taken the chest and thrown it away. But then he would have lost. He wasn't brought here to throw it away. His father could have done that. Anyone learning the legends and hearing the stories could have done that. In fact, they tried and failed. It needs more. It needs to be taken. He needs to take them, the thirty pieces, Judas' soul, to where it should always have been.

And if he fails, then it will take Ben.

'I knew you were stronger than me. I had faith in you, son.' He hears his own father's voice, but doesn't look at him.

He has to save his son.

With a desperate yell of defiance Chris tears his feet away

from their rooted spot. He falls to his knees, he crawls to his son, knocks the gun from Sarah's hand and the action wakes her. She registers that he is there. He grabs Ben's arm. Tears stream from his eyes as he pulls the boy's hand away, lifts his head to look at him.

'Ben,' he says. 'Ben! Look at me. Look at your father.'

The boy's eyes register and he blinks. He looks at Chris and smiles, weakly.

'You know that stuff that your mum keeps on about, all that stuff about seeing people in heaven?'

Ben nods.

Chris picks up the cap and places it on Ben's head. Then he holds his son to him for the briefest, saddest moment.

'She was right,' he says. 'I'll be seeing you.'

He mimes taking Ben's photo. Ben mimes taking his.

'Chris?' It is Sarah's voice, clear but afraid.

He gives her a kiss on the forehead.

'Change of plans,' he says, and stands up. He walks to the well with the pouch of coins.

The voices start up, chattering excitedly now, defiantly confident. The dead on the far side of the pit jostle and nudge. It's their time to move on at last. Chris steps up onto the edge of the well and looks across at Stavroula. She too steps up, and holds out her hand, smiling.

But, suddenly, a great blast of foetid air sweeps in from the high window and sweeps Chris away from the edge. A swirling black fog of filthy darkness rises up out of Frank and his body falls to the ground. The force, released and furious, rushes to the child, making Ben pick up the saw again. This time, he turns it to rest across his throat.

Then the presence swoops away and blasts into Chris,

throwing him against the wall and filling him with evil thoughts of betrayal.

He feels his mouth move. 'Too late.'

He sees Ben rise to his feet and start to walk towards the well, the saw pressed tight against his throat, his hand outstretched, ready to take the coins from his father. Ready to die in his father's place.

Chris forces himself away from the wall, his eyes fixed on his son. He makes himself imagine Ben taking the coins, walking to the pit, falling in. The thought crushes his heart. He knows he can't let that happen.

The coins bounce in his trembling hand as Ben reaches out for them, and their hands touch.

But the presence knows what they intend and Chris feels it surge from his body back into the room. It can't beat Chris but it can beat the child. On the loose again, it swirls and then dives towards Ben, ready to possess him instead. Ready to do whatever is needed to keep the coins from being lost.

But as it swoops down towards the child, Chris lets go of Ben's hand, grips the coins in his own, and steps up onto the rim of the well.

He hears the voices screaming for him. He hears Judas roaring. He reaches out for Stavroula.

He sees Frank, a tear in his eye, a proud look on his face.

He no longer fears falling. He relishes it. He lets the drop take him and pull him over the edge. He steps into the void, taking his inheritance with him.

A massive confusion of black mist and swirling dust, screaming, laughing, whispers, shouts, and a great drawn out howl from the Judas voice as everything is sucked towards the pit. The dead start to fade and vanish, their candles extinguished one by one. Frank is drawn to the edge and vanishes into the smoke. Helen, smiling across at Sarah, fades away. Stavroula is gone. The father grips his son's hand, and they share a smile. Petros' eyes are restored as he vanishes.

Clawing, spiteful fingers reach out from the well and grab the edges of the swirly black of betrayal, and slowly, painfully, gloating and laughing, they pull Judas screaming into the pit.

5

You are in darkness. Your eyes are closed. You can't see but you can hear. A strange kind of whispering sound, like voices from another room, frantically chattering, excited, hushing each other, gasping, begging, all mixed up. And fading away now, going to their rest. The sounds of visitors leaving after a long day, making their tired way home.

You open your eyes and see your son lying deathly still on the ground.

Thirty-two

Outside in the lanes the light returns as clouds evaporate and the sky calms, white and cold. A shutter is opened cautiously, a courtyard gate creaks, a bird starts to sing nervously. A woman peeks out from behind her door, looks up and down the lane. She sees a neighbour hanging out sheets, but it is only washing going out to dry in the returning sunshine. She leaves her house and heads off into the village.

᠌᠊᠌J

Sarah opens her eyes and sees Ben on the ground. For a moment she is about to scream, but then she sees him moving and she takes a deep breath. Her limbs ache, her heart aches more, and she tries to make sense of what just happened, what she saw, what she thought she saw.

No. She saw it all. She believes. She always has. The events flash through her mind quickly as she starts to recover her senses. But then she sees Ben on his feet and walking towards the round stone circle across the room, towards the well.

'Daddy?' he says, and steps up onto the edge. The stones crumble beneath his feet and he teeters, his arms out of balance, about to fall. Sarah grabs him and pulls him back. She lifts him up and cradles him, tears in her eyes, but there are no words in her throat. She moves towards the door.

'Wait,' Ben says, and she stops. He is pointing to the small metal chest that held the coins and a shiver runs through her.

'Please,' Ben says.

She picks it up and gives it to him. It seems to give him

comfort, something to remember his father by, perhaps? She will think about it all later. Right now she just wants to collect their things and get out of this place.

As they leave the room Ben looks back to the well and smiles at a presence unseen. Sarah doesn't see but he raises his hand and mimes taking a photograph.

Outside, the lanes are now sunny and bright and she shields her eyes as they leave the house. Which way was it? She starts walking, Ben at her side holding her hand. In the other, he clutches the casket.

5

Late afternoon. The sun has slipped behind the mountain, the long shadow has been drawn across the hillside. They sat and watched it as the rocks up there turned from dusty pink to dark grey, as the sun slowly slid away towards night.

They wait by the ferry. They have been told they can board in a few minutes. They can hear people making the boat ready. Some villagers have come down to pass on messages, letters to be taken to the mainland. "Send food. We are still here."

She has told herself to act normally for the boy. There will be questions and shock and things to work out, but that can all wait until they are off the island and on the way home. Until then, things must carry on as close to normal as possible.

On the way down from the house, Sarah was befriended by a tall youth who carried Chris' bags for her. He said he worked at a café and was going across on the boat to get more stock. The café was opening up again. She was only half listening.

She'd gathered up Chris' notes, his cameras and photos, what she thought Ben might like to see when he was older. It seems he had written a message for the boy, the start of a story, his 'adventure' as he put it. It would, one day explain to Ben what took place, and the reason his father is not around. It might help her make sense of the story. Maybe.

Beside her, Ben toys with the casket. He seems to be intrigued by it. He keeps opening it and peeking inside, only to close the lid again and laugh.

'What are you doing?' she asks.

Ben looks up at her, shows her the closed chest.

'There is something inside,' he says.

'Don't be silly. It's gone. They have all gone. But let's not talk about that now. Are you ready to go home?'

'The coins have all gone, yes,' Ben says, and his face looks ridiculously serious. 'But there is something else. Daddy says so.'

She was expecting something like this, but not straight away. She imagined that he would stay in shock, as she is now, for some time before he started asking questions. Before they could start to make sense of it all.

'Now then, Ben,' she says, putting her arm around him. 'It's not going to be easy but we will talk about daddy. It is going to be difficult, but we'll get through it together, okay?'

'Oh, I'm fine with that mummy,' he says. 'I know daddy's alright. He's told me. But it's this chest that's the problem.'

'I know darling. We'll talk about it when we get back.'

'You don't understand, mummy,' he insists. 'You see, the chest holds things that are dangerous, like those coins were dangerous, and old of course. But the coins have gone now.'

'Yes, I know that, Ben. Look, people are starting to go aboard. Let's go.'

But he hasn't made himself clear yet.

'No, mummy. Daddy says that this is very important. He says that the coins brought the bad man to earth...'

'Now stop this, Ben.' It is her time to insist, but it does no good. What her child has to say is very important, to him, at least. He resists the tug of her hand and grips the chest more tightly.

'He says it was this chest that brought them here.'

'Yes, Ben, they were brought here in it many years ago. We will get a museum to look at it when we get home, perhaps. We should see what it is worth. It is your inheritance, after all. Now, come on.'

'The chest brought them here.' He repeats himself for emphasis. His voice is cold. He almost sounds like someone else.

She has a creeping suspicion that something is not yet over. 'And?'

'Daddy says he missed it. Granddad missed it. They all missed it.'

'Missed what?' She is feeling very uneasy.

He holds out the silver casket to her, his big eyes wide with the excitement of a secret known.

'This chest was made from the same silver. It brings evil things to earth. And now there is something else inside.'

5

LONELY HOUSE

by James Collins

PROLOGUE

'Just do it, Pete. Shoot me now.'

Pete is crying. He can hardly see his best friend, but he can feel the shotgun in his hands. He is shaking his head. He can't shoot his friend.

Blood everywhere. On his face, on his clothes, on the gun. He can smell it. He has never smelt so much blood before.

'Do it, Peter!' The girl is also screaming. 'There's no time left.' She is crying, desperate, hysterical.

He points the gun towards her.

'No, me!' His best friend yells through his sobs. He is covered in blood too, it drips from his mouth as he chews and swallows. 'NOW!'

Pete swings the gun back to his friend. He grips it tight with one hand while he quickly wipes the tears and blood from his eyes. His eyes are stinging, his lids want to stay closed but he must force them open. He has to aim. There is only one cartridge and one of the two people in front of him has to die.

'I don't know what to do.' He screams it as he sobs it as he chokes on the words. 'I don't know what to do!'

'Me, Pete. Pete, look at me. Look me in the eye.' His friend is calmer now. That's the voice Pete likes to hear, the one that tells him what to do. 'You gotta kill me. I deserve it. You know that. You know what I did now, you know it, Pete. Kill me and it's over. Look.'

His best friend, his only friend, holds out the human heart he is eating and shows Pete the last remaining piece.

'It's nearly cold, Pete. You gotta do it now.'

Pete shakes his head and back off slightly.

The girls screams, 'Now! Kill him.'

'I can't.'

'I have to die, Pete, it's the only way.'

'I can't kill you,' Pete sobs, desperately. 'You're my friend.' Pete, slow and dim-witted, knows what is right and what is wrong. He has always known. He has grown up knowing exactly what is right and what is wrong. Killing his only friend is wrong.

At least, it would have been, a few hours ago. But, now?

'It's the only way,' the girl shouts again.

He doesn't like her shouting. He doesn't like to see her upset, but she is crying. She is watching his friend eat the last pieces of a human heart, and he is listening to her begging him to pull the trigger. He feels it, slimy with blood, under his finger.

'Choose her, Pete. It's what you want. She's what you always wanted.'

It's his choice. Pete's slow mind tumbles thoughts from back to front. He only has one choice. His friend or her. But it's not as simple as that. No. There's another choice. He could throw down the gun and run away, but then he would be abandoning his mate and Pete knows that would be wrong. He could kill Drover and escape with the girl. He wants to do that. He likes the girl. She likes him. They'd have the money. Whoever found what was in the house and whoever found Drover dead would say nothing. There would be nothing to say.

But then, he remembers the ghost train. Which way would he go when the time came? Down and down and never come back? Or back through the doors to the world? Yes, he'd come back because he should not be in this position. He hasn't chosen to be in this position. It's not his fault.

'It's nearly all gone, Pete,' Drover is saying.

Pete's mind won't settle on an answer. He can't decide. The ghost train. Which way? Is it right to kill his friend and get what he wants? Drover wants it. He has been begging him. He has given Pete no choice. He can't leave Drover alive once he has finished eating that heart. And if he kills him he will have the girl he always wanted, and the money. And Drover wants to die.

'Peter, there's no more time. Kill him.'

'No! It's wrong.' He shouts. 'What should I do?' He shouts it into the dark, gloomy barn and his words are absorbed by the blood soaked straw. There's no echo. No answer comes back.

'Look, Pete,' Drover says.

Pete is shaking his head. His friend is swallowing the last piece, his face taught and grimacing and not just because of what he is doing. It is what the heart will soon be doing to him that sickens him.

'Now, before it takes hold. Before it comes back,' Drover says, wiping his mouth with the back of his hand. 'There's no other choice, mate. It's in me now.'

'Please, don't kill me,' she says.

He swings the gun to aim at her. Her voice is softer, calming him. She has stopped screaming at him now. She is holding out a hand. 'Please, Pete, do it. It will go away and we can leave. It's all over.'

'Pete,' Drover's voice is calmer too. 'It's done, mate. You know what you have to do. Shuck it, Pete, there's no way out for me now, yeah?'

Pete looks at his friend while holding the gun on the girl. Drover's hands are empty. The heart has gone. He has eaten all of it, swallowed it. It is in him now and he knows what he has to do. He slowly swings the barrel back to face his one and only friend.

And Drover is smiling.

'That's it, mate,' he says. 'No worries, eh? It's all you can do. Here, aim it at my head. I'll shut my eyes.'

Pete's finger tightens around the trigger.

'That's it, Pete,' the girls says, inching closer. 'Just us, eh? Just you and me and all that stuff you've dreamed of.'

'Quick, Pete,' Drover says and his voice suddenly sounds different. 'I can feel it starting. Pete, quick!'

Pete grips the shotgun more tightly, pressing it against his shoulder. He closes one eye completely. Through the other he sees a clouded, red vision of the only person he ever loved until now. Drover. His friend.

'I forgive you, Drover,' he says. 'I'm sorry.'

Tears start to pour down his face, washing away the blood. 'I'm sorry.'

ᛏ

Outside, in the forest, a silver-white hint of dawn approaches. Through the tightly packed trunks of tall, sinewy trees a tentative light can be seen far in the distance. Something stirs, an unsettled leaf falls, swaying gracefully through the cold, dew-dripping air to settle softly on the carpet of moss.

Silence.

And a single gunshot.

ᛏ

The rest of

LONELY HOUSE
by James Collins

coming soon

Printed in Great Britain
by Amazon.co.uk, Ltd.,
Marston Gate.